ANNADYOMENE

Tiffany Leahy

Jaden

What's your secret?

Tiffany Leahy

BOOK PUBLISHERS NETWORK

Book Publishers Network
P.O. Box 2256
Bothell • WA • 98041
Ph • 425-483-3040
www.bookpublishersnetwork.com

10 9 8 7 6 5 4 3 2 1

Printed in the United States of America

LCCN   2010910123
ISBN10   1-935359-42-8
ISBN13   978-1-935359-42-5

A percentage of the net proceeds will be graciously donated to a children's charity chosen by the author.

Editor: Julie Scandora
Cover Designer: Laura Zugzda
Typographer: Stephanie Martindale

To my wonderful mom, Shalawn Leahy.
Thank you for being the first to read this book, and for
always listening.
And most important: for believing in me.

CONTENTS

Acknowledgements   vii

Introduction   ix

1. Meet Annadyomene   1
2. The Great Arrival at Brownstone   5
3. Shocking Blue Eyes   16
4. Fire!   27
5. Things Get Rough   34
6. A Scar to Remember   40
7. Hoshi Is But a Fire in the Bark   53
8. I Won't Tell Liam   59
9. Did You Get Her Name?   62
10. A Dress for Nature   67
11. Who's Cheating Whom?   73
12. Much More Than a Car Crash   78
13. Children Are to Be Seen ...
    Definitely Not Heard   84
14. Bullfights, Secrets, and Surprises   98
15. Fire Tricks and Dragons Galore   106
16. Being Followed?   111
17. Six Siblings in Hoshi   121
18. A Trip to the Beach   126
19. Anth Has a Message   145
20. Saturday Night's Costume Party   152
21. A Poison No One Can Stop   158
22. Seemsly and the Giant Oak Tree   163
23. Someone's Missing   171
24. Traveling through Myths   177
25. Captured   190
26. My Name Is Mary   199
27. Becoming the Sacrifice   204
28. Magic Mirror   212

About the Author   219

You are never too old to set another goal
or to dream a new dream.

※ C. S. Lewis

ACKNOWLEDGEMENTS

My mom was the first one to read this book, she's the one I share all my ideas with. Without her my stories would still be in my head, unfinished for no one to read. In fact, my mom, is the one who brought all my characters to life. The way she makes everything seem so magical, and tells me I can believe in anything I want to. She makes me see everything so differently. I just hope, in my stories, people can feel that kind of passion I feel while writing.

Also a special thanks to:

My dad for being there, and for just being my Dad.

My older brothers Billy and Brandon, my puppy Fionna, and last but definitely not least my best friend my older sister, Tara.

Also to my friends who are just as important as my family is. One of my best friends in the world, Woody McGowan, from Leitrim, Ireland. Thank you, Woody, for being there when it counted the most. You are the kind of friend that everyone should have in their life, thank you.

And a special thank you for those who made this book happen:

Sheryn Hara, Publisher – who has the patience of a saint with those who are so ignorant to what really goes into making a book.

Rob Resing, Photographer – you made taking pictures so fun.

Julie Scandora, Editor – Forgiveness ends all suffering and loss.

Laura Zugzda – the cover design you hit the nail right on the head.

Stephanie Martindale – who laid out my book so beautifully.

Justin Smith, from Bang Printing, thank you for all your effort in printing my book.

Laura Danforth for distribution of my beautiful book to all the many carriers.

INTRODUCTION

ANNADYOMENE'S CREATION

I was 12 when I first started writing. Having been an avid reader myself, I personally observed that there was little, if any, novels involving my age range for pre-teens.

Through my travels throughout many countries of Ireland, England, Spain, Holland, Africa, Canada, and the United States, I have observed that preteens are often the most neglected and ignored in this area for available reading material. I found either books were insultingly immature and geared for younger audiences, or the other novels threw me into a high school level with situations of which I had not experienced yet. So I was definitely in a quandary of what to read.

This preteen age range is forced by our society to grow up too fast, and accept situations beyond their scope. As a society, we are losing a most precious milestone in our youth. My crusade is to tell the preteens not to be in any hurry to rush through it to get to the other side.

My hope with "Annadyomene" is that it will not only get new pre-teens reading, but that they find a little of themselves within the adventures and then look forward to the sequel.

With my book I want to send the message to all my readers that it is definitely a beautiful time in your life. Your first crush, your first date, your very first real kiss, your first understanding of what it means to have friends at your back when trouble arrives, and that it is an awesome time to have the imagination of fun and fantasy that many people lose as they get older.

Meet Annadyomene

"**A**nnadyomene Ribbon ... come down those stairs right now," my mother shouted. "Do you want to be late for your first day of school?"

"I wouldn't mind staying at home reading," I whispered to myself.

"Anna ..." My mother started to shout again.

"Okay, I'm up, jeez!" I said before she could say anymore.

Reluctantly, I got up from my bed and started to walk to the closet, throwing aside my bright pink comforter. I loved the colors of my room and being able to choose them myself. When I finally got a room to myself (I used to share one with my sister), it was my space so I decided to make my room fun. Now as I opened my closet, stuff tumbled out all over. My closet was another issue because it was always a big mess. Like most sixteen-year-olds my age, I just didn't care what my closet looked like, just as long as I could find my stuff. I had more important issues to deal with. And anyway it wasn't that bad. At least not according to my standards.

I started looking around, trying to find the right outfit for my first day at Brownstone Boarding School. I couldn't believe I was going to such a place. Nobody in my family had gone to a boarding school, but the people at Brownstone thought I was some kind of genius or something. So here I was, going off to a bunch of stuck-up rich kids that use their mommy and daddy's money to buy everything.

I had packed all my personal bags, but I was checking to make sure I had everything. I had my school backpack with all my required schoolbooks and a few books for fun. I could hear my family waiting for me downstairs to say goodbye. They seemed so anxious to get rid of me, but I knew deep down that it wasn't true. I'm too much fun; they wouldn't want to get rid of me that fast.

With a sigh, I knew I had to hurry and get dressed or I'd be late.

"What should I wear ... what should I wear?" I asked myself over and over.

"Come on Anna! Mom and Dad are ready to go, and they're not even going to this school!" my older brother Billy called from the kitchen.

"Okay, let me get dressed first. Can I do that? Or do you want me to go in my PJs? What a great first impression that would make on those rich snobs!" I said sarcastically, not even waiting for an answer. I snatched my favorite pair of blue jeans. They had different colored flowers with rhinestones running down the sides. Then I picked a red long-sleeve, v-neck top with a black under top. Last, some red heart earrings, a double black pearl necklace, and my white and black sneakers. Now the last thing to do was brush my teeth and my hair. Oh no! I forgot about my hair—should I wear it up or down or just leave it for now? I voted on leaving it for now.

After ten minutes in front of the mirror in my room, I thought I had the right hairstyle. I took my black and white clip and pinned the sides of my raven black hair back. So now I was ready. Before I left my room, I turned around and looked at its bright colors one last time. My bright pink fuzzy comforter was thrown over my bed in a lazy way, as were my pillows. My rainbow heart pillow lay in the middle with the others. It was my favorite just because it was. Posters, flyers, and anything else I found cool covered my once white walls.

I left my room, walked downstairs into my living room, and found everyone waiting for me: my mom, my dad, my two older brothers, Billy and Brandon, my older sister, Tara, and last but not least, my best friend, Fionna. Okay so she has four paws and a tail and spots that make her look like a cow. But that didn't matter. Like people always say, "man's best friend." She is definitely my best friend.

As if leaving weren't hard enough, my mom had to make a big deal about my going to boarding school. And then just to make it worse, Mom started to mess with my hair, saying how much she liked the sides down.

"Mom ... please. My hair is fine. Leave it alone, pleeeese!" I cried.

"My youngest baby is going away to boarding school. I'm going to miss you every second you're gone. Are you going to miss us?" Mom asked, looking at me with a little smile on her face.

"Yes, I'm going to miss all of you," I said and then hugged everyone before my taxi came to get me. Fionna was first. She isn't that big, but when you pick her up she is a load. Then there's my dad, Bill, who's right off the boat from Ireland. My oldest brother, Billy, who loves to read like I do. My second brother, Brandon, who loves music and plays guitar and piano. My only, and older, sister, Tara, who's my best friend for life, no matter how many times we fight. Then there's my mom, Shalawn, who always listens, always cares, and always knows when something is bothering me, like now.

"You'll do fine, don't worry," my mom said as she was hugging me.

"I know that, Mom," I said, trying to sound happy while knowing how much I would miss them and all their noise too.

"Well, honey, your eyes are green, and when they are that green, that means you're nervous," my mom said. You see, unlike normal people whose eyes can't change colors, my eyes can. They change with my mood, so I have no control over what color they will turn next.

"I'm just a little nervous about this new school," I said.

"They would be crazy not to love you there at Brownstone," my mom said, choking back her tears; then she closed her eyes and kissed me on the forehead. "Love you, baby; have a great time," my mom whispered in my ear.

"I love you too, Mom. Bye," I said with a half smile as I walked outside to my cab.

"Anna, remember they'd be crazy not to love you," my mom said.

I nodded with a smile and said, "Thanks, Mom. Bye." Then I walked down the path to the driveway, looking around our large front yard with the orange, light pink, yellow, purple, and blue flowers I remembered planting with my mom. The lawn looked a beautiful green as the sun reflected off it. For once it was a sunny day, but I knew it wouldn't last for long. I had mixed emotions getting into the cab. On one hand, I was sad to leave everyone at home, and on the other, I was so excited to see what awaited me at the school. And of course, I still felt a little nervous to see what the kids were like. My dad and brothers finished loading my bags in the back of the cab, and after many more waves from everyone, I was on my way.

Once I had settled into the cab and had left behind the vision of my family waving, I could take a deep breath and try to relax a bit from such a hectic morning and all those goodbyes. I knew a long trip to the school lay before me, so instead of worrying the whole way on what I might expect from my first day at Brownstone, I decided to relax and fill my mind with one of my favorite pastimes—reading. So reaching into my backpack, I retrieved my latest novel and once again got lost within the pages.

The Great Arrival at Brownstone

"Miss, we're here," the cab driver said after our endless ride as he got out of the car to unload my bags. Running through the rain, he dropped them at the front door for me.

I looked out my window, through the rain, which I had predicted was inevitable. My first impression of this place was that it looked rather creepy at night with its big empty windows, large trees, and brickwork covered in green moss. I knew it was dark and rainy, but beyond that, this place looked as if nobody had inhabited it in years. The enormous building looming over me and the cab driver made me feel as if I was at that point in a horror film when the audience is screaming, "DON'T GO IN THERE!"

"Are you sure this is the right place?" I asked the taxi driver, covering my eyes from the pouring rain, hoping he had the wrong address and wishfully thinking that the boarding school I was going to was a lot happier than this one.

"Yes ... this is the right address. Have a good night, miss," he said as he ran to the driver's side of the cab. He couldn't wait to get out of there either.

Well I couldn't stay outside forever, no matter how much I wanted to. As I slowly walked up the stairs to the huge double doors of Brownstone, I wondered if even the gargoyles had run off, since none were in sight.

BOOM, BOOM, BOOM the knocker sounded as I rapped on the door. *Why not wake up the whole neighborhood while I am at it?* I thought. As I waited for a response, ready for almost anything, I half expected the doors just to open on their own. I stepped forward slightly and took a closer look at the doors in front of me. They were old but very thick, and they looked strong too. I reached out to touch them to see if they were as smooth as they looked when...

"Who's there?" someone asked in a booming voice on the other side of the double doors.

I gave a little jump. "Hello, my name is Annadyomene Ribbon. I'm a new student here at Brownstone," I said, then waited.

After I said my name, I could hear a deadbolt being moved inside the door, and then the right door opened. Standing to the side of the door and holding it open was a woman in a dark blue robe, with a big flashlight in her left hand.

She spoke not a word, and I felt very uncomfortable because of her sizing me up one end and down the other. It was as if she was inspecting a new car or pony she was about to buy. After staring at me for what seemed like forever, her face formed a grim smile, which accentuated all the many years of wrinkles.

"Welcome, Miss Ribbon. We are so glad you could join us here at Brownstone. I'm Mrs. Horn, your headmistress here at Brownstone."

She started talking to me as she walked away, so I picked up my luggage and followed her and her ever-so-dim flashlight down a dark hallway. As we came up to a staircase, I let my bags drop to the floor because they were dragging me down so much I thought my back would snap in two.

"Who is she?" I heard a voice above me ask as I stood, dripping wet from the rain, near the staircase with all my bags on the floor. Mrs. Horn was out of sight and probably still talking to herself.

"Where do you think she's from?" I heard yet another voice from above me ask. This time I looked right above my head and saw the enormous staircase winding up to a small point at the top. Many little faces hung over the rails, looking as curiously at me as I looked at them.

"I didn't know our school was taking on charity cases," said a young girl, probably around my age. From what I could see looking up, she had beautiful, blond, Barbie-looking hair, a sour look on her face, and one of those perfect bronze tans that could only have been acquired through a tanning salon where they spray that look into your skin.

Another kid leaned far over the railing and asked, "How's it going, new girl?" This guy had a sneaky smile and dark brown, almost black curly hair that hung into his face. I just gave him a half smile, which made some of the other younger kids start to giggle.

"Hey, new girl," the Barbie-look-alike shouted from the staircase.

"Yeah?" I said back as sweet as possible.

"Did you buy your clothes at a flea market or something, cuz looking at that outfit you're wearing, we all have to wonder," she said while giggling to her friends around her, which made all of them giggle too.

"No, I didn't go to a flea market for this outfit, but if I had, then I guess I would look just like you," I said smugly smiling back at her and her infamous minions.

Barbie-girl stopped giggling and stared right at me with such contempt in her eyes. Her little minions froze in place, daring not to laugh or giggle. Finally one of them just let out a low "oooooow."

"You better watch yourself and know your place ... new girl," she warned through her pursed lips. And then turning to her friends, she whispered, "Shut-up you idiots! Don't you have something else to do—like your nails or your hair or just zipping up your lips? Get out of my way," she said as she pushed by them.

"What's going on here?" said Mrs. Horn, coming out of the shadows and walking towards my bags and me, as if she had been waiting in the wings of a theater for her grand entrance in a play.

"I had to put my heavy bags down for just a minute; they were hurting my arms," I explained as I picked up and readjusted the bags on the side of my shoulder again.

"I was not referring to your trivial bags, Miss Ribbon; I was referring to your conversation with our Miss Fair," stated Mrs. Horn in her low but ever-demanding tone.

Barbie-girl spoke right up, instantly grabbing the conversation away from me, "I was just welcoming our new girl to Brownstone, Mrs. Horn, and we," signaling to her cronies, "told her how much fun she should expect to have here and that we should become great friends."

"How terribly nice of you, Miss Fair. Always such a sweetheart you are," said Mrs. Horn.

"Heed those words, Miss Ribbon. Miss Fair can show you quite a lot while you reside with us here at Brownstone," said Mrs. Horn.

"Yeah, I bet she can," I said looking sarcastically up the staircase.

"Did you say something, Miss Ribbon?" asked Mrs. Horn.

"What?" I asked with a clueless look as Mrs. Horn looked around.

"Yes, well, Miss Ribbon, we have a lot to discuss in my office, and it's late, so follow me," Mrs. Horn said after a moment of silence. Then she started walking back down the hallway. Before following Mrs. Horn down the hallway, I looked up the staircase one last time. The girl named Miss Fair and her gang were gone, and I was about to turn away when I noticed two guys staring at me. One had dark brown hair, green eyes, and from the way he looked at me, I didn't know if he was trying to be nice or if he was telling me I had one more enemy at Brownstone. The other guy had blond hair with almost white tips, brown eyes that looked black, and he looked familiar, but I didn't know why.

"Come along, Miss Ribbon," Mrs. Horn called to me, so I started walking down the hallway past a bunch of doors that probably led to Mrs. Horn's secret crematorium.

When I reached Mrs. Horn, she was just walking into her office, so I followed her inside and waited for her to say or do something. It seemed to take this woman forever to find the right key within her big military-style office, and after staring at her cabinet full of keys, she finally picked a pair out and turned around to face me.

"Well, Miss Ribbon, sorry about the delay, but you were, after all, not excepted until much later, as you yourself know. Never mind about that now," she said, clearing her throat as if she had a fur ball locked up inside her vocal cords. "You are here with us now," she continued, "and that is all that's important. Here are your keys to your new room, and tomorrow morning I will see you in this office at 7:30 a.m. sharp before your classes start at eight twenty so I can give you your class schedule. Please do not delay. I am not used to waiting for anyone, especially a student. I have a very demanding schedule and expect promptness from everyone," Mrs. Horn said, clearing her throat again.

"Okay … I mean, yes Ma'am," I stuttered, feeling especially uneasy and tongue-tied in her presence.

"Well, I think that will be all for tonight, Miss Ribbon. You may go. Heavens knows a woman of my means needs her beauty sleep. After all, tomorrow will be another hectic day," Mrs. Horn said almost in a demanding tone. She then looked down at some paperwork on her desk, as if she had totally dismissed me and I was to leave.

"Thank you, Mrs. Horn … um… I mean, Mrs. Horn. Excuse me, Ma'am. How do I get to my room?" I asked, trying to put a smile on my face, but all I really wanted to do was to put my bags down and get to bed.

Mrs. Horn, not even bothering to look up from her desk of papers, said, "Do you know the staircase by the front doors that you just came in from?"

"Yes," I answered, thinking about all the snobs I had just met and her secret crematorium.

"Take those up, and they should lead you to your room. But then I suppose you think I should escort you there personally?" Mrs. Horn said, glancing up momentarily from the papers on her desk.

"Ah, no, I think I can find it just fine on my own," I murmured.

"Speak up, child! My goodness. You'd think you were deaf by the way you murmur," retorted Mrs. Horn with just a hint of anger in her voice.

"Sorry," I said, kind of bowing my head.

"Good night, Miss Ribbon. That is all," Mrs. Horn said.

"Ah … goodnight, Mrs. Horn," I said and walked out of the office.

After I found the stairs and walked up to the first floor, the kids crowding the stairs didn't make my struggle with the heavy bags any easier.

"Excuse me," I said, trying to get past group after group of kids around my age, just sitting or standing on the steps. Then I looked at the keys in my hand and saw a number on them.

"Okay, Room 216," I said to myself, as I pushed past a boy and a girl kissing. Then I realized, walking halfway down the hall that I was actually on the first floor and the numbers were getting smaller rather than larger. I needed to go up one more flight to the second floor.

"Ah ... that stupid Mrs. Horn couldn't direct a marching band down a one-way street," I whispered to myself.

I turned back to the staircase and started climbing more steps, still carrying all my heavy bags while holding onto the keys to my new room. By the time I reached the second floor landing, I was exhausted and so ready just to drop on my new bed.

"Of course, my room would never be close to the stairs. Those are probably saved for all the kiss-ups or rich kids," I muttered out loud but to myself.

"WOW!" I said, dropping my bags and falling to the floor as I felt a foot trip me. Then as all the kids around me started laughing, I looked up to see Barbie and her "friends" (or should I say followers?) laughing at me as well.

"I guess fashion isn't the only thing you have to learn here, new girl. Being poised isn't everything, or in your case it might be. Consider yourself warned, Miss Ribbon," Miss Fair said, and her followers laughed as I lay there on the floor, my bags sprawled next to me.

"Well I should tell you, Miss Fair, I'm not intimidated by you. In fact, I like a good challenge, so maybe you should watch out as well," I said with a smug smile, still looking at Miss Fair as I got up from the floor and picked my bags up. Then before Miss Fair or her followers could say anything to me, I got all my bags and walked away.

"Let's see—213 ... 214 ... 215 ... 216. Here we are," I said as I tried to open the door. At first the key didn't work.

"Oh great, now the keys don't work, and I'll have to go back down to fur-ball throat again and tell her the keys are wrong, can't she get anything right," I said again to myself, not caring if someone was listening.

Finally after the third attempt and pulling the handle along with twisting the key, I heard the click of the door and walked inside, dropping my bags right at the door's entrance.

"Oh! I'm so sorry. I didn't know anyone was in here," I said shocked and a little bit annoyed that they hadn't helped with opening the door when they had probably heard my struggle with the key.

In the middle of the room stood a couple, whispering between themselves, which abruptly stopped upon my entrance.

"Well, Treelea, I guess you have a new roommate," the guy said to the girl next to him, a smile on his face.

"Hi, my name is Annadyomene Ribbon, but you can just call me Anna because my name is so long people forget it anyway." After a small pause, I said, "And ... I'm sorry. Did you want me to step out and give you guys some time?"

I considered my limited options. I had nowhere to go, unless I hiked it back to old Horn's office and helped her rearrange some of the wrinkles on her face. No couldn't do that either, because by now old Horn would be snoring away, enjoying her "beauty sleep." And heaven knows she needed all she could get.

"No, that's okay, Anna. I'm Martin Rivers, and ..."

"I'm Treelea Castle."

"So Anna, how do you pronounce your name again?" Treelea asked, looking genuinely interested.

"Oh, ah ... Anna-dime-a-knee," I said as I dragged my bags on the floor next to the empty bed.

"Oh, how do you spell it?" Treelea asked, moving to a desk in the room.

That's when I noticed the room was bigger than I had thought it would be.

It had enough space that you could walk around even with the two twin beds and two desks.

"Anna ... din ... no, sorry, Anna. Spell it for me?" Treelea asked, this time holding a note pad in one hand and a pen in the other.

"A-n-n-a-d-y-o-m-e-n-e, Annadyomene." I spelled it out to her slowly so she could get it right.

"Well, Anna, I'm sorry to leave so soon, but I have to get back to my dorm," Martin said.

Then he turned to Treelea and said, "I'll see you tomorrow, okay?" And then he kissed her.

Knowing that this was an embarrassing situation, I pretended that I was unpacking my bags.

"Bye, you guys," he said, looking at me for a second, and then staring at Treelea as if she were his whole world. Then he was gone, leaving just Treelea and me.

"So how long have you and Martin been together?" I asked Treelea, looking up with a smile on my face.

"Ah ... a year or two," she answered putting away something I couldn't see.

"How did you two meet?" I asked as I started unpacking all my stuff.

"Martin works for Liam's father," Treelea said, sitting on her bed with a dreamy look on her face.

"Who?" I asked.

"Liam's an old friend of mine. He's really nice. I'll introduce you two sometime, maybe tomorrow if you want?" Treelea said.

"Sure!" I said with a smile as I unpacked a wooden locked jewelry box.

"What's that box?" Treelea asked.

"This is my special jewelry box. I put everything in here," I said, putting it on the desk by my bed. Then I asked, "So what's the story behind you and Martin?"

"Oh ... well I met him while he was working, and so we both got to talking. Then he asked if we could hang out, and I said yeah," Treelea said looking at her hands with a dreamy smile still on her face.

"Can I ask you a few questions? But the first question you can't tell anyone, promise?" Treelea asked me suddenly.

I nodded, waiting while also thinking this was kind of odd to ask a favor from a new roommate she had just met a second ago. But I still waited for her to ask.

"Okay ... How do you feel about animals?" she asked a half smile on her face. Then her light brown hair with maroon stripes got in the way, and I couldn't see her expression.

"I love animals ... Just as long as they don't attack me ... Why?" I asked.

Then I saw something move under her bed.

"Well, would you like to meet Dillard and Carson?" she asked, a big smile lighting up her face. Then she bent down on a mat on the floor and reached under her bed and pulled out two furry things.

Taking a closer look, I realized one of the things was a ferret, all black with a white spot on its forehead.

The other was a gray and white mouse with long whiskers.

"This is Dillard," Treelea said, holding up the ferret. "And this is Carson," she said and held up the mouse. "They're friendly and won't bite ... So what do you think?" she asked, looking at the animals with a smile, and then looking at me.

"They're so cute. Of course, I won't tell," I said as I petted Dillard and Carson.

"This is great! My last roommate couldn't stand them. That's why she moved to a new room," whispered Treelea. Treelea then started to explain to me everything about her old roommate. The girl's name was Sara Pen, and from what I heard from Treelea, who was very easygoing, she was a difficult roommate. Sara hated animals, always left their room a giant mess, and never let Treelea have anyone in their room. But Sara would always bring her friends in, and if Treelea didn't like it, Sara would start yelling. So then, Treelea told me, one night while they were sleeping Sara woke up screaming. I could see Treelea trying not to laugh when she described Sara, waking up to about fifteen mice in her bed. I laughed a little just thinking about it. Then I wondered why Treelea didn't freak when all those mice were in her room, but I shook the thought off. I mean, Treelea owned a mouse herself; she wouldn't freak to see more. Treelea then said the next day Sara talked to Mrs. Horn and got another room.

"WOW," Treelea said after finishing her story and seeing the time on her desk. "It's eleven thirty. I better go to bed. Good night, Anna."

I already know that we are going to be good friends," Treelea said as she got into bed and turned off her light. That was the second time tonight someone said that to me, but hearing it come from Treelea made me smile.

Since I was already unpacked and not really ready for bed myself, I took the opportunity to make a phone call. I knew some of my family didn't sleep until one or two in the morning, and they all probably were wondering if I'd made it okay.

"Hello," someone said on the other side of the phone when I called my house.

"Hey ... it's me, Annadyomene," I said softly so I wouldn't wake Treelea.

"Hey, Anna, it's Brandon. Are you there? How is it?" he asked.

"It's too soon to tell if I like it here. I met my roommate and her boyfriend. They seem nice. I also met the headmistress here, Mrs. Horn. Boy, if looks could kill," I said with a bit of a laugh.

"Ha! So, Anna, Mom's up. Do you want to talk to her?"

"Yeah."

"No? Okay. Well, good night, Anna."

"Brandon, hand the phone over!" I said a little too loudly with a laugh, and then looking over to the other side of the room, I saw Treelea move a bit, but that was it.

"Hello, Anna. Are you still there?" my mom said on the other end of the phone.

"Hi, Mom. I just wanted to say I made it to Brownstone and everything is fine. I checked in with Mrs. Horn, and I have a meeting to get my schedule in her office at 7:30 a.m. sharp, and she warned me not to be late. And I met my roommate Treelea and her boyfriend and ..."

"Anna, Anna, slow down. You are going way too fast, and I can't keep up with you. You sound so excited."

I gave a little giggle. "Sorry. You know how I am when I get excited, have to tell everyone everything."

"Yeah, I know," my mom said with a little laugh.

"Mom, I just wanted you to know that I arrived okay and I'm all moved in and I have a really nice roommate and ... and ... I love you, Mom. Good night."

"Ah, baby, I love you too. Hugs and kisses and have a good night," whispered my mom. Just before I got off the phone I heard her call my name.

"Mom, did you say something?" I asked.

"Yes, I said be careful, Annadyomene. Remember to control yourself. You know what I'm talking about, right?" my mom asked.

"I know, Mom. I'll try to control myself," I whispered to her softly. "Night, Mom," I said, trying to change the conversation.

"Night baby, sweet dreams," my mom said before she hung up the phone.

I shut my cell and started getting ready for bed. When I finally got my PJs on, I crawled into my bed and stared out the window right above it to look at the sky, so dark and filled with such bright sparkling little twinkles of stars. I don't know why, but whenever I look up at the sky, I feel at peace and free.

3

SHOCKING BLUE EYES

One second I was staring out at the moonlit tree next to my window; then the next thing I know, music was booming out of my alarm clock. I forgot I had set it to a song I knew would wake me up, even from a deep sleep. I smiled to myself as the song kept playing.

Then I realized what time it was.

"Oh no—7:20 a.m.!" I almost screamed as I jumped from my bed to the dresser to find something to throw on. "I have to be at Mrs. Horn's office at seven thirty. I'm not even sure how to get there; it was so late last night," I said to myself as I threw on a khaki skirt, with a purple top (one sleeve elbow length, the other a spaghetti strap) with my own saying on the front. "Don't talk behind someone's back if they're behind yours."

I ran a brush through my hair as fast as I could, grabbed a scrunchy and white butterfly hair clips, and did my hair up in a ponytail, putting the clips on both sides of my head. Then I grabbed my backpack, key, and cell phone and ran out the door as fast as I could.

While racing down the hall to the stairs, I focused on remembering my way back to Mrs. Horn's office. Reaching the last stair, I turned to go down the hallway I had seen last night, not even looking where I was going. Big mistake.

WHAM! I knocked right into someone. Papers flew everywhere, and I with them.

"Ow ... oh," I said, lying on the floor.

"I'm so sorry. Are you okay?" I asked, getting up to help the other person I had hit who was trying to collect his papers from the floor.

"Where's the fire, toots?" he asked, looking up at me with a smile on his perfectly tan skin.

He looked into my eyes, and I can't explain why, but I felt excited, embarrassed, giddy, shy, and happy all at once.

Oh no! I thought, *I didn't put on my makeup. I must look like a car crash victim. No wonder he's staring at me.*

"Hi," I said, trying to hide my face by looking at my watch. "It's 7:28 a.m. Oh no! ... I'm going to be late!" I said, frantic, getting up so fast I almost tripped again.

"Late for what?" the guy asked, trying to organize the papers he had finally finished collecting from the floor.

"I have to meet Mrs. Horn in her office now, and she warned me not to be late. Err! I can't do anything right this morning," I said twisting my head around, trying to find her office.

"Here, follow me," he said, still smiling his gorgeous smile at me as he started walking down a sun-lit hallway, which seemed to gleam an aura around him that only I could see.

I remained in a trance until he turned around and said, "Aren't you coming?"

"Sorry ...," I said, walking up to him.

As we walked down the hallway, he turned his head and said, "I'm Liam." His dirty blond hair looked beautiful in the sun light, and I saw his eyes move from mine to my top, reading the words.

"Ha," his laugh also perfect, "that's funny. Where did you buy that top?" he asked, looking at me with those shocking blue eyes.

"I made it," I said looking down the hallway.

"Really? ... Wow! That's so cool. So where did you get the saying?" he asked.

"I made the saying up," I said.

"Do you like making things?" Liam asked.

"Yeah ... I like to make my own stuff sometimes," I said.

Silence echoed through the hallway and finally he said, "Here we are, Mrs. Horn's office."

"Thanks, Liam," I said, looking up once into his eyes, then turning to go into the office. "By the way, Liam ... what's your last name?"

"Huh?"

"Or don't you have one?" I asked

"Oh yeah, Angel," he whispered back.

"What did you call me?"

"No ... no, my name is Angel. Liam Angel," he said.

I thought, *How ironic. This nice, hot guy's last name is Angel.* Pushing away any more thoughts about Liam, I took a deep breath and opened the office door to the waiting doom inside. As I entered Mrs. Horn's office, I felt the coldness before I saw it. Mrs. Horn sat in her chair behind her desk, looking very upset and ready to explode, which I would have given anything to witness, but now didn't seem to be the appropriate time and place. Pity.

"Hello, Mrs. Horn," I said, sitting down in a chair in front of her desk.

"You're late, Miss Ribbon," she said, anger showing on her face.

"I ... I don't think I'm late. It's only ...," I said looking at my watch, "7:32 a.m., Mrs. Horn. I don't th—" I stopped talking when I saw her face. She looked as if I had just slapped her.

"Miss Ribbon, I have a lot to do today without waiting for you, a mere student at that, to show up when you feel like it, and then coming here and trying to pass off some kind of flimsy excuse on top of an already insulting behavior. Do you understand what I'm saying?" she asked as she was leaning over her desk and right into my face.

I just nodded, stunned at what she had said. Now I felt as if I had been slapped.

"Good. Now here's your map to the school and your class schedule. Try not to get too lost in your adventures," she said as an evil smile crept up on her old face.

"Yes, Ma'am."

"You can go now, please, PLEASE, *PLEASE*. I have way too much work to do without anymore from you," she said, staring at me.

I got up and walked to the door.

"Thank you," I said, truly grateful our session had ended.

"Oh, Miss Ribbon," Mrs. Horn said.

I turned around, "Yes?"

"Have a nice day, dear."

What's up with that? As if we're friends? No wonder kids go crazy with all these double messages that adults send them.

I walked out into the hallway. "Ahhhh!" I said to myself just barely more than a whisper. Well, now my face definitely felt like a piece of clay, or at least like a beaten-down piece of putty.

Outside of Mrs. Horn's office, I finally unfolded the paper that the old prune face had said was my classes, and I looked at my schedule.

1st Period: World Mythology 8:20 a.m.–9:20 a.m.

2nd Period: English 9:30 a.m.–10:30 a.m.

3rd Period: Japanese 10:40 a.m.–11:40 p.m.

Lunch: 11:50 p.m.–12:30 p.m.

4th Period: Math 12:40 p.m.–1:40 p.m.

5th Period: P.E. 1:50 p.m.–2:50 p.m.

6th Period: Fashion 3:00 p.m.–4:00 p.m.

Okay I have some time; it's only seven forty. What to do? What to do? I said to myself as I walked down the hallway. "Grrwl." "Ha ha," I laughed. In my rush, I had forgotten to have breakfast, and my stomach had to remind me. Time to eat. I looked at my map of the school to find the lunchroom. "Okay, so I'm here at Mrs. Horn's office and ...," I said, again talking to myself. *I seem to do a lot of that kind of thing lately.* Gliding my finger across the page, I continued searching. "Oh, it's down the next hallway," I said, walking to the end of the corridor and going down the next hallway. Before I even reached the doors, I could hear the kids inside. Once in the huge lunchroom, I could feel eyes running all over me. I didn't look at anyone as I walked to the line and tried to tune out their comments about my outfit. I just stared ahead, waiting in line.

"Look at her clothes."

"Where'd she pick up those things?"

"Weird."

"Where's she from?"

All around me, even when I left the lunchroom with a bag of barbecue chips, I could hear them talking. By the time I walked into World Mythology, my mood had lifted significantly and I felt happier because, for one, if people tried to talk about me, they would get in trouble with the teacher, and two, no one was in the class; I was the first.

So I sat down at a desk, took out my book for the course, and started to read. I had read only a few pages when I heard someone walk in. I turned to see if it was the teacher, but it wasn't; it was Liam. I looked at him, wondering if he remembered me at all. He glanced around the empty room, and then his eyes stopped on me.

"Hey," he said.

"Hey, where is everyone?" I asked.

"You know I never got your name," he said, taking the desk next to me.

"Yeah, I know," I said and then just sat there, staring at him as if he was about to break in two.

"Well?" he leaned over closer to me.

I could almost smell his aftershave. Mmmm, so clean smelling. "Well, what?" I said.

"Well, are you ever going to tell me your name, or do I have to drag you all over this school and then beat it out of you?"

Laughing I said, "Oh, ah ... my name is Annadyomene, but people call me Anna. My name's so long; people just forget ... I'm boring you, aren't I?" I asked.

"Uh, no. Why do you say that?"

My mind went racing. Ugh. *What to say?* That people seem to daydream when I start talking? No. He was probably the first guy to be this close to me and still listen to what I was saying without nodding off or trying to get me to stop talking. And his eyes—would he ever take them off me? "Ah, no reason," I finally blurted out. "I just thought I was; that's all."

"No ... not at all," he said, still staring at me. Then he asked, "So, Annadyomene, can I ask you something?"

"Sure."

"What color are your eyes?"

"Ah ... what color do you see?" I asked as he looked into my eyes again.

"Well, right now, your eyes are green. But when I first met you, I thought they were blue, and then I could have sworn I saw a beautiful shade of purple. So what color are your eyes?" he said, almost plunging into my eyes as his head rested barely an inch from mine.

"Hey, Liam, why are you talking to the new girl?"

Some girl who looked as if she had just stepped out of a fashion magazine sat down beside Liam, rubbing his arm in a familiar, loving way. I should have known a guy like this had a girlfriend. They looked perfect together. How stupid could I have been, to think that he would see anything special in me? Gorgeous blond hair, designer jeans, makeup done to perfection. And those nails—she probably had them done at least once a week. And—ouch—I realized she was the Barbie from last night that had made fun of me and my outfit.

And with her sat Liam, equally perfect but in a much nicer way. What more could I say about Liam? Err ... I felt like such a fool.

"Let's get started, everyone."

The voice shook me out of my thoughts about Liam. I hadn't even realized until that moment that the other students had come into the room.

"Welcome, class, to World Mythology," the teacher continued. "My name is Cumare," he said in a loud voice, making himself heard above the chatter of students.

I made it through that class intact, managing to stay in the background most of the time and just watching what went on among the students.

My next class, English, worked in my favor. With more than half the class girls, the focus seemed more on the teacher, Mr. Tenth, and certainly not on me. And the reason for the attraction? Hmm. What can I say? About thirty years old and single (I guessed since he wore no ring and never talked about a wife or kids), Mr. Tenth looked in shape and had great chocolate-brown, wavy hair. I could barely hold in my laughter, though, when the girl next to me leaned over in the middle of class and whispered, "Isn't he soooooo dreamy?"

"What?"

"Ah ... Mr. Tenth, isn't he dreamy, you know, cute?"

"You're joking, right?" I said back to her. I don't think she even heard me because during this whole little exchange she never took her eyes off Mr. Tenth as he walked back and forth in front of the class.

"Ahh ..." was her only response.

I laughed to myself, realizing how serious she was. Meanwhile, my mind floated a thousand miles away, thinking about someone else. That's probably why I didn't find Mr. Tenth as attractive as the other girls seemed to find him.

"Oh get over it; he's probably taken," I whispered to myself when English ended and I was walking out the door. *We probably won't see each other that much, anyway. It sure doesn't look like I'll have him in any of my classes*, I tried consoling myself. Just as I was thinking all this, I heard someone call my name and turned around.

"Anna, hey, how were your classes?" Treelea asked as we walked outside to the beautiful courtyard.

"Ah ... they were okay, I guess," I said trying to smile when we sat down at a bench.

"Who is it?" Treelea asked a smile on her face.

"Who is it? Who is what? I mean what are you talking about?" I asked looking at her, trying to look confused.

"I know that look. You met some guy, didn't you? ... Who is it? Maybe I know him," she said, looking around at everyone in the court-yard. "Come on; you can tell me. I won't tell anyone."

"Well ... I think he already has a girlfriend," I said, looking at my English book.

"I'll tell you if he has a girlfriend. I know everyone here. So what's his name?" Treelea asked a little excited, turning back to look at the kids one more time before looking at me.

"His name is ... Liam," I said, looking down again, waiting for Treelea's reaction.

"Ha ha," she laughed.

Ouch! That hurt. I certainly hadn't expected that.

"No .... I'm sorry. I'm not laughing at you. It's just so funny," she said, still giggling.

"Well, I don't see what's so funny," I said, more than a little upset. *And why is she still laughing?*

"Ha ha ... Didn't you say you thought he had a girlfriend?" she asked the giggling dying down a bit.

"If I say yes are you going to start laughing again?" I asked, looking her in the face.

"I'm sorry. I just find it ironic. I was going to introduce you and Liam, but it turns out you guys met on your own. And to answer your question, no! Liam doesn't have a girlfriend," she giggled.

"Really? Well in World Mythology this morning, there was a girl that acted very friendly to him, and I just thought that the two of them were ..."

"Well, you thought wrong, Anna. I know the exact girl you're talking about, and let's just say … mmm ... no, they are not going together. I swear."

"Yeah, really? I mean, you know her?"

"I'm pretty sure you're talking about Jenny, Jenny Fair," Treelea said.

"Oh, are you guys friends?" I asked.

"Jenny and I? No! She's so rude," Treelea said.

"Well, that's good to know. I met Jenny—or as I like to call her, Barbie—last night," I said.

"Oh really? What did Jenny-Barbie say?" Treelea asked, smiling when she said "Jenny-Barbie."

"Before or after she made fun of my outfit?"

"She made fun of your outfit? What did she say?"

I took a deep breath and told Treelea pretty much everything that had happened my first night. Treelea looked angry when I told her what Jenny had said about my outfit, looking as if it had come from a flea market. But she laughed when I said how I had shot back that if my clothes had come from a flea market I would look just like her. Then I filled her in on everything up to this point.

"She's going with Trent Stone, but she's always had a thing for Liam. I mean ALWAYS!" Treelea said, rolling her eyes.

"So do you know if Liam likes anyone?" I asked, trying to get more out of this conversation.

"No ... he never goes out with anyone," Treelea said.

"Why not?" I asked.

"I don't know. All the girls in the school love him. But he doesn't ask anyone on a date. He'll talk to everyone, but no date. I sometimes feel bad for him," Treelea said, deep in thought.

"Why do you feel bad for him?" I asked.

"Well ..." Treelea said, looking around us, "I feel bad because we all go on group dates and he doesn't have a date ... and there're other reasons, but I'm not allowed to say."

"We?" I asked wondering how many people were in the "we" part and what was Treelea not allowed to say?

"My other friends, Kara, Andy, Demaid, and my twin brother, Nicky, Sparnik, that's Demaid's brother, and Sandy, but they're older than we are, and Martin and I make an even eight. So Liam sometimes doesn't come with us, because it would be uneven," Treelea said, looking a little sad.

Until hands from behind her covered her eyes and a voice said, "Guess who I am, and if you get it right you win a kiss."

Then I turned around and saw Martin with a smile on his face.

"Hmm ... Tony," Treelea said with a smile on her face.

Martin quickly faced her. "Who's Tony?" he asked, concerned.

"Oh, it's my other boyfriend. I didn't want you to find out this way, but now that you know …," Treelea said sarcastically and shrugged.

"Oh, so you have another boyfriend, do you?" Martin asked, a smile returning to his face. Treelea nodded with a smile. "Well, I guess I should find another girlfriend," he said, looking around the courtyard. Then he looked back at Treelea and said, "But first I have to dump my old one." Then Martin picked Treelea up in his arms and said, swinging her around, "Hmm ... Anna, where do you think I should dump my old girlfriend?"

"Okay, okay, I give up!" Treelea said, laughing, so Martin put her back down on the ground.

"You two ...," I said, shaking my head with a smile, as both Martin and Treelea were laughing.

While all this fun and excitement was happening, I looked down at my watch. "It's almost ten forty ... I have a class starting soon, Japanese, Room 47. Where's that?" I asked Martin and Treelea as I gathered my stuff.

"Here, we'll show you, Anna," Treelea said, holding Martin's hand as we walked to another brick building.

By the time we made it to the classroom, I could hear the teacher inside, already talking.

"The class already started. What should I do?" I asked, peeking around the open door.

"Go in, Anna," Treelea whispered.

I took a deep breath and started sneaking into the room. Halfway to a seat, I heard a voice announce my whereabouts.

"Ah ... I see we have a new student here today," the teacher said to the class, making everyone turn to look at me. "Why don't you introduce yourself to everyone?"

I felt my cheeks burn. "I'm ... I'm Anna, Anna Ribbon," I stuttered, looking around the room at everyone silently laughing. Well not everyone was doing that. One person in the classroom just looked at me with sympathy, Liam Angel. He was sitting in the second row, staring at me like everyone else was at that moment. When I thought I'd had enough punishment, I sat down at the first empty desk and kept my eyes glued to the floor.

"Miss Ribbon ...," the teacher called.

I looked up. "Yes?" I asked.

"This is not your full name; am I correct?" the teacher asked, sounding pleased.

"Yes, Ma'am, you are correct," I said, looking only at the teacher. A short, somewhat chunky Japanese woman, she looked forty-something, with black hair. She also had a kind and gentle smile on her face.

"How do you pronounce your full name?" she asked with genuine curiosity. Her kindhearted smile told me she wasn't trying to be mean, but this question at that moment felt very mean and cruel to me.

"Anna … dime … a … knee. Annadyomene," I said, looking down again.

"What a nice name. And now, class, on today's …"

FIRE!

The rest of my Japanese class melted into one big blur. Until I heard a voice next to me and I snapped back into reality.

"Hey, Annadyomene."

I looked up to see Liam standing in front of me. Class had ended, and everyone else had left.

"So did you want to have lunch?" Liam asked, smiling a sweet smile.

"Sure," I said, gathering my books and walking out the door.

"So how do you like the school?" Liam asked as we walked outside past the courtyard to the building with the lunchroom and dorms.

"Good ... Well ... it was a bit weird in my English class," I said with a little laugh.

"Why's that?" Liam asked.

"Well, apparently every girl in my English class is in love with the teacher, Mr. Tenth, so when this one girl asked me, 'Isn't he dreamy?' I laughed, thinking she was joking," I confessed to Liam.

Just as we walked into the lunchroom, both of us reached for the same soda at the same time. I quickly pulled my hand away, and Liam commented, "You like root beer, too?"

"Yeah, I do. Hey, what kind of pizza do you like?"

"I'm really into sausage with black olives," he said.

"I ... I can't believe this. That is my absolute favorite, too, I swear!"

After we both got our pizza, we looked at the tables filled with students.

"Hey, Annadyomene, you don't mind if we sit with my friends, do you? It's okay; I understand if you don't want to since this is your first day and everything."

"No, no that's fine," I answered although I had secretly hoped that we could have just sat and talked between ourselves. I was also hoping that Jenny-Barbie wasn't going to join us. I wasn't sure if I could handle her attitude throughout the whole lunchtime.

Liam led the way and headed for a round table towards the corner with eight people talking to one another. I recognized Treelea and Martin so, when they looked up at me, I waved slightly.

"Guys, this is Annadyomene," Liam said.

"Hi ... but you can just call me Anna," I said, nervously looking around the table. All the kids looked about the same age as I was, around sixteen, except for a boy and a girl across the table who appeared to be about eighteen.

"Okay, guys, quiet for a minute. I want Annadyomene to meet you all. Okay, Anna, this is Kara Lawnie in the dark red top; this carrot top is Andy Woods. And just to let you know, these two have been together since birth."

Everyone laughed and did a little teasing back and forth.

"This guy here is Nicky Castle, and his better half is the marvelous Demaid Newberry ... who can never figure out what color she wants her hair. She's tried so many varieties that we've all forgotten what her real color is."

"Very funny, Liam," said Demaid. "Don't mind him, Anna; he doesn't know what he's talking about half the time."

"When it comes to your hair color, no one knows how to talk about it," Liam said back, and we all started laughing. Then we have Martin and Treelea over there," Liam said and then continued, "which brings us to the last part of the table. These two are Sandy Jones and Sparnik Newberry."

"Nice to meet all of you," I said, sitting down next to Liam.

Then everyone started chatting and laughing again. Even Liam and I talked a bit about nothing, really. But with him, the words didn't matter ... I felt a bit giddy. We'd only met each other that morning, so I felt weird feeling so taken with this guy. How could anyone feel that way with someone she'd known for hardly three hours? But he didn't seem like a stranger ... not to me. I felt I'd known him all my life, and yet I still had a lot to learn about Liam Angel.

"So, Anna, we're going to the movies tonight. Do you want to come as Liam's date?" Demaid asked looking at me with a mischievous smile on her face. That quickly brought me back to reality. She never even noticed Liam choking on his slice of pizza.

"Uh ... what?" I asked, my cheeks burning.

"Demaid," Liam said, looking irritated at Demaid.

"So, Anna, do you want to hang out with us tonight?" Demaid asked.

"Ah ... sure, if I don't have too much homework to do," I said, giving myself an escape if Liam wouldn't want to hang out with me that night.

"Homework ... homework, who does homework anymore? In fact who gives homework anymore?" piped up Sparnik with a huge grin.

"This could explain your grades, Sparnik," Martin said with a chuckle.

"Trust me, Anna; he wants you to go," Demaid said, looking at Liam with a smug smile. Liam looked back at her with an annoyed look on his face.

"No, Annadyomene, you should come," Liam said, letting a half smile sneak over his face before turning back to eat.

Why do I do this to myself? Maybe he doesn't like me, I thought. *Maybe he likes someone else.*

"You're wrong," Demaid said, looking at me. Everyone at the table stared at Demaid, then at me.

What is she talking about? Did I say something out loud? I asked myself. And then to Demaid, I said, "Excuse me ... why did you say that?"

"What?" Demaid asked, trying to look innocent, but I could see right through the weak cover up.

"You said, 'You're wrong,' to me. Why?" I asked, looking only at Demaid. Then she looked up at me, all serious and determined, and I felt a headache coming. It hit so hard I had to grab my head to stop the spinning.

"Demaid, stop! You're hurting her!"

I heard Liam's angry whisper next to me, and then I felt it coming.

"Oh no!" I whispered, waiting for the screaming.

"FIRE!" someone in the lunchroom screamed and in the garbage bin, a little ways away from the table where I was sitting, a small but contained fire blazed, smoking up the area. I had tried to hold it back, but sometimes I just can't stop it from coming, like then. You see, the fire was totally my fault; I couldn't control it when I got that headache. *But, how did I get that headache?* I asked myself.

I watched as my English teacher, Mr. Tenth put out the fire and asked, "Who did this?"

Yeah, as if we were all going to raise our hands and confess to it. He might have really good looks, but I just wondered how much he had between those ears of his.

Looking around the lunchroom, I saw not a single body move.

Mr. Tenth let out a big sigh, and dropping his shoulders in his disappointment with having no willing confession, he walked out of the room, more than likely going to Mrs. Horn's office to tell her about the whole scenario. The poor guy really lacked in the brain department. Didn't he realize Mrs. Horn would just use him as her sounding board in her aggravation—for having no culprit, for having to replace that garbage bin? And did he have any idea how expensive those bins are and blah ... blah ... blah ... Not one word would be exchanged about any students getting hurt or burnt during the fire—for nobody cared.

Back in the lunchroom, everyone was looking back and forth at each other, questioning what had just happened.

"What was that?" Liam asked, staring at the table near the bin.

I looked up at him, still holding my head. What if he knew? Would he still talk to me, or would he think I'm a nut? Then I noticed my math class was going to start soon.

"Well I have to go, you guys, or I'll be late for another class. Talk to you later. Bye." I waved to everyone. Some waved back, but others looked nervous, still not knowing or understanding what had just happened.

As I walked away, Demaid's voice—a mere whisper—said, "I didn't mean to hurt her. I don't know what happened. It was out of my control."

I made it to math just in time to hear my teacher, Miss Brook, call my name. As I responded, I settled in behind an empty table; everyone else had a partner. Then just before she called the last name on the list, Demaid walked in.

"Sorry I'm late," Demaid said to the teacher. Then she looked straight at me. "Yeah, there was a small explosion in the lunchroom, and half the school is gone."

"That's all right, Demaid," the teacher said with a smile. I could tell the teacher was real easy-going and a little preoccupied, to say the least.

Demaid sat down in the seat next to me, put her bag on the floor, and stared at the teacher.

Did I do something wrong? I asked myself. *Why is she acting weird around me? And why did I have that headache attack in the lunchroom? What is going on around here? I haven't had one of those episodes in a long, long time. Something ... or someone ... triggered it, but who?*

"Class, today you and your partner are going to take a test together," Miss Brook announced with a smile. Then she looked at my table with an almost glazed over look and said, "Demaid, you and Anna are excused from the test today because Anna is new here, and I don't want you to take this test by yourself. You may do whatever you want."

Demaid turned towards me with a smile and asked, "Do you want to go somewhere?"

"Sure. Where?" I asked with a shrug, smiling but also thinking how weird it was that the teacher would just let us go anywhere.

"It's a surprise; come on," Demaid said as she grabbed her backpack and stood up. I grabbed my bag and started walking to the door with Demaid. As I did, I could hear a few of the kids in class mumbling. They were probably jealous that we were skipping class and they had to stay. When we were outside, Demaid started walking behind the building.

"Where are you going?" I asked.

Demaid looked over her shoulder at me with a smile. "I told you it's a surprise." She picked up her speed and just kept walking after that, so I followed her. Then after a few minutes, she stopped and sat under a big, beautiful cherry tree.

"Come, sit down," Demaid said, patting the ground next to her, so I joined her. "I wanted to ask you something. That's why we're out here, alone," she said, looking up at the blossoms on the tree. "If I ask you something, will you tell me the truth?" she asked, looking at me with a serious look on her face.

"I'll try ... ask away," I said, wondering what could be so important that we had to come all the way out here behind the school.

"Did you start that fire in the lunchroom today?" she asked, looking at me in a funny way, as if she were reading a book.

"What are you talking about?" A pause dangled as I tried to figure out what to say next. "How could I when I was next to Liam?" I looked at her, blocking my true answer from my mind.

"That's what I'm wondering."

"Can I ask you something?"

Demaid nodded.

I took a deep breath and then said, "This might sound silly but ... Did you ..." Before I could ask my question, a frown appeared on Demaid's face. "What's wrong?" I asked, waiting for her to say something.

"Nothing ... nothing at all. Keep going," Demaid said, twirling a cherry blossom between her fingers.

"Ah ... what I want to ask is, and this might sound nuts but, did you do something to me today at lunch before the fire?" I asked.

"What do you mean?" Demaid asked, still looking at the cherry blossoms between her fingers.

"Well, first you said, "You're wrong," to me when I said nothing, and when I asked you about it, you acted as if you were confused. Then when I looked you in the face, I got a horrible headache, and I heard Liam whisper, "Demaid, stop you're hurting her!" So that's why I'm wondering what's going on. Can you tell me?"

When Demaid didn't answer, we just sat under the cherry tree in silence for a while. Finally Demaid asked, "So what's your next class?"

"P.E. Why?" I asked.

A smile crept up her face. "If you have P.E., we have to go now. This is great! Everyone in our group has P.E. together. So come on; this should be fun," Demaid said, getting up and slowly walking away.

I followed her with a million new questions rolling around inside of me. But knowing Demaid wouldn't answer any of them because she hadn't answered my first one, I kept my mouth shut.

Once we got to the gym, Demaid started talking non-stop about our P.E. class.

"You can do anything you want for thirty minutes, then we all go swimming, okay?"

"Okay ...," I said looking around the enormous gym.

"Here," Demaid said, handing me a pair of blue shorts and a T-shirt, then a blue swimsuit. "Now, let's go get changed." And Demaid led the way to the locker rooms.

When we were finally dressed in our not-so-beautiful gym clothes, we walked out to the gym.

5

THINGS GET ROUGH

"**H**EADS UP!" someone shouted in the gym as a volleyball came towards my head.

Startled, I jumped back and lost my balance. Thankfully, someone behind me blocked my fall and caught me, keeping me from falling straight on my butt, which would have made a very embarrassing situation. As I pushed forward from the person's hold, or should I say catch, I could feel his arms, very muscular, nice and strong. *This person really must work out*, I thought

"Obviously, you're not a sports girl," Liam whispered in my ear.

He was so close at this point that I could feel his breath on my neck, sending chills right through me.

Straightening myself up, I turned and said, "Well … who said I was?" Both of us started to laugh a little.

"Okay, you win. Maybe I'm not a sports girl, but I can fight," I said, teasing him into a challenge.

"Well, then come right this way," Liam said, taking my shoulders in his big strong hands and leading me toward some doors.

When we walked through the doors, I knew it was a fighting class. And I was the only girl there. Forget a challenge. I had entered the slaughterhouse.

"Do you think you could fight anyone here?" Liam asked me, trying not to laugh.

My eyes swept the room, taking in all the guys. Then I turned and looked at Liam, into those eyes. Ah yes, I bet those eyes had a melting effect on many a girl. But they didn't stop me. "If it's a challenge, I accept," I said with a smile.

"Who's first?" I asked, teasingly running circles around him.

Liam looked shocked at first. Then walking over to an empty mat, he said, "Bring it on, sweetheart. I'll try to go easy on you."

"You'll take it easy on me? Really? That's funny I was just thinking the same thing about you. Come on then. I'll try to do the same, but no promises."

I knew by the look on Liam's face that we were both going to enjoy this little bit of sparring.

"Now before we get started and get a little too physical, did you want some head gear or knee pads?" Liam asked.

"No, I'm fine. Do you need some? I can wait until you get them," I said, tilting my head to one side with a smile.

"You ready?" Liam asked.

I nodded, still with a smile.

Then he ran towards me and grabbed my shoulders, trying to take me down to the floor. I used his momentum, and grabbing his shoulders while I put my foot on his stomach, I fell on my back, making him flip over my head. THUMP!

Oh no! I killed him! How could I be so stupid, stupid, stupid. The first guy I think I could get together with and I go and kill him on the mat, in the gym, while showing off my wrestling. How stupid!

I got up as fast as I could and crawled to him.

"Liam! Oh my gosh! Liam say something to me, ANYTHING, please …," I said. "Ah, come on, Liam; say something."

"Something," whispered Liam, rubbing the back of his head and trying to right himself into a sitting position.

"Oh, you clown. I really thought I had kil—I mean—hurt you."

Liam started to laugh, "You didn't think you had killed me, did you?"

"Of course not. I knew you were playing around with me. I was just joking back, that's all. Anyway, what's so funny about getting hurt?" I asked looking down at Liam's pathetic position on the mat.

"Well for starters, I can't believe you flipped me. I thought you were going to be easy to take down." Liam stood up and smoothed back his hair where he had been rubbing the sore spot. Then he poked his finger into my side arm and said, "I want a rematch."

"Anytime you want, buddy."

"How about … right now!" And Liam swung into action, trying to catch me off guard.

This wrestling move is just weird. Why is he doing the same thing he did the last time? I asked myself. Then, like before, I flipped him and again crawled to his side. Why was he replaying everything we just did?

"Surprise!" he whispered. Then he grabbed my shoulders and pushed me down on the ground. When he was on top of me, pinning my arms over my head, he said with a smile, "I win."

I giggled a little, but then I noticed his eyes looking down, and I realized my T-shirt was showing my stomach and exposing my scar. He looked back into my eyes, and I saw through his eyes not only questions but the concern he felt within.

"What happened?" Liam asked as he released my arms and looked back at my scar.

"I don't want to talk about it," I whispered now with a frown. Then I turned my head.

"Why?" he said.

"I said I don't want to talk about it," I repeated firmly, trying not to be mean to Liam but having no desire to bring back those haunted memories.

"Come on, kids; it's swim time," I heard Coach Clayborne say. I twisted myself from Liam's body and walked to the locker rooms, not even looking back at him. When I walked into the locker room, I met up with Kara, Treelea, Sandy, and Demaid.

"What's up?" Treelea asked when I walked in and sat down on the bench.

"Nothing. Why do you ask?" I looked up as Treelea shrugged.

"You coming?" Sandy asked with a big smile as she shut her locker. "Coach gives us only a minute to get our suits on."

"Yeah. I'll be right there," I said, smiling back at all of them. Demaid looked at me with a kind of sad smile as they all left the locker room. When they were gone, I sighed and said out loud, "Finally, some peace."

By the time I walked out of the locker rooms, a couple of kids were already in the massive pool, and everyone else was standing in a line facing the water.

"Hey, Anna, over here," Treelea called with a smile.

I walked over and stood next to her and Demaid.

"So, are you a good swimmer?" Demaid asked.

"Yeah ... you could say water and I are best friends," I said, smiling at my private joke. *Of course, we're best friends. Just like fire, don't I control it?* I thought to myself. *It would blow their minds to know that, but then they would really bust if they knew—*

"New girl ... Hey new girl!" Coach Clayborne called.

"Yes sir?"

"You're next; get ready."

"Yes sir," I said as I walked over to an open lane and slowly slipped into the water. Dunking my head under to wet my hair, I joined the others, matching my strokes to theirs. It seemed a snail's pace to me, but if I went my normal speed, people would've wondered how I could go faster than a shark. So while the others struggled to go as fast as they could, all out of breath and gasping for air, I just swam leisurely along, having my fun—that is, until I got out of the pool.

Liam was staring at me, but I loved the thought of him looking at me. Then looking over Liam's shoulder, another student was staring at me with the most evil smile on his face. I thought I recognized him, but I couldn't quite place him. Where had I seen that face before? And that grin ... that wicked, wicked grin ... And then I remembered. How could I forget? The last time we saw each other, we both gave each other scars. *Breathe, Anna, just breathe*, I told myself as I walked over to Treelea and Demaid.

"You okay, Anna? You look pale," Treelea said, concern in her voice, as she turned to see what I was looking at to make me go so pale.

I nodded. What else could I do? My mouth was dry, and I felt numb all over. After a few moments of toweling myself off, I whispered, "Maybe you guys could tell the coach I don't feel very good and I have to lie down in my room."

"Sure. Do you want some help getting back to the room?" Treelea asked.

I shook my head no and started walking away. Then I heard someone behind me whisper in my ear.

"Don't you remember me, darlin'? ... Do you still have your keep-sake? I have mine. It looks real cool, all the way up my arm, one perfect line from my wrist to my shoulder."

I just kept walking, not even looking at his evil face. The thought of him smiling about this disgusted me. I wanted to turn and slap the grin right off his smug face.

"Oh, come on ... Stop for a minute ... Come on, baby. You know you like me. You know you do. Don't fight it," he said, rubbing my arm and then giving it a bit of a squeeze.

"Ugh! You are so gross. Don't touch me. I mean it!" I said in a growl of a whisper. Without looking at him or letting any of the others see, I made a face directed straight towards him. He caught it, and then he did a really stupid thing and grabbed my left arm and swung me around to face him.

"Stop it," I said. "You are such a pig. I don't want you to touch me. Understand?" I said in a low voice right in his face, which was now within inches of mine. He tightened his grip on my arm. "I said let go, you scum-bag."

"And what are you going to do if I don't? Cry like a baby? Or, better yet, run and tell Mommy and Daddy on me?" he whispered sarcastically.

"Isn't that what *you* do best, call on your mommy or daddy when things get rough?" I said in a cool voice and with a smirk.

He looked angry at first, then he squeezed my arm more, and pulled me closer to him.

"I told you to stop. That's hurting me. I warned you ..." WHACK! I hit him hard in the face, and—I won't lie—it felt good to hit him and see the complete shock crawl over his stupid face.

"You asked for it," I said.

"Why you bit—" He didn't get to finish because of the yelling.

"Hey! Hey! What's going on over there?" Coach Clayborne yelled.

"Oh great. Here comes the coach," I said.

"Come on, students. I asked what is going on over here. Now I need some answers. I'm waiting, and somebody better start talking," Coach said.

"Go ahead, baby. Why don't you explain to Coach Clayborne what we were just talking about?" I said, tilting my head to one side, a mocking smile on my face.

"What happened here? Are you bleeding, man? ... Did this girl hit you, Trent?" Coach Clayborne asked.

"Nah ... we were just clowning around. Huh, honey?" This time Trent looked at me with his head tilted and a stupid-looking grin on his face.

"You sure? ... You're okay? Nothing happened?" asked Coach.

"Nothing happened, just got a little carried away with horsing around; that's all," Trent said.

"Okay ... The pool isn't the place to be horsing around, you know, Trent. See to it you knock it off in the future, or I'll have you benched. You got that, son? Okay ... okay ... everyone back to your swimming. Go on. Back to your swimming. Nothing to see here," Coach Clayborne yelled. He then held up his whistle and blew an ear-splitting sound that echoed throughout the pool area. Everyone squealed and held his or her ears because of the sound.

"You ... you make me sick. Stay away from me. You hear me?" I said.

"Ahh, come on. It was just a little joke. Don't you have any sense of humor? Anyway, I want to ask you—"

6

A Scar to Remember

"Liam! Hey, Liam!" I shouted over to the side of the pool. "Can you help me get back to my room, please?" I asked before Trent could finish his sentence.

Liam smiled at me as he walked up to face me, turning his back purposely on Trent, who was now fuming and trying to move closer to me in order to finish his sentence.

"Sure. Come on," Liam said. Then he took my arm and led me to the door to the girls' locker room.

"Go ahead and get ready, and I'll wait for you outside the locker area. Don't worry about that jerk; he won't bother you again today. I'll make sure of that," said Liam.

"What a shining knight you are, Liam," Trent mocked as he passed Liam on his way into the boys' locker room

"Drop it, Trent. If you weren't such a jerk already ..."

"You'd what? Drop me? I doubt it, Liam," said Trent with a low laugh.

"You know what, Trent?" Liam said, balling his fists.

"Liam," I said, shaking my head no.

"Just knock it off; that's all," said Liam.

Then we both entered our respective locker rooms to change. Within a few minutes, after I had showered and gotten dressed, I went out to meet up with Liam again.

"I'm sorry I'm late. I couldn't get to the mirror—too many girls around trying to get beautiful, which should take them another couple of hours if not longer," I said. "Sorry ... I shouldn't have said that. I'm not in a very good mood."

"I understand. Trent has a way of bringing out the worst in people," said Liam.

❧

When we were safely in my dorm room, alone together, Liam sat down next to me on my bed. I felt so good with him, and I didn't want to ruin the moment by talking, especially about Trent.

Liam finally broke the silence. "So tell me how did it feel?"

"How did what feel?" I said.

"You know, how did it feel to punch that jerk?"

"Oooh!" I whispered. "It was … yeah … it felt really good." I started to laugh as I said that.

"What did he do anyway?" Liam asked.

I stopped laughing and looked into his eyes. Could I tell him everything? I asked myself. Yes, I could. I could see it in his eyes; he won't make fun of me.

"You're sure you want to know? Really?" I said, giving him a chance to back out and run for the hills.

"Yeah, I do. Go ahead. I'm all ears, and I've nowhere to go for awhile so tell me everything you want me to know," he said with a slight smile at the corner of his lips, saying to me that it really couldn't be as bad as I made it.

So I took a deep breath and poured it all out. "Well, about a year ago, I was hanging out with some friends when five guys jumped us, and we all ran. I wasn't as fast as my friends, so the guys cornered me. I thought maybe I could talk to them and just work out whatever problem they had with us. But I never got the chance. One of the guys pulled out a knife, two grabbed my arms, and another covered my mouth. The first guy ... swung the knife ... and ... got me. The knife ... cut me ..."

Saying not a word, Liam reached for my hand and held it. With our hands touching, I felt a tremendous connection between us, a feeling I had never experienced before. I knew that Liam understood what I was saying—not just the words of the story but also how much I needed someone to listen to me. He sensed what mattered to me, and I felt safe in continuing even though the memories still hurt.

"It sliced ... my stomach ..., and ... I hadn't started to bleed that bad, or ... I didn't think so. I thought it was a small cut, but ... then the blood ..."

Liam leaned over and lay sideways on the bed. "Don't stop, Anna. I want to hear everything," he whispered.

I swallowed hard and kept going. "Well, I'm not the only one with a scar. The guy who cut me also got one that night. Only his scar is on his arm, right above his wrist."

"You mean the jerk was Trent?" asked Liam, sitting up straight on the bed again and releasing my hand.

"Yeah, it was Trent, but I didn't know that then. I'd never seen him before that night," I said, searching in Liam's eyes for what he was thinking.

"Anna, please tell me the rest. I need, I mean, I want to know what this jerk did," said Liam.

"When the blade cut into me, something happened, something snapped inside me. I was so hot and angry all at once. The next thing I remember was the fire."

"Fire?" asked Liam.

"Yes, fire ... fire went up the blade of his knife and right up his arm, burning that line of a scar he has."

"No harm to him," Liam said with a touch of contempt in his voice.

"I didn't know what happened at first. He grabbed his arm in pain and was yelling, calling me every name imaginable. Someone from the neighborhood called the cops. Hearing the sirens, he and his buddies ran off just before the cops arrived. Before they ran, one of them called out Trent's name and said for him to run, too."

Liam sat on the bed for a few minutes, taking in all he had just heard. Finally, he broke the silence. "So you think you burned him. But how?"

"If I tell you that part, you'll think I'm nuts."

"Stop saying that. I won't. I want to know, Anna," said Liam, taking my hand again just like before and giving it a little squeeze for extra reassurance.

"Anna, you're shaking," he said.

"I'm afraid."

"Afraid of what?" he said.

"I'm afraid you'll think I'm crazy," I said, choking back the tears.

"No, I won't. I promise," he said.

"I can do … things, Liam … And the things I do aren't normal, well, not by most people's standards. Like my eyes … You noticed them. My eyes aren't normal."

"I love your eyes, Anna." And Liam touched my cheek ever so gently, as if I were the only person in his world at that moment. I felt so safe and so secure with Liam. I only hoped that when I woke up I would remember this sweet dream because nothing like the way Liam was looking into my eyes with so much love could ever be more than a fairy-tale dream. How well I knew that all girls have such dreams and, however wonderful, we must wake up and realize that what we thought was real can never be. But Liam … Oh Liam was real. I felt his hand in mine, I saw his eyes with mine, and I heard his voice gently run through my whole body. I knew Liam was more than just another fairy tale.

I closed my eyes and smiled. When he was with me, I forgot everything bad. How could you know someone for a day and like them so much? Just then the door opened and Treelea and Martin had broken the magical moment. They remained standing in the doorway, staring at Liam and me with big smiles on their faces.

"What?" I said, wishing for our privacy for just a few more minutes. I hoped that my voice didn't give that away. After all, I was the new kid and Treelea had as much right to the room as I did. I certainly didn't want to seem rude.

"Nothing."

"Okay," I said back, standing up and smoothing down my top, anything to look away from the situation.

"Sorry if we interrupted anything ... but I have to get ready for the movies. You're still going, right, Anna?" Treelea asked. I could feel my cheeks burning.

"Yeah, I'm still going ... Wait—what time is it?" I asked.

"It's six o'clock."

"Oh no. I missed my fashion class," I whispered more to myself than to anyone else.

"What's had you guys so distracted all this time?" Martin asked a sarcastic smile on his face.

"Martin, you know as well as I do how time flies when you're having a good time," Treelea said, returning his sarcastic smile.

"Ha ... ha. Oh, you're so funny," Liam said, shaking his head.

"We'll meet you guys by the cars, okay?" Martin asked.

Treelea nodded and then kissed him on the check.

Liam got up. "See ya," he said with a smile for me.

"Bye," I said with the same smile. Then the two left.

"What was that?" Treelea asked.

"What do you mean?" I asked.

"I mean, what's going on with you two? I've never seen Liam look like that before."

"Look like what?"

"You should know," Treelea laughed. "You have the same look on your face."

I blushed and turned my face away quickly before she noticed and said something about that too.

"So what's going on?"

"What's going on is ... I don't know what to wear," I said giving a half laugh.

"I think I have something for you," Treelea said mysteriously, and I knew she wasn't going to let me off that easy.

At six twenty-five, Treelea and I walked to the parking lot to meet the others.

"Are you sure I look okay?" I asked Treelea, still feeling a bit odd in her clothes. I was wearing her light blue sandals, knee-high jean skirt, and a white T-shirt under a wavy, light blue, spaghetti-strap top. But I had my own jewelry—silver heart earrings and a necklace with a penguin on it—and wore my hair flipped to the right side.

"You look hot. Plus Liam's favorite color is blue," Treelea confessed.

"That's why you told me to wear all blue," I said.

Treelea just smiled and looked ahead.

"Ah ... who's driving?" I asked.

"Sparnik and Liam."

"Liam can drive? How long has he been driving?"

"A year. And wait till you see his car," Treelea said as we approached our group. She went into Martin's open arms, and they kissed. Then someone whispered into my ear, "You look hot." I turned around and looked into Liam's eyes, tilting my head to the side in a loving way. He was wearing a black T-shirt that showed off some of his muscles and a pair of blue jeans.

"You don't look so bad yourself," I said to Liam, and he came closer to me.

"Okay, so, Liam, you're taking Martin, Treelea, and Sandy ... 'Kay?" Sparnik asked with a smile. Everyone turned to look at Liam and me.

"Ah ... what? I thought I was taking Annadyomene," Liam said, looking away from me for a second to look at Sparnik.

"Just making sure you're listening. Anyway, I'll take Sandy, Demaid, and Nicky. Okay, let's go," Sparnik said, getting into a shiny black Ford pickup.

"So why am I going with you this time?" I heard Demaid whisper to Sparnik before they got into the truck.

"Because I don't want a repeat of the lunchroom," Sparnik whispered back.

Then Liam grabbed my hand and pulled me toward a dark blue Dodge Charger.

"Sweet car," I said as Treelea and Martin got in the back.

"You like it?" Liam asked, getting in behind the wheel, a smile on his face. I couldn't help but smile, too, sitting in the front seat, looking at him.

"What?" Liam asked.

"Nothing," I said, looking out the window on my right so he couldn't see me blush. He had that effect on me, and I loved it.

"Are we ready?" Liam asked.

We all nodded and said, "Yeah," and Liam drove out of the parking lot and headed down the main street.

"So what movie are we going to see?" I asked, breaking the silence in the car because nobody was talking and I hated the silence.

"We're going to Kara's house to watch some old movies. I don't know the names," Martin said, shrugging.

"Oh ... so you guys like to see old movies. Like which ones?" I asked, looking at Liam. He held my gaze for a second and then turned back to look at the road.

"*The Graduate, West Side Story, Romeo and Juliet, The Color Purple, My Cousin Vinny, Somewhere in Time*, stuff like that. What do you like?" Liam asked.

"I like those, too. And others—*The Scarlet Letter, The Birds, Ever After*. And I love musicals like *The Wizard of Oz, Sound of Music, The King and I, Fiddler on the Roof*. And let's not forget the infamous *Animal House*. When I said the last one, Liam started laughing so hard Martin had to remind him he was still on the road.

"Sorry," Liam said, drying his eyes because he was laughing so hard.

"So I guess you've seen it," I said.

Liam nodded and then said, "Yes, but I find it double funny because you're the only girl I know who's seen *that* movie."

"Oh ... Treelea, you've seen *Animal House*, haven't you?" I asked.

"No ... I don't think so. What's it about?" Treelea asked.

Liam and I started laughing.

"Liam, why don't you tell her what *Animal House* is about?" I said, still laughing.

"Oh no ... I'm not telling," Liam said, like me, still laughing. "You'll just have to see for yourself, Treelea."

"How about *Somewhere in Time*? Did you see it? Like it?" I asked Liam, looking at him while he drove.

"Yeah. You?" he asked.

"I loved it. Especially the part when Christopher Reeves meets Jane Seymour on the once beautiful beach. So romantic. What a classic."

"That was a good part," Liam said, nodding his head in agreement.

"I learned something from that movie," I said.

"And what was that—people in love stay together even after death?" Liam asked.

"That, and if I were in that movie, I would never pull a penny from my pocket," I said looking at Liam with a smile.

"You are so comical. Are you always like this?" Liam asked.

"Not always."

"What do you mean 'Not always'?"

"I'm not comical if people don't get my jokes, which is 90 percent of the time."

"Oooh, I see," Liam said with a smile, looking at me.

Then we pulled up into a driveway of a two-level brown house and got out of the car. Andy and Kara were already inside making treats when Kara's mother, Grace, escorted all of us inside.

"Hey, guys, you can head downstairs if you don't want to help with the treats," Kara said, acting like a mom talking to her kids. Everyone headed down stairs, except Andy, Kara, Liam, and me.

"I don't mind helping. I have a big family so I know it must be hard to make treats for everyone. What can I do?" I said.

"Thank you. Um.... You can check on the egg rolls in the oven. Just don't burn yourself," Kara said, decorating a plate with cupcakes of different colors.

I tried not to laugh about her 'Don't burn yourself.' Fire would never do that to me.

"The cupcakes remind me of Demaid's hair; they don't know what color to be," Liam whispered in my ear, laughing a bit.

"That's not nice. What if she could hear you?" I playfully scolded him while checking on the egg rolls.

"I think they're done, Kara," I said looking over my shoulder.

"Okay. Can you take them out? Here; use these," Kara said, handing me a pair of mitts.

"Do you need some help?" Liam asked me with a smile.

"I can do it. Thank you," I said, pulling the mitts on, opening the oven door, and taking out the egg rolls. But as I put them down on the counter, fire shot up from the stove. Immediately, I backed away, not sure if I had caused the fire. Even though I can control the elements, sometimes, like in the lunchroom, they act on their own.

"You okay?" Liam asked.

"Yeah. Why do you ask?"

"You ... oh … never mind."

"Hey ... could someone help me get that bowl?" Kara asked, pointing to a bowl on the top shelf.

"Here, let me get it," I said, walking toward the shelf and reaching for the bowl. Even with stretching and standing on tiptoes, I couldn't touch it. Then I felt Liam's body behind me.

"Can I try?" he asked in my ear and, not waiting for me to move, grabbed the bowl over my head.

"Thanks, guys," Kara said, taking the bowl from Liam.

I turned around slowly, feeling Liam's body still against mine. Coming fully around, I looked up into his gorgeous eyes and waited … for … whatever might come. As if in slow motion, Liam's face came closer to mine, and I felt chills run down my spine.

"So, you guys seeing each other or what?" Andy asked, eating popcorn out of a bowl, before Kara could scold him.

"Ah ... what?" I asked, blushing, looking at Andy, who had a wicked smile on his face. Liam turned around and gave Andy an irritated look, but Andy just kept smiling and eating.

"Oh, Andy, stop making Anna feel so uncomfortable with questions like that. I'm surprised Anna's still here," Kara said wiping her hands full of flour on a towel.

"What! I'm just curious about the two of them. So, are you guys dating?" Andy asked again.

"Err! Andy! … Why don't you guys head downstairs with some plates of food before he can think of something else to ask you," Kara said shaking her head at Andy, as he came up behind her and kissed her on the cheek.

Taking her advice, Liam and I grabbed a dish.

"Sorry. I don't know what got into him," Liam said behind me as we headed down the stairs.

"It's okay. They're probably just worried about you being with me, that's all," I said.

"Why would they be worried about my being with you?" Liam asked with a little chuckle.

"I don't know. Maybe they see something in me that makes them worried and ask questions," I whispered as we walked into a large room with the others there. As soon as we walked through the door, everyone stared at me.

"Liam, everyone's staring at me, and I don't think it's because of the cupcakes I'm holding," I said quietly.

Liam looked at his friends, and they all looked away.

"Don't let them get to you. They're ... shy."

"*They* are shy around *me*? I'm only one person; they're a group. Do the math," I whispered sarcastically.

"The math tells me it was just nine of us until you came along, and I'm glad you make an even ten," Liam whispered in my ear, touching my hand gently.

I looked up at him, wondering why he liked me when he could have the pick of any other girl he wanted. Why me?

"Hey, Liam, you think you're so funny about my hair, don't you?" Demaid said coming closer to the treats with a tone of playfulness.

"Yeah, I do," Liam said, enjoying the light exchange.

Demaid flipped her colorful hair in retort and walked away from us.

"How does she know you made fun of her hair?" I half whispered into Liam's ear, more excited about the closeness of his body to mine than an answer to my question.

Liam chuckled a bit, but he didn't answer my question.

"Okay, let's pick a movie," Sandy said cheerfully, walking to a wall with shelves of movies.

"Anna, do you want to pick it?" Sparnik asked, and like clockwork, all eyes turned to me.

"Ah ...," I hesitated, looking at all the movies. Then for Liam's benefit, I said, "Do you have *Animal House*?"

"Hey, come on! What's *Animal House*?" Treelea asked with a bit of frustration.

"We got a new movie today. Do you guys want to see it?" Kara asked, coming through the door with the rest of the plates of food.

"Sure. What's the movie called?" I asked, helping Kara with the food.

"I think it's called *Ever After*," Kara said.

My jaw dropped. "Show of hands. How many of you have seen *Ever After*?" I said, holding up the only hand in the group. "You guys have never seen *Ever After*? … I know that movie by heart. I can't believe it," I said, shocked, looking around at each person.

"Do I hear a unanimous no for *Ever After*? Liam asked sarcastically.

"Let's watch it," I said smiling.

After everyone filled a plate with food, we all settled down to enjoy the movie, and I sat down next to Liam in a love seat. Andy put the movie in, and I almost forgot who was sharing the couch with me. As soon as the movie began, I started mouthing the lines. I completely lost myself in the part where Danielle says to the prince, "Forgive me, Your Highness. I did not see you," and the prince replies, "Your aim would suggest otherwise." Suddenly, I became self-conscious and noticed Liam looking at me and with a huge grin on his face. In utter embarrassment, I put my head down, my hair in my face.

"Don't stop; it's cute," Liam whispered, wrapping his big arms around me and pulling me towards him.

My beating heart picked up the pace as I leaned into him. And when he grabbed my hand, it began racing, and I felt warm, nervous, excited, and happy all at the same time. I smiled, resting my head on his shoulder, and I could see him smiling, too.

When the movie ended, I turned around to face Liam and asked, "So what did you think?"

"It was good. How many times have you seen this movie?" Liam asked, his thumb rubbing the top of my hand.

"More than a few times. Why?" I asked, enjoying his touch and watching his hand work over mine.

"Just curious," Liam said, shrugging. Then he added, "You ready to head back to school?"

I sighed, not wanting the night to end. "Sure."

Liam laughed a little at my sigh; then he got up and held out his hand for me. I took it, and we all walked out to the cars.

"Night kids. Drive safe," Kara's parents called from the front door. We all waved goodbye as we got into the cars and drove off.

"How did you guys like *Ever After*?" I asked, turning my head to see Treelea and Martin all lovey-dovey in the back seat, whispering to each other in low tones I couldn't hear.

"Okay, never mind," I half laughed. When I turned back around, I saw Liam put in a CD, and I couldn't believe what I heard. "You like Nickelback?" I asked, stunned.

"Yeah. Why?" Liam asked, nodding his head in perfect rhythm with the song.

"I love Nickelback," I said, thinking, *He's perfect*.

"I guess that's another similarity we have," he said, looking at me with that gorgeous smile before turning back to the road.

I gazed out my window, holding back a giggle, and then saw Brownstone come into view. We parked the cars, and then all got out and walked toward the dorms.

"Night, you guys," Sandy whispered as she and Sparnik got off on the first floor.

"Night. See you tomorrow," I whispered back as the rest of us went to the second floor.

"See you guys tomorrow," Demaid said with a wicked smile on her face as she and Nicky went all the way down the hall—and I had thought my room was far off!

Then Treelea, Martin, Liam, and I stood together for a few uncomfortable moments.

"Well, good night," Treelea said after several seconds of silence had passed, and then she and Martin started kissing goodbye.

Liam and I remained in awkwardness. Wanting the night to last forever but hating the emptiness of no words, I finally said, "Good night. See you tomorrow."

"Yeah, same to you." Liam nodded, and we both let another awkward moment descend upon us.

"Good night, Martin," I said, hoping he would get the hint. But he and Treelea just looked at us with smiles, said "Good night," and then started kissing again. "You've got to be kidding me," I said in exasperation and turned my attention to finding my keys.

"Now you know what I have to go through," Liam said with a sigh.

"Come on in," I said, finally retrieving the keys and opening the door to my room. Liam walked in behind me, and I shut the door.

"How long are they going to be?" I asked, sitting on my bed, staring at Liam while he walked around the room.

"It could be a while. Hey, Annadyomene ...," Liam said and then stopped.

"Hey, Liam," I said with a smile.

"Are you doing anything tomorrow?"

"I don't know ... Why?"

"Just wondering if you want to do something," Liam asked in a cute way, like a kid asking for a toy, wondering if he'll get it.

"Sure, what do you have in mind?"

"I don't know. Maybe have lunch with me ... and everyone in our group again?"

Just then the door opened, and Treelea and Martin stepped inside.

"Well, I guess this is good night, boys," Treelea said, walking over to her desk and taking out her earrings.

Martin just stood by the door waiting for Liam.

"Good night," Liam said and gave me a wink as he walked to the door.

"Night," I said, following them, but I didn't shut the door right away. When they reached their room, only four doors down, Liam looked back and smiled. I returned the parting gesture and then playfully stuck out my tongue. Laughing, he went inside his room, and I did the same.

Hoshi Is But a Fire in the Bark

A knock on the door woke me the next morning. Still groggy, I got up slowly and asked, "Who's there?"

"What? Forgot my name already?"

I opened the door to see Liam, standing in the doorway wearing a white T-shirt and black jeans.

"Ha! You're so funny," I said. But instead of meeting my glance, his eyes rolled over me, checking out my purple shorts and a blue tank-top—my PJs!

"Nice outfit," Liam said, still looking me up and down, evidently pleased.

"I'll be ready soon," I said before closing the door in Liam's laughing face. After some searching, I finally found an outfit—a black T-shirt with a rhinestone butterfly on the side and rhinestones that spell out "HOT ANGEL" on the front (I thought Liam Angel would appreciate that), blue jean shorts, some funky costume jewelry, and a hair band. When I opened the door, Liam looked me up and down once more and said, "It's okay, but I like the other outfit better."

I hit him playfully and then asked, "So why are you here?"

"I was going to walk you to class ... but if you want me to go," Liam said jokingly, about to walk away.

I quickly grabbed his hand, and he looked back with a smug smile on his face.

"I love my women fierce," he said sarcastically.

I gave him another punch in the arm as we walked to World Mythology.

And so it went, every day for weeks—I woke up, met Liam and the others, went to my classes, did homework, hung out with Liam, and read my books. As happy as I felt in that routine, I also needed more. For too long, before I came to Brownstone, I had stayed away from Hoshi. I had to go back, but I had to go without Liam. He would never understand. That's why I broke a date Liam and I had planned.

More than a month after starting at Brownstone, I just had to get away and prepared to visit Hoshi, or "star" in Japanese. So tonight I'm the masked enchantress Nature tomorrow I'll just be Annadyomene, regular girl, at Brownstone Boarding school. From my precious, locked, jeweled box, which I kept hidden under my mattress, I removed my mask and special stone. The purple eye mask identifies me to everyone in Hoshi as the enchantress Nature. But far more important, the colored stone from Hoshi lets me travel there and back. Only at night when the stars shine brightest can I move between other realms and Hoshi with the stone.

So that night I went outside and held the stone in my hand, looking for a particular tree stump that appears to anyone with the stone. I had to walk around a bit in the back woods of the school before I found the stump, shining brighter than all others around it. I walked up to it and felt the soft bark. *Yes, this is the one*, I thought. Next I closed my eyes and called for fire, and in no time, fire appeared in the palm of my hand. I laid my hand near the bark, and the fire rolled off my hand and into the stump.

WHAM!

"Owww ...," I said as I landed in Hoshi on my back, dropped from the sky.

"I really have to work on my landings," I said out loud to myself as I put my mask on. Then I looked around the beautiful field in which I had fallen and all the different colored flowers and the trees so big you can't see the tops of them. *I've stayed away too long*, I thought. I also noticed that for once I was close to Gardenia, the main castle of Hoshi.

"Nature?" I heard a voice call from behind a huge tree.

"Rose ... is that you?" I asked, walking closer to the massive tree. Rose, one of the nymphs in Hoshi, had beautiful, flawless skin, dark red hair, and was wearing a dress with magnificently striking colors. Every time I see the dresses of the Hoshi nymphs, their radiance and beauty awes me. Nothing in the other realm compares.

"Nature, thank the gods you're here. Where have you been?" Rose asked, hugging me like a dear sister.

"Oh, I am sorry, Rose, for keeping you waiting, but in the other realm, my schooling has demanded too much of my time," I said smiling and giving a huge hug back. Just seeing the nymphs reminded me how welcoming all creatures in Hoshi treated me, and I felt instantly at home.

"No worry. We are just glad you are back with us. Come along. The others are waiting," Rose said, taking my hand and leading me into the spectacular woods of Lycia (lie-SEE-a).

Few had the privilege that was granted to me by the nymphs. Because they trusted me, considered me like a sister to them all, they willingly revealed their hideout to me. Too many people had given them reason to distrust—some had treated them like slaves, others called them a nuisance, others tried to hurt them, and some even wanted them annihilated altogether.

"She's back, our lady Nature is back!" someone shouted as Rose and I walked to the center of the hideout and stood near the waterfall.

"Nature you came back to us," said Cat, a blond nymph who had a soft touch for stray cats. She walked up and hugged me as did all the others, one by one. Then they fussed over my hair, arranging it on top of my head and decorating it with flowers, leaves, anything they had. I loved the attention and realized how I really had stayed away too long.

"Nature, how have you been?" a little nymph named Rasie, hardly older than ten years, asked me while pushing her strawberry-blond hair out of her face.

"I've been fine, but I have missed all of you so much," I said, picking up a flower on the ground. Then I looked around at everyone, and noticed Cat staring at me with a smile.

"What?" I asked.

"You always dress so funny Nature," Cat said with a giggle, and soon everyone had joined in. I looked down at my boring jeans and plain white T-shirt; then I looked at their beautiful dresses (all of them different colors), and started to laugh at myself.

"Don't worry. We'll find you something to wear so you don't look like an outsider. Rasie and Scarlet, why don't you show Nature the dress we made her, please?" Cat said.

Rasie, the strawberry blond, and Scarlet, the brunette, both the same age, got up and disappeared behind some trees. When they came back, they were holding a light blue dress, so beautiful I couldn't take my eyes off it. It almost glowed with its brilliance.

"This is for you, Nature. Do you like it?" Rose asked, as she took the dress from the two girls and gave it to me.

I looked around with my mouth wide open. Finally, I managed to speak. "Thank you ... It's gorgeous; I love it!" Everyone looked so pleased and wore such a big smile that I felt completely at peace in that moment. To their delight, I put on the dress, barely touching my knees, and stroked the soft silky material. I did a little twirl, letting the bottom flare out, and then sat down on the grass next to Rose and Cat.

"Nature, did you hear?" Rasie asked, coming to kneel next to Cat.

"Rasie, she just got here. She wouldn't know," said Scarlet, who had also joined them, resting beside Rasie.

"Know what?" I asked.

"There's going to be a party at the castle, and they invited you!" Rasie said with a big smile.

"We heard some people from town talking about it. So you're going, right? And you'll wear that dress, right?" Scarlet said, pointing at my new dress.

"Why are they having a party?" I asked.

"Who knows? But one thing is for sure—they want you there to do your tricks," Rasie said.

"So are you going or not?" Scarlet asked with wide eyes staring at me.

"What do you girls think? Should I go?" I asked. Everyone nodded her head in agreement.

"Okay, I guess I'm going. When is it?" I asked.

"Two days from now," Cat said.

"Oh ... so you all think I should wear this?" I asked, getting back up and spinning round and round. Everyone clapped and nodded again in agreement, and we all shared a laugh together.

"So what tricks are you going to do at the castle?" asked Diana, a nymph a few years younger than I, with light brown hair.

"Oh, I don't want to tell you," I said, and all the younger girls' heads went down in disappointment. "I want to show you!" And they all popped back up in delighted surprise.

So I showed them the tricks I was planning on showing at the castle.

By the time I finished, the sun was setting in spectacular streaks of deep purple, magenta, red, pink, mango, and gold. I knew I had to return to the other realm, and reluctantly, I put my jeans and T-shirt back on.

"I must go. But I will be back in two days for the celebration," I said, hugging everyone. "Until then, goodbye."

As I was walking away, Scarlet and Rasie ran up to me and asked, "Can we help you get ready for the party?"

I nodded yes, and they excitedly ran back to the hideout. Returning to the empty field, I held the stone in my hand ready to take off. But before I could do anything, a large blue dragon appeared out of the sky and landed right in front of me. He spread his lips wide and showed off his massive sharp teeth. But I knew better than to feel any fear.

"How are you doing, Nury?" I asked.

"I'm fine ... You weren't going to leave without saying goodbye to me were you, Nature?" he asked, looking intently with his big greenish gold eyes and bowing slightly with his huge purplish-blue head.

"No, of course not. I'm sorry, Nury," I said, tilting my head to the side with an apologetic smile. Then I sat down on the grass and so did

Nury, although when Nury settled down, the earth below him shook, much like a small earthquake.

"So I hear you're invited to the Gardenia Castle for the celebration. Are you going?" Nury asked.

"Yes, I'm going and wearing a dress made by the nymphs. Why do you ask?"

"I would like you to meet my master and his family. He has twins, a boy and a girl that are the same age as you ... You are sixteen, aren't you?" Nury asked.

I nodded.

He continued. "The twins are friends to one of the king's sons, the one in line for the crown. And I think they would like to meet you. What do you think?"

"Nury, you are a great friend of mine. Of course, I'll meet them," I said, and Nury smiled even wider. Then I said, "Nury, not to be rude, but I have to go. I'm running late, as is, but I'll be back in two days for the celebration. Maybe I can meet your master and his family then at the Castle Gardenia."

"Yes, yes, go. I have kept you too long. Goodbye, Nature," Nury said, as I got up and held the stone in my hand. Nury also rose, causing yet another trembling sensation upon the ground where we were sitting.

Finding this ordeal laughable, I waved and yelled out, "Goodbye, Nury," blowing a kiss to this most lovable dragon. Then turning to see the tree stump, I put my fire inside and before I knew it, I was back in the other realm—SMACK!—landing in the middle of a street I didn't know. I heard the traffic and freaked out, so I ran to the sidewalk before an oncoming car had a chance to run me over.

I Won't Tell Liam

I quickly removed my mask and just started to walk, not really knowing where I was going. Not more than a few minutes later, a car drove beside me and rolled its window down. I didn't even bother to look and said loudly so whoever was in the car could hear me, "Back off, buddy." Then I whispered, "What else could go wrong tonight?"

"Is that you, Anna?" a familiar voice from the car asked.

I stopped walking and turned to face the vehicle, a black Ford truck.

"Sparnik?" I asked, looking inside the window, and there he sat.

"Need a ride?" Sparnik asked.

"Yes, thank you," I said, opening the passenger door and getting inside the truck. When I got my seat belt on, he started driving; then he looked at me and barely held back a laugh.

"What?" I asked.

"You have flowers in your hair," Sparnik said, looking straight ahead at the road again as I pulled and tugged to get them all out of my hair.

"So what are you doing out here, looking like that?" Sparnik asked.

I looked at him stunned. "Do I look that bad?" I asked, looking at my reflection in the window, hair falling onto my face, which was quickly turning a bright, hot flushed red.

"No, no, I didn't mean anything by it ...," Sparnik stuttered. Then he said, "you didn't answer my question; what are you doing out here?"

"Would you believe me if I told you I wanted to go for a walk?"
I asked.

"Almost a mile from the school? Come on! Do I look stupid?"
Sparnik asked, looking at me with an eyebrow raised.

"Uh, well, the reason is ... Wait a second. What are you doing out
here?" I asked, trying to switch the conversation from me to him in
order to avoid answering his questions.

"If you must know, there's a place I like to go around here."

"Oh? ... What kind of place?"

"Just a place, that's it. I don't really want to talk about it," Sparnik
said with a shrug. Then he glanced at the bundle in my hands, the dress
the nymphs had made me and my mask.

"What's that in your hands?" he asked.

"Just a dress," I said, trying to hide the evidence by holding it
closer to my body.

"So how are you and Liam doing?" Sparnik asked after a moment's
silence.

"We're good. How are you and Sandy doing?"

"Oh, Sandy's amazing. She's just so much fun to be around.
Everyday ...," and he paused, almost closing his eyes at the thought,
"she does something crazy that I love," he said with a sigh.

"That's great," I said with a genuine smile.

"Yeah," Sparnik said with a smirk. Then he suddenly turned to
me and asked, "Hey, Anna ... you're not seeing another guy besides
Liam are you?"

"No! ... Why? Is he seeing someone else?" I asked, stunned by
Sparnik's question. Then I remembered Jenny Fair, and the thought of
Liam with her made me furious and sad at the same time.

"No, Liam's not seeing anyone besides you. I just don't want you
to break Liam's heart, as if he's nothing but a toy," Sparnik said.

"Oh, I would never treat Liam like that. He's so kind, sweet, and
beautiful inside and out. When I'm with him, it just feels so right. And
it may be silly, but when I see him, I just want to run into his arms
and tell him never to let me go," I confessed. Then I realized Sparnik
was smiling. I turned my face so he couldn't see me blush. I probably

sounded like a silly schoolgirl with a crush, and I was beginning to think I had let out way too much information.

"Why are you smiling?" I asked, wanting to know, even though I suspected he was thinking the schoolgirl crush thing.

"I know how you feel about Liam because I feel the same way about Sandy."

When he said that, I turned back to face him. Then we both started to laugh at ourselves.

Sparnik then said, "Here we are," and he pulled into the school parking lot. "So you're not going to tell me what you were doing over there today, are you?" Sparnik asked with a smug smile on his face as we both got out of the truck.

"I can't. Sorry," I said, looking at the buildings of the school.

"That's okay," Sparnik shrugged.

Then we both started walking toward the school.

"You won't tell Liam about this, will you?" I asked, thinking of how crazy it would seem to Liam.

"If you don't want me to, I won't tell Liam." he said, raising and lowering his eyebrows so fast I almost didn't catch his subtle reaction.

"Not anyone, please. This is really embarrassing for me," I said as I grabbed Sparnik's arm like a begging child.

"Don't worry; I won't say a word," Sparnik assured me as we walked up the stairs to the dorms.

I sighed, thankful that he would say nothing to the others.

"Well, goodnight," Sparnik said, going to his room on the first floor as I continued on to mine on the second.

"Good night … and thank you for everything," I said, walking up the stairs while I looked back at Sparnik. He nodded, and then he was gone.

I opened my door and found I had the room to myself. Quickly, I put away my dress and mask and placed the magic stone in its secret, special place. Then I changed into my PJs, grabbed my reading book, and sat next to the window, letting the moonlight fall onto the pages while gently and quietly allowing sleep to overtake me.

Did You Get Her Name?

Next thing I knew my cell phone was ringing.

"Hello," I answered as I stretched.

"Anna, is that you?" said a voice I recognized right away.

"Hey, Brandon, what's up?"

"I was just wondering, are you in your room?"

"Yes. Why?"

"Open your door and find out," Brandon said, and he hung up.

Filled with curiosity, I quickly put on my favorite jeans and a pink tank-top and opened the door—to find my brunette brother standing in front of me wearing a huge grin

"Surprise!" Brandon said.

I felt so excited I wrapped my arms around him in a tight bear hug.

"Not that I'm not happy to see you, but what are you doing here?" I asked, leading Brandon into the dorm room.

"Billy and I wanted to see your new school in all its glory," Brandon said with a little laugh. Then he continued with saying, "We kind of felt bad that we didn't drive you down here your first day."

"You two had work, I understand," I said.

Brandon just nodded his head once.

Then a thought came into my head and I asked, "Billy's here? Where is he?"

"Oh, he found a bookstore, so he said he'll see you later on today," Brandon said, rolling his eyes as he said "bookstore" because he's not a big reader like my mom, Billy, and I are.

"Of course! How about you? Do you want to see the school?" I asked.

"No, Bill and I drove all the way here to find a book store," Brandon said sarcastically.

"Shh … you," I said with a laugh, lightly hitting him with the back of my hand.

"Don't you have classes?" Brandon asked, looking around the room.

"I can skip a day."

"You sure a nun won't come out and hit you with a ruler?" Brandon said, smiling.

"No nuns here, although some of the girls here would be great ones," I said laughing. "The others will fill me in."

"The others?" Brandon asked as he stopped looking around the room.

"Oh, you'll meet all of them at lunch. Anyway, do you want to see the school or not?" I asked, happy that both my brothers had come so I could show them the magnificent Brownstone Boarding School.

"Let's go," Brandon said, and we both walked out of my room.

"How did you find my room?" I asked as we walked down the stairs.

"I asked the first person I saw when I walked into this building, some blond girl."

"Did you get her name?"

"No. Why?"

"Just wondering if it was one of my friends." I shrugged it off.

I took Brandon all around the school, showing him everything except the classes I was skipping. But I did get him to some of the empty classrooms—the ones for English, the fashion room, and the gym.

One moment we were talking in the courtyard, and the next it was lunchtime. Eager to introduce Brandon to my friends, I led him to the lunchroom and saw all my friends at their usual spot.

"Do you want to get something to eat?" I asked, getting in line for lunch.

"Sure," Brandon shrugged and joined in behind me.

After we got our food, I walked Brandon over to the table with all my friends—and then some. I almost exploded when I noticed one extra person in the group. Sitting just a little too close to Liam, Jenny Fair was rubbing his hand and wearing the most satisfied look on her face.

"Hey, guys, what's up?" I asked as Brandon and I walked up to the table and sat down.

"I have class," Liam said and stood up in an odd way and grabbed his stuff, never once making eye contact with me.

Then Jenny Fair looked at me with an evil smile and ran off after Liam.

"Hey, that's the blond that showed me where your room is, Anna," Brandon muttered to me.

I looked at him; then I looked at the others. "What's wrong with Liam?" I asked.

"He's wondering why you felt you needed a new boyfriend," Treelea said, her words laced with anger and her eyes shooting between Brandon and me.

"Why would he think that?" I asked, looking around at everyone.

"Hello? You spend all morning with this guy and then bring him to our table. If that doesn't give Liam the hint, I don't know what will," Martin said, glaring at Brandon and me.

I looked from Martin to Brandon, confused, and then I realized what they were saying. I laughed a little, but I didn't feel very happy.

"Oh, you guys! This is my brother! Brandon and my other brother, Billy, made a surprise visit today," I said. Then I introduced Brandon to everyone at the table. But even after that, everyone looked uncomfortable, and no one seemed willing to meet my eyes.

Finally Kara took the brave step and said, "Sorry, Anna, we didn't know." Her warm smile helped to lighten the mood, but I knew we would need more than that to put all bad feelings aside.

"It's okay, but Liam doesn't know. Does he hate me?" I asked.

"He doesn't hate you; he's just upset," Demaid said.

"Leave it to my 'best buddy' to jump at the chance …," I said. "Somehow her last name just doesn't fit, does it?" I said, shaking my head.

Everyone just squirmed, and they still kept their eyes lowered. Treelea, especially, looked remorseful about what they had thought about me.

"I'm sure Liam will talk to you soon; then you can explain everything," Sandy said smiling.

"I wouldn't have to explain anything if it wasn't for Jenny," I said. Everyone looked remorseful now, so I added, "I'll text him." I took out my cell phone and sent, "Where are you? We need to talk." I waited, but I never got a reply.

Later on in the day, Brandon and I met up with Billy, and we all went out to the Rock 'n' Blue diner. I enjoyed spending time with family, hearing what I had missed at home, and telling them about Brownstone and my friends.

"So you like this Liam guy?" Billy asked, finishing his 7-Up so we could go.

"Yeah, he's really nice," I said, looking at the table with a smile. Then I said, "But right now, he probably hates me because he thinks Brandon is my boyfriend."

Billy looked confused and asked, "Wha—? Dating your brother?"

"This one girl, Jenny, told him and my other friends that Brandon was my boyfriend. No one knew who he really is, and she was more than glad to give them her opinion. As you can tell, she doesn't especially like me," I said.

"He won't stay mad at you. You're too crazy not to talk to," Brandon said with a mocking smile that made me smile.

"Come on. Let's get out of here, and maybe you can talk to him," Billy said.

"Yeah … well, yeah … maybe. I already texted him, but that didn't help. Maybe I'll call him," I said as we walked outside. While Billy went to get the car, I called Liam. I never should have bothered. Hearing a noise behind me while the phone was ringing, I turned, and there stood Liam and Jenny in a passionate embrace, kissing. I froze, as if time had stood still. I couldn't believe Liam was doing this to me.

"Anna, the car's here," Brandon said. I turned away from Liam and Jenny and got into my brother's shinny black Ford Mustang. We drove off, but only one scene passed before me on the whole way back.

My brothers had to get back home for their jobs the next day, so I said goodbye after they dropped me off at the dorm. Wanting to see absolutely no one, I ran up to my room, slammed the door, and dropped on my bed just in time for the tears to begin falling onto my pillow. Then as I lay on my bed, trying to forget everything that I had seen that night, my phone rang. The name appeared on the screen: Liam Angel.

A Dress for Nature

"Hello," I answered in a cold voice, trying to hold back my tears. "Hey, you texted me about something. What's up?"

"I just want to say the guy I was with today was my brother, and I hope you and Jenny have fun," I said, my anger building up inside me.

"What's that suppose to mean?" he asked, getting a little mad himself.

"Tell me did you enjoy kissing her?"

"Annadyomene, what are you talking about?"

"I'm talking about you and Jenny Fair kissing at Rock 'n' Blue diner."

"I don't know what you saw, Anna, but that wasn't me."

"I saw you with my own eyes."

"Well, I'm telling you it wasn't me. Please believe me, Anna."

"You know what, Liam? I don't know what to believe."

"Believe me."

"Then tell me where you were tonight," I said.

"I ... can't," Liam said in a defeated voice.

"Mm ... I see."

"Annadyomene, please—"

"Goodbye, Liam," my voice broke into a kind of sob when I said that. Then I turned off my phone so he couldn't call me back. I sat there in my room, alone, on my bed, feeling a little angry at myself for being so foolish but mostly feeling really sad. I had opened up a little to Liam and what had I gotten in return? He had turned around and kissed Jenny ... Or had he? Well I saw him with my own eyes; there was no mistaking that. Then as I was thinking all that, I had an idea of how to make my sadness go away. The nymphs would make me feel better. So I grabbed all that I would need and was going to head out the door when someone knocked.

"Annadyomene, open up. We need to talk," Liam's voice came from the other side of the door. I froze, not knowing what to do. Then I turned around and opened the window. It was a pretty long way down, but with the tree, I could get down in no time.

"Come on. I know you're in there," Liam said with a sigh.

I thought, *Not for long.* And two seconds later, I was on the tree. When I reached the ground, I ran as fast as I could toward the forest and the tree stump.

Once in Hoshi, everything felt a little better. The flowers and trees welcomed me with open arms. All around, the air, the colors, everything felt warmer. The sun and the moon, both in the sky, each had its own special beauty. After a moment of looking around this enchanting land, I went to the nymphs and told them all my sorrows. And like sisters, they tried to cheer me up.

"Oh, Nature, you don't need that boy," Rose said, and the others nodded their agreement.

"Thanks," I said as Cat did my hair.

"He sounds as if he doesn't deserve you; you're better off without him," Rose said.

I looked down at the grass, not wanting to say anything to that.

"Now I think it's time to rest," Cat said, putting a hand on my shoulder, and everyone went to their sleeping spots.

"You can sleep here, Nature," Rasie said, pointing to a pillow on the grass.

"Where did you get that pillow?" Rose asked sternly, putting her hands on her hips.

Nymphs don't use pillows. Why would they even have one?

"We found it," Scarlet said.

"Really? And how did you *find* it?" Cat asked with a knowing smile.

"Ah ...," Rasie and Scarlet both started but had no more words to finish.

Everyone else just smiled.

"Tell us," Cat said in a sweet but insistent voice.

"Some people from town were airing their clothes, and we found this pillow," Scarlet said.

"We didn't think they would miss one little pillow," Rasie said. Then Scarlet looked at Rasie, and they both put their heads down.

"Tomorrow you will return it," Rose said.

Rasie and Scarlet nodded. Then we all lay down and went to sleep. Or, at least, they slept. I couldn't stop thinking—about Liam, the others, my family, going to the castle in a dress made by nymphs. Then I must have drifted off because I was dreaming of Nury, the nymphs, and all the other creatures in Hoshi, all the beautiful fairies, elves, flower dwarfs, unicorns, dragons, and pretty much all the animals in Lycia Forest. But the dream started turning bad. I could see all the horrible creatures of Hoshi, and then I heard a dark voice call my name, "Anna." I looked all around but couldn't see anyone. Hands grabbed my arms, and I froze. Then I heard the thing that called my name laugh a most hideous laugh.

"Nature ... wake up. Nature." I heard Rasie's soft voice. Then someone was pulling my arm hard.

"Ow ... my arm is still attached to my body, thank you," I said as I got up and found both Scarlet and Rasie staring at me.

"What?" I asked.

"You said we could help you get ready." And they both smiled at me.

"When do I have to be at the castle?" I asked.

"Maybe an hour from now," Rose said, sitting right next to me.

"Okay, let me get my dress on, and then you two can do whatever," I shrugged.

Then they shrieked in delight and ran off.

"That was a big mistake," Rose said with a smile when they were out of sight.

"Oh, I think it's a very nice thing Nature's doing," Cat said, sitting on the other side of me.

"I didn't say it wasn't nice, but the girls will go crazy," Rose said, and we all chuckled, knowing exactly what she meant.

Preparing for the worst, I got out of my jeans and tank-top and into my dress. When I walked out, I got a most surprising reaction from the nymphs. Rather than expressing pleasure about my outfit, they all looked terribly worried.

"What's wrong?" I asked.

"Rasie and I were getting flowers for your hair, and someone came up to us and told us to give this to you," Scarlet said, pointing to a gold box on the ground.

I picked it up.

"They said it's from the castle," Cat said as I opened it, and everyone moved closer to see what it held. There in the box was a beautiful and elegant gold mask.

"Oh my!" Rasie and Scarlet said together.

"Put it on, Nature," Cat said.

Since no one there knows my identity, always seeing me only in a mask, I went behind a tree and took off my old mask and then put on the gold one. It fit perfectly, covering only my eyes. I stepped out from behind the tree, and everyone gasped, and then they smiled.

"You look magnificent, Nature," Cat said as Rasie and Scarlet began fussing with my hair.

"Thank you all for everything," I said.

When Rasie and Scarlet felt satisfied with their work—and I felt I could take no more—the time to go had arrived. I hugged all the nymphs, we said our goodbyes for now, and then I was off to the castle.

At the gate, soldiers bowed their heads to me in respect, and so did everyone else.

"Good day, Nature," people said as I passed by, and I nodded with a big smile in return.

Then I finally made it to the castle. It was enormous and beautiful at the same time, suited to its name, Gardenia, a flower of simple elegance.

"Right this way, Nature," said a soldier with mouse-brown hair and a sword at his hip as he led the way to the inside of the castle.

When we came to the main room, I nodded my head and thanked the soldier. Then I made my entrance. All around me, ladies in spectacular dresses danced with their partners, and some looked my way. Drapes of gold, silver, dark red, and royal purple, each with a gardenia in full bloom, hung on all four walls of the massive room. Long dining tables lined two opposite sides of the enormous room. Waiters moved smoothly in and out amid the lords and ladies, filling their drinks and offering tasty refreshments of all kinds.

In the front of the great room, by the windows, stood ten chairs, all magnificent with their dark red velvet seats and beautiful carvings of different creatures. But one stood out from the others, obviously meant for a king. Like the nine, it had the same fabric, carvings, and overall shape. But gold inlay covered the wood, and the size dominated the others.

While taking the big room in, I noticed two children with light brown hair sitting in chairs at one of the long tables on my right. They looked bored out of their minds, so I walked over to them.

"Hello," I said, standing in front of them.

They looked up and gave a half-hearted smile. Then they noticed my gold mask, and their grins broadened.

"It's Nature," the girl said in awe.

The boy just stared at me.

"What are your names?" I asked, still smiling.

"I'm Lily, and this is my brother, David," the girl said.

"How old are you two?" I asked.

"My brother's eight, and I'm six," Lily said with a proud smile on her angelic face.

"I'd like to see a magic trick. How about you?" I asked.

"Yes, we do! Yes we do!" Lily said, jumping up from her seat with an excited look on her face. Her brother did the same.

"You two sure you're not too old for this?" I asked, trying to keep a serious expression on my face.

"No!" they both said.

"Okay, now I will need your help. Are you up to the challenge?" I asked almost in a whisper, smiling at them.

They nodded their heads and waited.

"Watch this," I said, cupping my hands over both of their hands.

"Now don't be afraid because this special fire won't burn you," I whispered. Then I let go of their hands. In Lily's, a fire rose glowed, and in David's, a fire bird flickered.

"Wow!" both of them said at the same time.

"Lily, David, where have you been?" someone said behind us.

I turned to see the queen with her light brown hair perfectly arranged on top of her head, some gray strands here and there. Her beautiful maroon gown lightly brushed the floor as she approached, and I bowed. She looked at me with a smile.

"Hello, Nature. I hope these two haven't been bothering you," Queen Vanessa said, gently holding Lily's and David's free hands.

"Mom, look at this," David said jumping up and down, holding the tiny fire bird in his hands while Lily did the same with her rose.

"That's lovely dear," Queen Vanessa said to the children but kept glancing around the room as if looking for someone.

Who's Cheating Whom?

"May I help you find someone, Your Highness?" I asked.

Queen Vanessa looked at me with a little hope.

"Oh, yes, dear … perhaps you could help me find my third oldest son. I don't know where he's run off to. Probably with his friends," she said with a sigh.

"It would be no trouble at all, Your Highness," I said. Then I conjured the fire to take the shape of a border collie.

"Go find Queen Vanessa's third oldest son and lead him here, please," I said to the fire dog, and then it was off.

"Oh! Nature, you always surprise me," Queen Vanessa said.

Over the years, she and King Bryan had seen enough of my clever tricks to know what I could do, but somehow I still managed to impress them with new ones. But, despite our long relationship, I hardly knew their children. They always kept to the background at royal functions, and we just never really met.

"Is that all, Your Highness?" I asked.

"Yes, that will be all. Thank you," Queen Vanessa said.

I bowed my head.

Then Queen Vanessa said, looking behind my back, "Ah, here he is now."

"Liam!" Both Lily and David ran behind me.

I turned around and gasped. "Liam!" I whispered.

"Liam, this is Nature. She showed us a fire trick," David said.

"Oh, really? So is the dog yours?" Liam asked me, with a half smile pointing to the fire dog.

I nodded. Then I called the fire back to me, and the fire dog disappeared.

"You are some enchantress," Liam said, looking me up and down but in a comfortable way. Then he turned to his mother and asked why she had called him.

A flash of panic raced through me. Would he recognize me? Then I remembered the spell that I had cast on my mask to help disguise my true identity. The spell shortened and waved my hair, making it so different from my usual style that no one would ever recognize me in a million years.

"I called you because I didn't know where you were. Also your father wants you to meet with some of the creatures," Queen Vanessa said. Then she saw someone and excused herself. Lily and David also ran off with their fire bird and fire rose.

"Liam! Hey, Liam!" a group called, and as they got closer, I gasped a second time. I knew every single person.

"Hey, guys," Liam said, "this is Nature and Nature this is—"

But I stopped him before he could say their names.

"Oh, I already know all of you," I said with a half smile.

"You do? How?" Treelea asked.

"I hear and see more than most people realize. Let's just leave it at that," I said.

They all looked at each other. Some of them shrugged; others looked at me with questions in their eyes.

"So just asking, Treelea and Nicky, does the name Nury ring a bell?"

"You know Nury, too? How?" Treelea asked in awe.

"I met him a long time ago. I was with the nymphs when he came by," I said, thinking of the day I had met Nury by a stream. The nymphs and I were picking wild berries, crystal berries too, the special ones that turn into edible crystals at the touch of a person's hand.

"What are the nymphs like?" Sandy asked.

"They're gentle creatures and fun to be around," I said with a smile, thinking of all my nymph friends and wondering what they were doing right then. Probably having a lot of fun dancing, singing, and just playing around.

"I hear you're the only one they let near them. Is that true?" Martin asked.

"Yes, that is true," I said in a cool voice, adding a single nod of my head for emphasis.

"Why is that?" Sparnik asked.

"Too many people have tried to catch them and hurt them," I said.

"Not all people try to catch them. I just don't see why they have to go into hiding," Andy said with a shrug.

"True, but some have tried. Now tell me, would you not hide if even some people were trying to take away your freedom?" I asked.

"You have a point there," Martin said.

I smiled, and then I turned to face Liam and the disheartening look on his face stung me deeply.

"Is something wrong?" I said to Liam, careful not to say "Your Highness" because it would have been just weird for me to have used that title for the guy I liked.

"It's nothing," Liam said, shaking his head.

"Oh, I know what it is. Liam, don't worry. Anna will come around. Just give her some time," Sandy said with a kind smile for Liam.

"I don't know ... She seemed really angry at me," Liam said with a little sigh.

"What is the problem?" I asked, knowing perfectly well the answer.

"This girl in the other realm thinks Liam cheated on her," Treelea said to me. Then when she felt everyone staring at her, she asked, "What?"

"You don't have to tell everyone," her brother Nicky said.

She waved at him as if he were an annoying fly and then rolled her eyes with a smile at me.

"Did you cheat?" I asked Liam, trying to stay cool

Liam looked up with kind of sad puppy-dog look.

"No ... I would never do that to her," he said in a firm voice.

"Then I wouldn't worry about it. Just tell her the truth," I said, happy to know Liam hadn't cheated. From the way he looked at me when he answered, I knew he was speaking the truth.

"How can I tell her the truth when she doesn't even answer my calls?" Liam asked, folding his arms, over his chest in defeat.

"Don't give up. As your friends said, she'll come around," I said with warm assurance.

"Okay," Liam said with a half smile.

"Give me your hands," I said to Liam.

"What?" Liam asked, looking at me in confusion.

"Give me your hands," I said again, holding out my hands.

"Why?" Liam asked.

"Just do it," I said with a little laugh.

"Okay," Liam said, and I placed my hands over his. When I pulled my hands back, a cute little fire mouse with a little sundress on was dancing in Liam's hands.

"Wow!" everyone in the group said at once.

"Go ahead, you guys; you can touch it. This fire won't burn you," I said, and they all started to pet the fire mouse.

"The fire's almost cold," Sandy said with a giggle.

I nodded and watched them get almost as excited as Lily and David were.

"Now if you ever need anything, just close your hands over the mouse, and ask for what you need. When you open your hands again, there will be fine powder. And all you have to do is blow the powder to the wind," I told Liam when he looked back at me with that million-dollar smile I love so much.

"Thank you, but ... why did you do this?" Liam asked, still smiling.

"I like to make people happy," I said and then continued. "Also, if the mouse gets lost, just call to it," I said.

Liam looked confused. "How do you call to a fire mouse?" he asked.

"How would you call humans?"

"By their name," Liam said.

I nodded my head yes. "Her name is Cora," I said with a little laugh.

"Hello, Cora," Liam said, and the mouse curtsied, holding her dress with her little paws.

"Oh, Cora, you are such a darling," Treelea exclaimed.

"And so polite," added Sandy.

We all had a good laugh at cute Cora's manner, but we made sure she understood we truly appreciated her pleasant display and were not laughing at her. Although the others did not realize the danger, I knew that even a little fire mouse could turn from a friendly, cool fire to an angry one that burns if it thinks you're making fun of it.

"Your turn," I said. "I showed you guys half of my powers. What kind of powers do you all have?"

12

MUCH MORE THAN A CAR CRASH

"Here I'll show you, and don't be freaked if you hear me talking to you every once in a while. I'll just be telling you some facts," Liam said, gently grabbing my hand.

Then like a flash of light, I saw everything I needed to know about my friends. Like a movie trailer, important scenes from their lives flashed before my eyes. First I saw Sparnik, Demaid, and their parents in a car driving down a back road. ["Sparnik was two and a half, and Demaid was a baby. That's their parents, Alex and Sky," Liam said.] The trees that surrounded them in the darkness and the absence of streetlights told me it had to be a country road. Out of nowhere, something on fire hit the car and made it slam into a tree. Alex got out first, made sure the kids were okay, and then ran to his wife on the passenger side.

"Sky, are you all right?" Alex asked in a soft voice, pushing Sky's blond hair away from her face.

"How are the kids?" Sky asked, rubbing her forehead.

"They're fine," Alex said.

"Then I'm fine," Sky said, and Alex smiled, brushing his dark strawberry-blond hair out of his face.

Suddenly, I heard a noise from the road. It sounded otherworldly, like something moving incredibly fast, more than any human. And then I heard laughing. *The same laughing I heard in my dream*, I thought.

"Now take the kids and run. Can you do that?" Alex asked, helping Sky out of the car. She took Demaid in her arms, and after Alex helped Sparnik out of the car, Sky took Sparnik's hand.

"Go! Hurry!" Alex said, pushing his family away from whatever was making the sounds, towards the forest.

"What about you?" Sky asked.

"Don't worry. Just GO!" Alex said. He kissed his family and rushed back to the road. WHAM! A dark almost human shape knocked Alex down to the ground.

"Alex," Sky whispered in the dark, remaining where he had left them.

Slightly stunned by the first strike, Alex rolled and then staggered up. Attacking his opponent with his fists, he seemed sometimes to make his mark for I saw pauses in his actions. I could still barely make out the dark shape he was fighting, but I saw Alex flinch or move unsteadily on his feet every once in a while. Soon Alex began to show signs of weakening, hitting less often and recoiling backwards more and more each time the dark shape struck him.

"Sparnik, watch Demaid," Sky said as she put the baby in his arms. "And if anything happens to me or Daddy, take this stone and think of Hoshi. Okay, baby?"

Sparnik nodded, holding Demaid.

Sky petted the top of Sparnik's head, kissed both the children, and then went out to help Alex.

"Sky, get back to the kids!" Alex shouted as he saw Sky coming closer.

"No, we're doing this together," Sky shouted back, and she pushed the dark shape off Alex.

"Go! I can handle this," Alex said, nodding his head toward the dark shape.

"And I can help you," Sky said.

Then the most unusual thing happened. The dark figure took the shape of a dark-haired, bearded man with a dirty pair of pants and a jacket.

"Rata," Alex said, shocked.

Rata only smiled.

"Hello, Alex. Long time, no see. Ah, I see you found a wife. Madam …," Rata said, bowing his head in a mocking way to Sky.

"Alex, who is this?" Sky asked, looking back and forth from Alex to Rata.

"He's a demon. We used to be friends when I was a demon," Alex explained, looking at Rata with an angry stare.

"If I'm not mistaken, Alex, you *are* a demon. You still have your powers," Rata said with an evil grin. ["It reminds me of something, or someone," I told Liam.]

"What are you doing here, Rata?" Alex demanded, and Rata's grin reached from ear to ear.

"Finbar has sent me to kill a demon, a mermaid, and their magical children. But you wouldn't know anything about that, would you?" Rata asked.

Alex and Sky's eyes widened.

"Why did Finbar send you to kill us?" Alex asked, standing in front of Sky.

"He sent me because I know you," Rata said.

"Who's Finbar, and why does he want us killed?" Sky asked after a moment's silence.

"You don't know who Finbar is?" Rata asked.

"No ... why should I?" Sky asked.

"Finbar is fear itself. You can never hide from him because as long as you have fear he will always find you," Rata said.

"So now what are you going to do? Try to kill us?" Alex asked. Then he turned his head and whispered to Sky, "The kids are okay, right?"

Sky nodded yes and said, "I gave them the stone from Hoshi so if anything happens they'll be safe."

Alex nodded his head once, and then faced Rata again.

"You guys ready to fight?" Rata asked.

"I'll use my power to see what he'll do," Sky said. ["She has premonitions," Liam said.]

"Okay. Be careful," Alex said.

"And you, too. I love you," Sky said.

"I love you, too." Alex said, and they kissed.

"Enough!" Rata said with impatience, and he struck the first blow, an upper-cut to Alex's chin that sent him reeling backwards. Recovering quickly, Alex moved forward, about to throw a punch to Rata's stomach, but Sky yelled out, "Danger on your right." Alex used the momentum of his arm moving forward, instead, to twirl himself around and back out of the way … and then he was nowhere in sight.

"Oh, Alex ... up to old tricks, I see," Rata said. Then he reached his hand out.

"Alex, left cheek!" Sky shouted.

Rata must have missed since his fist kept going forward until he screamed and put both hands to his left side. Blood spilled from an ugly slice just below his ribs and oozed over his trembling hands.

Sky smiled at the turn of events, forgetting to keep aware of all around her and on what was coming. In seconds, her smile had contorted into a grimace. Looking down, she saw blood on her stomach. In confusion, she looked up at Alex, who had reappeared. He was shaking and whispering her name. Then Sky turned around and saw a woman robed in dark red, revealing only a hideous face.

"Now you and your husband can die," the woman said, holding up a dagger with Sky's blood on it.

"Rata, finish the job, now!" the woman shouted at Rata. Rata got off the ground and lunged toward Alex, but Alex was too fast and, as he stepped aside, again turned invisible.

"You senseless demon! Where did he go?" the woman again shouted at Rata.

"I don't know," Rata shouted back, holding his left side where Alex had stabbed him. Then Sky turned invisible too.

"Now they're both gone." The woman stomped her foot on the ground, causing her hood to slide down a bit and reveal thick white hair. Although her smooth skin gave the impression of a much younger woman, about thirty, her hair said otherwise.

"Not for long," a dark voice said, again, the same dark voice I had heard call my name in my dream.

Then a big dark shadow descended over everyone, and Sky and Alex became visible. But before the woman or Rata could do anything, the shadow became smaller and more intensely dark, as if concentrating its evilness, and remained over Sky and Alex.

"Sparnik, use the stone," Sky shouted toward the forest but said no more as the dark shape swallowed her and Alex and disappeared.

Sparnik grabbed the stone and, still holding Demaid, thought of Hoshi, not needing the fire since they were under the age of reason. Seconds later, he was standing near Gardenia Castle, holding the stone and Demaid in his hands. Frightened, Sparnik dropped the two and turned into a white dog. ["He's a shape shifter; he can turn into anything," Liam told me.] Then Sparnik gently picked up Demaid by her baby blanket with his canine teeth and ran to a corner of the castle wall where he sat down on the ground. But Demaid started to cry so Sparnik turned back into his human form. Retrieving his little sister and the stone, he rocked her until she stopped crying.

"I'll be right there, Amanda," a woman said as she came out of a doorway near the two children. Her fine clothes and confident bearing spoke to her royal heritage. But her smile when she saw Sparnik and Demaid gave all away—a younger Queen Vanessa.

"Hello," she said as she knelt down in front of them. Her light brown hair hung free on her shoulders with no gray streaks, and her eyes sparkled in kindness.

"Hello," Sparnik whispered.

"You can call me Vanessa. What's your name?" Queen Vanessa asked.

"I'm Sparnik, and this is Demaid. She's my sister," Sparnik said, holding Demaid up a little.

Queen Vanessa's eyes widened. "Where're your mommy and daddy?" she asked as she looked all around her.

Sparnik only shrugged. Then, after thinking a moment, he said, "A dark thing came out of the sky and took them. Mommy told me to come here."

"Sparnik, you better come with me, and I'll take Demaid," Queen Vanessa said, taking Demaid out of Sparnik's hands, and she led them inside to King Bryan, in the castle.

"Bryan, something's happened to Sky and Alex. I think Finbar ..." Queen Vanessa didn't finish her sentence but instead said, "These are their children, Sparnik and Demaid."

"Vanessa, take them to the playroom, and I'll have Amanda sent to watch them. We need to talk," Bryan said, smiling kindly at the children. [*Liam has the same dirty blond hair as his father*, I thought to myself.]

While Vanessa carried Demaid, Sparnik followed her to the playroom, and an attendant fetched Amanda to assist the maid already caring for another infant. ["Little Liam," Liam said with a chuckle. "You were so cute. What happened?" I asked Liam. "Ha, ha. You're so funny," Liam said back.]

13

CHILDREN ARE TO BE SEEN ...
DEFINITELY NOT HEARD

Next I saw a part of Kara's and Andy's life. ["You see them at the same time because they've always been together. This is January 15," Liam whispered to me.]

Grace was in labor with Kara, and Bob was rushing her to the hospital, accompanied by Sahara, her best friend, and Sahara's nine-month-old son, Andy.

["That's what you meant when you said they've been together since birth," I said to Liam.

["When did I tell you that?" Liam asked, sounding a little confused.

["Um ... well, you just said they've always been together. That means from birth, right?" I said, hoping I'd made a good recovery and he wouldn't remember when he'd used exactly those words in the other realm.

["Oh, yeah," Liam said.

[*That was a close one*, I thought. *I'll have to watch what I say.*]

Sahara and Andy remained in the waiting room while the nurses put Grace in a wheelchair and wheeled her to a hospital room, accompanied by Bob.

Seconds after Grace had settled into the bed, doctors and nurses poured into the room. Grace was going to ask something, but then a look of severe pain crossed her face, and she doubled up and cried out.

As she did, her arms flew out to grab her belly, and she accidentally hit her left hand on the side of the table. The force caused her ring to turn, but in her pain, she never realized what had happened.

["The ring holds the power to transport the wearer anywhere she wants," Liam told me. "If she wants to go into the past, she twists it counterclockwise. To travel to the future, she turns it clockwise.]

Bob did notice and saw a rose appear on the face of the diamond, like fire, burning into the precious stone. He was going to warn Grace, but it was too late. Although I was watching, I felt I was in the room with them, spinning, spinning, and spinning for several minutes. I looked at the clock in the room, and we had gone forward only five minutes. During that time, the nurse must've felt the spinning, because she tried to get to the door to go get help for Grace. Grace quickly turned the diamond in the opposite direction so the nurse couldn't ruin things, even though it was only a little into the future. The rose appeared, and again the room started spinning, spinning, spinning. When it stopped, they were back five minutes, and no one was the wiser.

At eleven forty-two, Grace gave birth to a beautiful baby girl. As the nurse brought the baby to Grace, she looked down at the infant and said, "She's so beautiful. What's her name?" Grace turned to Bob, turned to the nurse with a big smile on her face, and took the baby, holding her ever so gently. Gazing into her baby girl's face, she said "Kara … Kara Isabel Lawnie.

The next scene moved ahead four years with Grace and Kara in a kitchen. Grace was doing the dishes, and Kara was coloring something on the counter near her mom. Bob came in, and everything stopped when Kara saw him.

"Daddy!" she squealed.

Bob smiled and said, "How are my girls, today?"

"We are just fine. And how did your day go?" asked Grace with a big smile on her face.

"Oh, busy as usual, but good … Hey, honey, don't you have to be at work?" said Bob.

"What? … Oh my goodness! I have to go. Watch Kara, will you?" Grace said as she raced out of the kitchen.

"Yes, yes, go before you're really late," laughed Bob, who knew that Grace hated to be late for anything.

["Bob's a doctor, and Grace owns her own bakery," Liam told me.]

"Okay, bye-bye … Love you, baby," hollered Grace, leaving through the kitchen door.

"Okay, love you too," said Bob, still laughing as he turned to Kara and said, "So now what?"

"Color!" said Kara, and she was coloring again.

Bob decided to pick up some paperwork of his own, and just when he was going to read, the sheets went flying out of his hands. But they didn't fall to the floor, oh no. The papers seem to take on a life of their own and were zooming up over the furniture, past the cabinets, around the room, and everywhere!

Bob looked over at Kara, who was moving her arms with the papers as they whizzed by. She looked as if she were in an orchestra, waving her arms like a conductor. Then she stopped, and all the papers fell to the floor, but she still had a smile on her face, looking up at her daddy.

Bob didn't quite know what to make of this display of fun.

["As you can tell, Kara was a handful when she was younger," Liam said with a chuckle.]

Then a knock sounded at the door.

"Andy … Sahara … they're here!" said Kara as she waited for Bob to get up and get her off the counter.

"What … how do you know that?" asked Bob as he picked Kara up and placed her on the kitchen floor.

"Because it's a play date, Daddy. Hurry up. Come on!" squealed Kara. Before Bob could even take a step, Kara was already running for the front door, trying to twist the handle open. She managed to twist and pull at the same time, and the door popped open, and there stood Andy and his mother, Sahara.

"Andy!" cried Kara, and then she hugged him. Andy was just as excited to see Kara and hugged her back.

Bob then motioned for everyone to step inside. "Come on in. This weather changes so quickly; you'd think living in Seattle we would be used to this by now."

They had stepped inside before the horrible wind started howling away and rattling the front door. Looking out from the front room window, perched upon their knees on the back of the sofa, Kara and Andy could see the wind bending and blowing the trees. The neighbors' garbage can had blown over, and all the contents were flying in little hurricanes around and down the street.

As Bob came into the front room, the sight of the two of them on the sofa so serious and somewhat frightened by what they were seeing made him chuckle to himself.

Finally tiring of watching the wind's activity, Kara and Andy got down and sat on the floor with papers and crayons and a few chocolate chip cookies that Bob had brought out to them with some milk.

Meanwhile, Bob and Sahara had gone back into the kitchen area to enjoy a hot cup of tea and some scones, evidently left over from breakfast. Wanting to keep an eye on the two children while they talked in private, they had left the kitchen's swinging door fixed open with the stopper. At first they were talking in a normal tone of voice about nothing in particular. Then Sahara must have had a more serious issue to discuss with Bob because she started to lower her voice. That must've made Kara curious to find out what exactly they were talking about, and listening from the front room wouldn't tell her. So very quietly, she got up and moved to the side of the front room and along the wall of the dining room where she could probably hear much better.

Before another word was spoken, Andy popped up in the middle of the front room and yelled, "Hey, Kara what's ya doin'?"

Startled by this sudden intrusion, Kara gave a small jump and then looked down at the stopper in the kitchen door. Seeing it as a cover for her spying, Kara sent the stopper flying onto the carpet, and the kitchen door immediately swung shut—and then immediately opened. Behind it stood Sahara.

"What was that Kara? Did you use your powers just now?" Sahara asked.

Kara didn't speak and just stood there kind of silent.

"You have been warned before about using your powers, haven't you, Kara?" Sahara asked.

Kara nodded yes, looking down at her feet.

"This isn't the first time you've used your powers today, is it? You used them in front of your daddy, didn't you?

"What is so wrong about Kara using her powers around me, Sahara? It doesn't hurt anyone," said Bob, getting up to put his cup into the kitchen sink and looking out the kitchen window to the backyard just as a chair blew over on the porch.

"Bob, you don't fully understand. Times are very serious now. Things have changed; they are not what they used to be. We could be headed for dark and serious trouble, not just for Kara but for all of us. We are all at risk now. Every time someone uses his or her powers, it brings them closer to finding us. Don't you understand? You did hear about Sky and Alex didn't you, and their so-called accident? Right now, they could be watching …" Sahara let her voice trail off.

"Who's watching us?" asked Bob as he looked closer out the kitchen window and scanned the backyard one more time before sitting down across the table from Sahara.

"Sorry. I have said too much already. You would think by now I would learn to keep my mouth shut, especially in front of the children," whispered Sahara.

"Sahara, tell me more about this accident. We were told that they died avoiding a deer and the car flipped and ...," said Bob, looking over at the two children, who were now standing at the swinging door, listening.

"I'll not go into specifics right now," whispered Sahara, glancing over at the two children, "but I can assure you it was no deer. The ones I feel so sorry for are their two kids. They survived. And just a few of us know where they have been hidden for their own protection," said Sahara a little louder but still not above much more than a whisper.

Sahara turned her attention to Kara, "Are you all right, pumpkin. Don't look so worried. Daddy and Sahara won't let anything happen to you or to Andy, I promise."

Kara looked confused, as if she was trying to figure out a math problem or a very difficult puzzle.

"What is it, honey?" asked Sahara.

"You have powers just like me, huh?" asked Kara.

Sahara looked at Bob; Bob looked back at Sahara and just shrugged his shoulders.

"Yes …yes ... I do, Kara, just like you," sighed Sahara.

"What are your powers?" Kara asked.

"I can sense when other people have powers, and I can tell what their powers are, but they have to be close to me of course." Sahara said and she bent over to hold little Kara's hands between her own.

"WOW! Do you know what my powers are? Where do I get my powers? Who gave them to me? Do Mommy and Daddy have powers, too?" asked Kara.

"Yes, yes, honey, one question at a time," Sahara said. "Everything has an answer," Sahara said.

"Does Andy have any powers?" Kara asked, looking at Andy and Sahara.

"Yes," said Sahara, looking over at Andy and welcoming him to join them at the kitchen table.

"Mommy, can I show her? ... Please?" asked Andy, looking up to her with his fire red hair half in his eyes and a grin ever so wide.

"Okay, but nothing scary!" Sahara said. Then she turned and gave a wink to Kara. Sahara then turned back to Andy, and when Kara looked at Andy, she looked stunned at what she saw.

Andy stood in the middle of the kitchen and slowly raised his arms from his sides to waist level, creating a beautiful powder-blue aura all around him.

Something very slowly started to emerge from within the aura. Faint at first, it gradually became darker and took the shape of a person. Finally, it formed the figure of a woman, absolutely beautiful with an angelic face but dressed in clothes anyone would wear—blue jeans, blue denim jacket, and a green tank-top that accentuated her emerald green eyes that smiled so softly at the foursome in the kitchen that afternoon.

"Oh! My! Sky, is that you?" asked Sahara with a small bit of alarm in her voice. "I hadn't expected that Andy would bring you here. How wonderful to see you again, dear," said Sahara warmly. ["They were very best friends before Sky died," said Liam.]

"Yes, Sahara, and I am so glad to see you, too. How I wish I could have a bit of that scone there, but I guess that won't be possible from here," sighed Sky. "And who is this I see next to you? You're Kara, right?"

Kara looked over at her dad for approval, and he nodded and said, "Go on, honey; answer Sky."

"Yes, Ma'am, yes, I am," answered Kara shyly.

Now Sky's aura was shimmering back and forth, as if waving in the wind. Sahara said, "Please, don't leave us, Sky."

"Quickly, now, I have something to ask all of you," responded Sky just above a whisper. Sky started to talk and then stopped and looked all around, as if someone else was about to overhear what she had to say.

"Our two children …" Sky was fading even more now. "Our two children, Sparnik and Demaid, I need you to watch them for me, keep them safe, and especially—and this is so important, for I have never spoken to anyone about this …" Again she looked around the room. "Never, oh, never let …" And Sky faded totally away.

"Wait! Sky! Wait!" cried Sahara. "Finish it! Finish what you were going to tell us!"

Just then a huge wind hit the backyard and spun the lawn chair around, causing it to bang with a horrible THUD against the back wall of the house. Everyone jumped. Kara ran to Bob, and Andy was in Sahara's arms in a second, and then all the lights flickered and WHACK! All the lights blew out in one blinding flash. From a distance, through the wind, came a scream, a long and horrifying woman's scream.

I barely had time to take in the events in that scene when the next one started. Grace and Bob were decorating the entire house with streamers and balloons. ["It's Kara's sixth birthday. Nothing really important happens in this part, but I thought you might enjoy this," said Liam.]

As young kids entered the house, Grace put a red ribbon in Kara's blond hair.

"He's late, Mommy," cried Kara, looking out the front room window, her blond curls bouncing on her back. "You don't think he got sick or something. Maybe they got lost. Or … maybe ….." Kara let her voice fade off.

"Now, now, Kara," said Grace. "Andy is just running a little late. You worry too much for a six-year-old. Stop all that and come join your other guests."

"All right, Mommy," sighed Kara, dragging her feet off the sofa and heading back into the kitchen.

Just then the doorbell rang. Kara ran so fast to get the door that she slid on the small carpet in front of it and banged smack into the door.

"Ow! Oh, Andy, where have you been?" asked Kara.

As Andy and Sahara walked through the door, Andy held his present up high in the air so Kara would have to jump for it. But, instead, the present zoomed out of Andy's hands to Kara so fast that Andy just stood in the doorway, confused and a little disappointed.

"Kara! Did you just use your powers?" scolded Sahara.

Just then Grace came out of the kitchen. "Well, hello, strangers. Glad you could make it. What's wrong, Sahara?" asked Grace.

"Grace, I think Kara just used her powers in front of everyone," said Sahara.

"Oh! No! Did you, Kara? Tell Mommy. Did you use your powers just now?" asked Grace.

"Sorry, Mommy. I got so excited about seeing Andy that I took the present from him before he gave it to me. Should I give it back?" asked Kara with a small tear in her eye.

"Let's just forget it for now, but be careful, especially around other people. You never know who is watching and waiting for you to show and use your powers, honey," said Sahara as she bent over and kissed the top of Kara's head and then wished her a very happy birthday.

All afternoon, the house was buzzing with excitement. Everyone was playing games and running around, and then Grace called everyone to the backyard as she carried out the birthday cake decorated with blue, purple, and green circles all around the sides and top. [*Even then Kara liked those colors*, I thought.] Along the edges of the top of the cake ran white icing, and a graceful and lacy purple butterfly adorned the top, safely low enough from the six big green and blue candles all lit up and ready to be blown out by Kara.

"Go on, Kara. Make a wish. Wish for something that you really want," said Andy.

Kara held her breath and blew as hard as she could all around the cake, until all the candles were blown out. And then without any warning, she leaned over towards Andy and gave him one big kiss right on the cheek.

Everyone cheered and laughed, except one sitting in complete shock, wearing a grin and rubbing the side of his cheek.

["Two years later," Liam said as the scene changed again.]

"Aye, yes ... Hello, may I speak to Grace Lawnie, please?" inquired a woman's hard voice. [*I know that voice*, I thought to myself.]

"Yes, this is Grace Lawnie. May I help you?"

"Mrs. Lawnie, hello. My name is Miranda Horn. I'm calling about your daughter, Kara." [*No way! Mrs. Horn!* I thought.]

"What about Kara, Mrs. Thorn?" said Grace.

"Mrs. Horn ... Horn ... dear with just an H," demanded Mrs. Horn.

"Sorry ...," said Grace.

"As I was saying, dear, we are calling about Kara, your daughter, joining us at Brownstone Boarding School," said Mrs. Horn.

Mrs. Horn continued, "You know, Grace—may I call you Grace?"

"Aye ... yes, yes, of course, you may call me Grace ...," whispered Grace. "What is this all about? My Kara is only eight years old," sighed Grace.

"Well, Grace, we have received from outside sources very impressive recommendations about your little Kara. We feel that she is gifted in many ways beyond her years, don't you agree?" said Mrs. Horn.

"What? Well ... mm," Grace muttered, looking worried.

["Grace later told us she was afraid someone had seen Kara use magic and had told Mrs. Horn. She said, if Mrs. Horn had asked about it, Grace wouldn't have known what to say," Liam said.]

"Don't you agree, Grace?" asked Mrs. Horn. And then after a pause, she added, "Grace, Grace, are you still there?"

"I'm sorry, Mrs. Horn. What were you saying?" asked Grace.

[*So I'm not the only one who doesn't listen to Mrs. Horn's rambling. Grace doesn't either*, I thought.]

"I was … saying … how … in school … Kara … is very intelligent!" said Mrs. Horn somewhat frustrated.

"Oh! Yes, you are right. Yes, you are quite right. Kara is very bright," Grace said taking a deep breath.

"So what day should I make it?" Mrs. Horn asked.

"I'm sorry. I must have missed that part of the conversation. What day for what?" Grace asked back.

"Well … Mrs. Lawnie, for you, your husband, and your daughter, Kara, to come in and see our beautiful school," Mrs. Horn said as if Grace had asked a question with a most obvious answer, like how do you make ice?

"Well, of course, I will have to talk about this with my husband. Where exactly is Brownstone located?" Grace asked.

"Well, this is certainly a first, that someone doesn't know where Brownstone is," said Mrs. Horn, clearly put out. "However … Mrs. Lawnie, Brownstone Boarding School is located in one of the finest of neighborhoods, in Brier. I have September second available right now, that is, if you are interested. Be aware, Grace, we are filling our schedules and calendars up very fast, and you know what they say—the early bird does get the worm," stated Mrs. Horn quite frankly.

Grace rolled her eyes at this statement but went over and looked at her calendar nonetheless.

"Let's see, today is only the twenty-eighth …," said Grace.

"Is there a problem, dear?" asked Mrs. Horn.

"Hmmm … no, no ... not at all, Mrs. Horn. Looks like we have a date," said Grace.

"Good. Very well, Grace, we will see you and your husband and that bright little Kara on the second—at two o'clock, shall we say?" asked Mrs. Horn.

"That will be just fine, Mrs. Horn," sighed Grace.

"I look forward to meeting you then, dear," said Mrs. Horn, squeaking out a very small bit of sweetness in her voice.

Ten minutes must have passed after ending the call when Grace finally realized that she was sitting in the chair, in the kitchen, with the phone still in her hand. She shook her head as she walked into the dining room, still holding the receiver. As the cord popped her back, she then remembered to hang it up.

["Brownstone Boarding school," Liam whispered.]

I saw the three Lawnie's, Grace, Bob, and Kara sitting in the waiting area near Mrs. Horn's office. Grabbing at his neck and squeezing two fingers between his skin and the starched collar of his shirt so that he might be able to breathe, Bob said, "I hate wearing ties."

Grace shot Bob a look that would have stopped charging elephants—and put an end to his comments. Grace looked down at Kara with the same stern look but gave a quick wink, so Bob didn't notice and think it was okay to loosen his tie.

Immediately after that exchange, Mrs. Horn came out and looked their way. At first she said absolutely nothing and just looked each one, in turn, up and down, as if inspecting the troops.

Bob leaned over and whispered to Grace, "Who is she?"

"Shhh!" Grace whispered back.

Adjusting her glasses down her nose and peering over them, Mrs. Horn finally spoke out in a low but demanding tone, "You must be the Lawnie family, and this must be Kara, about whom I have heard so many incredible stories."

Kara did not answer; instead, she just looked at her parents.

Grace spoke first. "Mrs. Horn, I trust?"

Mrs. Horn turned her attention to Grace and said, "You trust right, and you must be Grace?"

"Yes, I am," said Grace, "and this is my husband, Bob, and daughter, Kara."

Bob stood up to shake her hand, and Mrs. Horn just ignored his hand and spoke directly to Kara.

"So you are here, Kara, to see your new school," said Mrs. Horn.

"Well, we are not sure about that; we haven't even seen the school," said Bob.

"Small technicality, I assure you, Mr. Lawnie," said Mrs. Horn as she straightened herself up and, pulling down on her jacket, forced a small smile to emerge on her puckered lips. "Well, shall we have a look at your new school? Isn't that why you came here today?" Mrs. Horn said with a half laugh. "Let's get started!"

Bob looked over at Grace, and they exchanged glances—fortunately, Mrs. Horn never saw—followed by Bob rolling his eyes and Grace mouthing, "Sorry ..."

"This school looks big. How many rooms does it have?" asked Kara.

"Excuse me, young lady. Children are to be seen, definitely not heard, in my book," said Mrs. Horn. "I will be quite happy to address any questions that your mother and father deem important, though."

"Well, then, how many rooms does this school have?" asked Bob, shooting a wink to Kara. Kara just smiled back and then gave a glaring look at Mrs. Horn.

"Kara ... Kara ...," whispered Grace. "What do you think so far?"

Kara looked up with sad eyes at her mother and then over to her father. "Are you serious about having me go here, Mommy?" whispered Kara with desperation in her voice. "This place is so big, and I might get lost, or ... or ... they might lose me."

"I don't think so, darling, and anyway, nothing has been decided. Daddy and Mommy still have to talk about many things before we can even think about your going here."

"Excuse me," said Mrs. Horn, clearing her throat as if she had something in it, [*Even then she had a fur ball in her throat,* I thought, holding back a little laugh.] "As we were saying, before we were so rudely interrupted by whispering ..." Mrs. Horn glared down at Kara.

"Yes .... yes, Mrs. Horn, as you were saying," said Grace.

"Brownstone Boarding School is one of the finest boarding schools in Washington State. You won't find anything like what we have here," Mrs. Horn said with a suspicious smile on her face.

They continued on down the sunlit hallway in uncomfortable silence.

Then Mrs. Horn turned to Grace and Bob and said, "Maybe we should discuss Kara's fees in my office." Turning around, she started walking back the way they had come, not even waiting to see if they were following her.

"Not much of a tour," Bob whispered to Grace.

"Excuse me, Mr. Lawnie, but you've seen all you need to," said Mrs. Horn, still walking.

"How ...," Bob was about to say but shook his head instead.

"We didn't get to see the rest of the school," Kara said, looking at her parents.

"I know, baby, but maybe later on we'll look around more," Grace said, smiling at Kara.

They finally came to Mrs. Horn's office, and she turned and said to Grace and Bob, "I think the child should stay out here .... for the time being, anyway." She had added that last part when she saw the look of confusion on both Grace's and Bob's faces.

Bob and Grace graciously went into Mrs. Horn's office. She waited for the two to take a seat in front of her desk before she turned towards Kara out in the hallway and gave a wrinkled smile so incredibly evil that you could almost hear animals running away in fear.

Kara sat in the waiting area, just swinging her legs back and forth, staring at her black shoes. After a few moments, she looked up and saw an orange cat sitting in the hallway. She called to it, whispering, "Here kitty ... here kitty, kitty." But the cat didn't move. Instead, it just stared back at her with its big blue eyes. Then quick as a flash, the cat bounded straight up and ran down the hall.

Kara jumped up from her chair, running out of the waiting area and after the cat. The more she ran so did the cat, becoming a game between the two of them. All of a sudden a growling sound came from the hall where the cat was heading, and Kara stopped dead in her tracks.

"Here kitty. Where are you?"

"Grr ..."

"Hello ...? Who's there?" Kara asked.

"Kara ... is that you?" said a familiar voice.

Kara turned around to see ... "Andy!" Kara whispered. "Andy, what are you doing here?"

"My mom got a call, and the next thing I know we're here. Are you coming here too, Kara?" Andy asked.

"I think so ... My mom and dad are talking to Mrs. Horn," Kara answered with a frown on her face.

Then a group of kids came up behind Andy.

"Andy, who are the kids behind you?" Kara asked.

"Oh, um ... Liam, can you help here?" Andy asked, and a boy the same age as Kara with dirty blond hair and a big smile on his lightly tanned face stepped up next to her. I giggled slightly as I saw eight-year-old Liam.

"I'll show you everything you need to know. Just take my hand," said Liam as he put his hand out for Kara.

Kara debated a second, but then she took Liam's hand and looked at Andy. Something happened, and she closed her eyes. When Liam took his hand away, Kara opened her eyes.

"You all have powers too?" Kara asked, stunned. Everyone nodded.

14

BULLFIGHTS, SECRETS, AND SURPRISES

Then everything changed and I was in Spain at a bullfight. And right next to me was a family of four, the two parents and a boy and a girl. *Nicky and Treelea*, I thought, since they looked like twins. [Treelea and Nicky are five years old," Liam said, confirming my guess. "Their mom's name is Eva; their dad is Tom."] The matador was going to kill the bull when Treelea froze everyone but her family. ["Treelea can freeze time and people. She can also talk to animals," Liam said.] When everyone was frozen, the bull got up from the ground, got out of the arena by knocking down a weak gate, and went to the hills.

"Oh, Treelea!" Eva said with a half smile. ["She's a nymph, but Eva doesn't really talk about being a nymph. I think she just wants to blend in," Liam said.]

"Mommy, Treelea used her powers," Nicky said, shaking his dark red hair like his mom's. [And Nicky can stop any power he wants," Liam told me.]

"It's not that bad," Tom whispered to Eva. [He's a dragon rider. That's why he has Nury," Liam said.]

"No, but I think it's time to go," Eva said, and when everyone else unfroze, the Castle family was gone.

We moved ahead several years, and in the next scene, Treelea and Nicky were teenagers, keeping to themselves while walking down what looked like a school hallway crowded with kids. A guy with an open soda came running down the hall. Someone tripped him, and his soda went up over Treelea's head, and then everything but Treelea and Nicky froze.

"Treelea!" Nicky turned to Treelea, looking upset.

"What?" Treelea asked.

"You did it again. Why can't we go to one school without you freezing someone or you talking to the animals?" Nicky said, continuing down the hallway with Treelea behind him and both of them moving around the people frozen.

"I can't help it if animals need my help and soda does not go with this top," Treelea said with a little laugh, looking at her white short-sleeve hoodie top. ["Some had a challenge in finding a school, as you can see," Liam said to me.]Next we switched to Martin, his mother, and his father in, probably, a room of their house. ["Their names are Owen and Irma," Liam told me. "And, boy, do they like fighting."] As Irma knit, Owen and Martin fought, as if for their lives. I could see they would not really kill the other, but they certainly took that exercise seriously. *They all have black hair a little lighter than mine*, I thought to myself. ["That's Martin's power; he can fight like any warrior he wants. That's one of the reasons I have Martin for my bodyguard," Liam said.]

I didn't know Martin was your bodyguard, I thought. *Of course that would explain why you two go everywhere together ... and share a dorm room ..."*

"Martin, concentrate on your power. Come on. You can do it," Owen said, tackling Martin to the ground. Martin got out of the tackle, breathless, closed his eyes, and like lightning, was gone. One second later, he was behind his father. "How's that, old man?" Martin asked as he got his father into a chokehold. Owen tapped Martin's arm for a tap-out, and when Martin let go, both he and his father were smiling.

"Not bad for today," Owen said.

"I totally got you, and you know it," Martin said.

"Really? You think you can take me?" Owen said, picking up a stick and Martin immediately doing the same.

"Oh, for goodness sake! Will you two stop fighting? Put the sticks down and come talk to me, for once," Irma said. Somewhat reluctantly, both put their sticks down and joined Irma, watching the fire and talking.

Again, the scene changed, but this one I could tell was a bit more recent.

I saw a man with the same sandy-blond hair as Sandy walk into a small living room and sit on a green couch next to a dog. ["Last, but not least, Sandy and her father, Aaron," Liam said.] The dog turned toward Aaron with its big blue eyes and put its head on the couch. Suddenly, the dog turned into an eighteen-year-old girl, and she sat down next to him. *Sandy and Sparnik are shape shifters*, I thought. *That explains so much...*

["So it's just Sandy and her father?" I asked Liam.

["Aaron's not Sandy's real father. He found Sandy on his doorstep when she was very young. She had changed herself into a cat, but when she saw Aaron, she changed back into her human form, I guess she could tell he was good or something." Liam told me as I watched Aaron and Sandy watching TV together.] They looked like the perfect little family, laughing and having a good time. Just watching them made me smile, as if I could feel their hopes and joys.

["Do you want more, or are you okay for now?" Liam asked.

["What?" I asked, not understanding

["Would you like to see anything else or what?" Liam asked.

["Thanks but I'm done, at least for now," I said.]

And next thing I knew, I was in front of my friends again.

"Wow," I said when my head stopped spinning.

"Too much?" Liam asked.

"No, it's just ..." I stopped trying to think of something to say, and then I noticed Liam and I were still holding hands. I slowly withdrew my hand from his grasp. "And your power is …?" I asked.

"I can touch anyone, or anything, and know its history," Liam said.

"So do you know my history?" I asked in a sudden panic.

"If you want me to, just take my hands again," Liam said, holding out his hands.

"That's okay," I said with a nervous smile. Liam nodded once in agreement, with a smile on his face.

"Are your secrets that bad?" Liam asked.

"Oh, I'm sure they would surprise you," I said, looking at Liam, wondering what he would do if he learned the truth about me. As we stood there, I could hear the music playing a soft melody.

"Would you care to dance?" Liam asked, holding out his hand. I smiled and then took his hand as we went to the dance floor. He then put his other hand on my waist, I put mine on his shoulder, and we started slow dancing.

"You remind me of someone," Liam said as we danced.

"Whom do I remind you of?" I asked.

"I don't know … You just do," Liam said, and I relaxed.

"It seemed like the hours were passing by when you were showing me all that about the others," I said.

"Yes, it seems so. But when I'm seeing—or showing—someone's past, time stops. What you thought took hours, I truthfully showed you all in the blink of an eye," Liam said.

"Oh," I said, trying to concentrate on his words and not get too lost in our dancing and his holding me and my being so close and …

"What do you do?" Liam asked, looking into my eyes.

I turned my head and pretended to be looking around the room, hiding my giveaway eyes or he would know me for sure.

"I do a lot of things," I said.

"Like what?"

"I talk to the creatures of Lycia Forest, and sometimes I do magic tricks for money," I said as we danced in a circle.

"What's it like?" Liam asked.

"Talking to the creatures or doing magic tricks for money?" I asked.

"Both," Liam said.

"Well you're the king's son. You probably already know about talking to the creatures," I said.

"Not really," Liam said in a low voice.

"Well some of the creatures are really nice, others not so much. But those others don't bother me."

"Why not?" Liam said.

"Because they know I have power over fire and other elements, and they don't want to test it," I said with a little laugh.

"What kind of tricks do you do?" Liam asked.

"You'll just have to see me do them someday," I said with a big smile.

"Hmm ... maybe I will," Liam said, smiling back.

"You should," I said with a slight giggle.

"How about your family?" Liam asked.

"They live far away," I said, looking at all the ladies around me and how they jealously eyed my dress.

"Don't mind them," Liam said.

I looked up at him briefly, keeping my eyes a secret still, as we danced. Then the song stopped, and I realized it was dark.

"I have to go," I said as we walked back to the others.

"Why?" Liam asked.

"It's a long story, but I'll be back. Look for me on the street. I'll be the one doing the magic tricks. And don't give up on your girlfriend," I said to Liam as I ran out of the castle, waving goodbye.

When I got back to my dorm, it was a half hour past midnight. I was late because my landing was off again, and I landed in bushes outside a house a block away from the school. I ran the whole way, and as fast I could, I grabbed my PJs and threw them on, put my mask and stone away, and got into my bed. Just in time. I had hardly pulled the covers over me before the door opened and Treelea walked in. I pretended to be asleep, but I watched through my eyelashes. She looked at me, making sure I was asleep, and then she changed into her PJs and got into bed. I relaxed a bit and let sleep overtake me, thinking of what I had just learned about my not so normal friends.

The next day I woke up, smiling and feeling good, knowing that Liam hadn't cheated on me. I brushed my teeth and put on a light pink and white sundress. *Nice sunny weather today for once*, I thought. I pulled out my sandals that matched my outfit, added silver butterfly earrings and a pink flower necklace, and grabbed my pink fuzzy bag (with my cell phone, keys, money, and makeup). Out the door I ran—WHAM!—right into someone. Then I noticed who I had hit, and I started laughing uncontrollably.

"Why are you laughing?" Liam asked, standing up and then helping me up.

"Don't you see? This is how we first met," I said, and then he smiled.

"I think you should stop running, or we'll end up in the ER," Liam said with a little laugh, and I laughed again.

"Annadyomene ...," Liam started but stopped.

"Liam, I know you didn't cheat," I said.

"I would never hurt you. You know that, right?" Liam said.

I nodded my head yes with a half smile. Then I said, "It just looked like you … Maybe my mind was playing tricks on me." When I stopped talking, Liam looked as if he had just figured out something. "Jenny," he whispered in a kind of angry tone. Just as I was about to ask what he was talking about, he started talking again.

"So why were you running?" Liam asked.

"I … I was going to see you," I said.

"I see," Liam said with a mocking smile, and I pushed him playfully.

"But Liam... where were you?" I asked.

Liam sighed slightly and after a moment he finally said, "I was with my parents."

"Liam ... oh Liam," Jenny Fair called from down the hall.

"*Baka* ('stupid' in Japanese)," I whispered, and Liam laughed.

"Liam, where have you been?" Jenny looked at me as she talked to Liam.

"I've been with Annadyomene," Liam said, looking at me with a smile.

"So, Liam, do you want to walk me to class?" Jenny asked, this time looking only at Liam.

"Sorry, Jenny, but I have to talk to Annadyomene," Liam said, taking my hand.

I felt a blush working its way up to my cheeks. Then Liam and I walked away together, leaving Jenny and all her meanness behind us.

"So what did you want to talk about?" I asked.

"I don't know. I just want some time with you," Liam said, looking at me with soft eyes.

"You really want time with me?" I asked.

Liam nodded his head yes.

"Then you have to catch me," I said with a smile, and I started running down the stairs, Liam after me.

"Catch me if you can," I said, laughing, as I ran outside to the courtyard.

"Anna, what are you doing?" Treelea asked as I ran past her and the rest of the group.

"Playing a little cat and mouse," I said, still running away from Liam.

"Are you two in the second grade?" Kara said with a smile.

"Yep," I said. Then Liam got me and picked me up off the ground. I started laughing as he swung me around.

"Miss Ribbon," Mrs. Horn called, and all the laughing stopped. Liam put me back on the ground. "What is this?" Mrs. Horn asked.

"I'm sorry, Mrs. Horn. It ..." I tried to talk, but it's pointless to try to communicate with Mrs. Horn.

"My office, Miss Ribbon," Mrs. Horn said.

I turned to say something to my friends, but she cut me off.

"Now, Miss Ribbon," she demanded, pointing to her office. I walked after her with my head held high.

"What were you doing out there, Miss Ribbon?" Mrs. Horn asked.

"Just having fun, Mrs. Horn," I answered, thinking the word "fun" was probably not in her vocabulary.

"Really?"

"Yes, Mrs. Horn."

"You were acting like a crazy girl. What if a new student came today and saw you like that? What would he or she think?" Mrs. Horn asked.

Before I could stop myself, I said, "Well, nothing because you would already have the student's brain in a jar, controlling them like you control everything else."

Mrs. Horn looked ready to kill. It was a good thing she didn't have a gun in her hand.

"You are never to act like that again. Do we understand each other, Miss Ribbon?" she asked.

"Yes, Ma'am. I won't ever do that again ...," and then I whispered, "in front of you."

"You may go, but don't forget I am watching you," Mrs. Horn said in a firm voice as I left the room.

When I met up with everyone, they all asked what happened, did I get in trouble, what did I say.

"No, I'm not in trouble," I said, leaning against Liam.

"Then why did she call you?" Nicky asked.

"I don't know, but I kind of slipped up in her office," I said.

"What do you mean?" Liam asked.

"She said, 'You were acting like a crazy girl. What if a new student came today and saw you like that? What would he or she think?' And I said, 'Well, nothing because you would already have the kid's brain in a jar, controlling them like you control everything else.'" Everyone in the group started laughing.

"She also said she was watching me," I said.

"What, like a stalker?" Liam asked.

"I don't know. She reminded me of the dean in *Animal House*. 'You've been on double secret probation since the beginning of this year,'" I said, mocking the dean.

A few moments later, Liam and I decided to leave the group and so we headed back to my dorm.

"So do you want to do something tonight?" I asked Liam when we were alone in my room.

"I can't; I have to meet with my parents. Sorry," Liam said with a sad smile.

"No, no, that's okay," I said, thinking of Hoshi.

"You sure?" Liam asked.

"Oh, sigh, without you here, I'll just die," I said in a damsel-in-distress voice, putting the back of my hand to my forehead.

"Okay, I get it," Liam said, and we both started laughing.

"Stop laughing," I commanded Liam, and he stopped.

"Why?"

"Didn't you hear? No fun for me—I'm being watched," I said, and Liam looked around.

FIRE TRICKS AND DRAGONS GALORE

"I better protect you." And with a laugh, he started tickling me.

"Liam ... stop ... I mean it ... Ha ha!" I said laughing. Then Liam stopped tickling me, and we both lay on my bed, his arms still around me. I looked into his eyes, and he looked into mine. He brushed my hair softly, and as he leaned in to kiss me—

RING!

"Sorry," he said and pulled his phone from his pocket.

"Hello," Liam said.

"Liam, where are you?" I heard Martin over the phone.

"With Annadyomene. Why?"

"Dude, we're going to be late," Martin said.

"Okay, okay. I'll be there in a second," Liam said and hung up the phone.

"I have to go," he said, getting up off my bed.

"Have fun," I said.

"Thanks. I'll see you soon."

"Sooner than you think," I whispered so he couldn't hear. Then he walked out the door and was gone. I grabbed my stuff and headed out the window for an unobserved return to Hoshi. When I made it back to Hoshi, my landing was softer than usual. Then I noticed glowing creatures around me.

"Nature, are you all right?" a blue fairy asked.

"Is that you, Hana?" I asked.

"You remember me?" The little fairy Hana sounded shocked.

"Yes," I said, trying to get up—out of a bed sheet? "What happened?" I asked.

"We saw you falling and grabbed this sheet," Tsubomi, a boy fairy with red wings, said.

"Oh, thank you," I said when I was back to the ground.

"You're welcome," all twenty fairies said at the same time.

"Well, not to be rude, but I have to go soon. So has anything new happened?"

"Oh, Nature," a green fairy said as she flew to a tree branch at my eye level.

"What?" I asked.

"We all feel something evil is approaching," Hana said.

"All the fairies feel this?" I asked, and the twenty fairies shook their heads no.

"No, just all the creatures in Lycia Forest feel this way," Tsubomi said, crossing his arms over his chest.

"I see ... Will you tell me if anything else happens?" I asked, and all the fairies nodded their heads yes.

"Thank you, my friends," I said, walking toward the castle. When I made it on the road near the castle, I set my stuff aside and when I turned my back to the castle wall, I saw people stop walking and look at me with excitement. Everyone was ready to watch the show; I could even see a few of the traders in the market-place look over.

"Hello, everyone," I said as I made fire appear in midair, forming the word "HELLO" for all to see. "Now for this trick, I will need a daring volunteer," I said, looking around at everyone as the fire greeting disappeared.

"We've got one," someone in the crowd shouted.

"Then come forward," I said, and Martin pushed Liam to the front.

"Don't worry. It won't hurt ... much," I said, and suddenly Liam looked a little freaked.

"I'm kidding. Just hold still," I said and then made a water dragon appear, which wrapped around Liam.

"Think of Cora," I said to Liam, and he smiled.

"Do you all like this water dragon?" I asked, and the crowd cheered.

"What if I told you I could change this water dragon into a fire dragon?" The crowd cheered more, and I transformed the creature into a fire dragon, still winding itself around Liam.

"How are you doing?" I asked.

"A little nervous," Liam said.

"I was talking to the dragon."

"Oh."

"I'm kidding ... I was asking both of you," I said, trying to hold back a laugh while also keeping Liam distracted as I worked on my finale trick.

BOOM! The dragon engulfing Liam had blown up, and beautiful, fresh flowers rained down everywhere. The crowd had gone wild, and everyone was trying to pick up as many flowers as possible. Then I opened up the little pocket bag I had with me and collected the money people were willing to give for my trick.

"That was so cool," my friends said as they came up to me.

"Thanks," I said.

"Nature, do you want to walk with us?" Treelea asked.

"Sure, but not for long. I have somewhere to go," I said.

"Where's that?" Andy asked, and Kara elbowed him in the side.

"One of the things I have to do is give some of this money to those who need it," I said.

"You're giving away the money you just worked for?" Treelea said, sounding confused.

"I don't need much money here, so I give it to those that need it the most," I said. Next time I was free in Hoshi, I would give it to the people and creatures; I had made that promise to myself. But I just told my friends I had to go, leaving out the detail that I wanted to beat them back to Brownstone so they wouldn't be wondering where normal Anna had gone.

"How come you don't need that much money? Don't you live here?" Sparnik asked.

"Um ... no, I don't live here," I said.

"Where do you live?" Treelea asked.

"I move around a lot in different realms," I said with a half laugh.

"That's cool," Liam said as we kept walking.

"So how did things work out with you and your girlfriend, Liam?" I asked, changing to a safer subject and one of more interest to me.

"We're back together," Liam said.

"That's good," I said as we walked. Liam nodded in agreement. "Isn't it?" I asked, concerned with his unenthusiastic answer.

"Yeah ... of course it is," he said without genuine feeling.

"Hear of anything new?" I asked.

"No why?" Liam said.

"I was talking with the fairies today, and they told me all the creatures in Lycia Forest feel something evil coming," I said.

"Like what?" Sparnik asked.

"I think ... I think it's Finbar," I said, and we all stopped walking.

"Are you sure?" Nicky asked.

"I just have a feeling of my own," I said.

"We have to tell our parents," Treelea said.

"Leave it to me," Demaid said, and she closed her eyes.

"What is she doing?" I asked Liam.

"Demaid can read minds and communicate with others through their mind," Liam said.

"I told them," Demaid said.

"Liam, does that mean she can read my mind?" I asked.

"Yes and no. Demaid doesn't like invading a person's mind. I mean sometimes she can't help it and she hears a person's thoughts. But that doesn't happen much," Liam whispered to me.

"But has she been in my mind?" I asked.

"No, but she does think you have some secrets you don't want anyone to know," Liam said.

"How does she know that?"

"Well, for one, you wear a mask to hide your face. And you always avoid questions about yourself."

"If anyone found out who I am, I'd be treated differently. I know it."

"You sure about that?" Liam asked.

"My friends would be upset because I kept this from them," I said.

"If they're true friends, then they'll understand," Liam said.

"So if you found out something surprising about someone you know, what would you do?" I asked.

"I'd try to understand that person's side of the story," Liam said.

"And you wouldn't get mad at that person?" I asked.

"No," Liam said.

"Sure, you say that now," I whispered to myself as Liam turned back to the others.

"Nature, we're going to watch the sunset. You want to come?" Demaid asked.

"Ah ... sure," I said, and we all walked out of the village to the hill. When we sat down on the ground, I put my hands in the soft grass and made flowers appear.

"What are you doing?" Liam asked, sitting next to me.

"Ah ... nothing," I said.

Liam picked up a gold lily. "This is nothing?" he asked, smelling the flower. Then he put it in my hair.

"Oh, look at the colors," Sandy said, and we all oohed and ahed at the changing display in the sky—bright reds and pinks turning to oranges, golds, and yellows and finally light purple and dark blue.

"What do you think?" Liam asked me.

"I think it's lovely," I said, careful to avoid letting Liam see my eyes. But I could feel him staring at me, and I looked down, pretending not to notice his stare.

The sun had completely dropped below the horizon, and only the faintest of colors remained in the sky. Soon darkness covered all.

"I have to go," I said, getting up, and Liam did the same.

"I'll walk with you, if you want." Liam said.

"No thanks. I have to go by myself. Goodbye," I said to everyone, and they said the same to me. Then I ran into Lycia Forest to give a safe distance from my friends for my return.

Being Followed?

I made it back to the other realm, landing near a supermarket five minutes away from school, and ran all the way to my dorm. I opened my door and slammed it as I ran over to my bed quickly.

"Hello," someone in my room said.

I gave a little yelp. Then I turned around to see Trent sitting on Treelea's bed.

"What are you doing here?" I asked in a shaky voice.

"I just wanted to say hi," Trent said.

"How did you get in here?" I asked.

"I've been picking locks for years," he said, getting up from Treelea's bed.

"Stay where you are," I said.

"Or what?" Trent asked, coming closer to me. Not even thinking, I went to the open window, and I stepped onto the window ledge.

"You're going to jump, is that it?" Trent laughed, and he came even closer.

"Get out of my room, now," I said and stepped onto a branch of the tree next to my window.

"Don't worry; I'll forgive you for being with Liam," Trent said, now at the window.

"Like I would ever be with you," I said, and you could see Trent getting angry.

"Come back inside, and we can talk about this, baby," Trent said touching my hair. I turned my head in disgust.

"Don't call me baby," I said, and that did it for Trent. He grabbed my arm to pull me inside, but instead I slipped off the branch.

"Ahhhhh!" I screamed as I fell with no time to use my powers. I hit the ground with an awful thud and yelled even louder. As I rolled on the ground in pain, holding my left arm, I heard a door open, and in a moment Mr. Tenth and Mrs. Horn were standing over me.

"What happened?" Mr. Tenth asked.

"I fell from my window. Ow! I think my arm is broken," I said. Mr. Tenth touched my arm, and I said even louder, "Owwww," wincing in pain and turning away from him and Mrs. Horn.

"I think she's right; it's broken. We better get her to the hospital," Mr. Tenth said to Mrs. Horn.

"Oh, all right," Mrs. Horn said after giving it some thought, as if falling from a two-story window was nothing a Band-Aid couldn't fix. Having done her part, she let Mr. Tenth help me up and walk me to his car, a 2006 tonic blue Ford Mondeo.

"Watch your head," Mr. Tenth warned me as I got into the passenger side of the car. He shut my door, then got in behind the wheel, and drove me to the hospital.

"So how did you fall out your window?" Mr. Tenth asked as we sat in the waiting room.

"Someone was in my room uninvited, so I went to my window and fell," I said.

Mr. Tenth shook his head and didn't ask any more questions.

Finally, a nurse called my name, and I went in for X-rays. After that, I met Dr. Masker, who first stopped the bleeding from my forehead and taped a large piece of gauze to the wound. Because of the pain in my arm, I hadn't even noticed I had also hit my head when I had landed. Then he put a cast on my left arm. When he briefly left the room to talk with the nurse, my cell phone started ringing.

"Hello," I answered.

"Hey, Anna, where are you? We were thinking of going some-where," Liam said.

"I can't."

"Why?" Liam asked. I could hear the disappointment in his voice.

"I'm in the hospital."

That brought a long pause over the phone. At last, Liam asked, "The hospital?"

"My left arm is broken, and I have a cut on my forehead," I said.

"How did that happen?" Liam asked.

"I kind of fell out my window."

"Annadyomene, how do you *kind of* fall out a window?" Liam asked.

"Your guess is as good as mine," I said with a little laugh.

"Is this a joke?" Liam asked.

"Yes, Liam. Ha ha! Got you," I said.

"You really fell out a window? How? ... Why? ... What? ..." Liam asked all at once.

"Well there's a little story behind this, but I have to tell you later. Dr. Masker needs to talk to me. Bye," I said, hanging up my cell.

"Well, Anna, great news, you have just a simple fracture. Your arm should heal in about six weeks. Make sure you keep the cast dry. And you be careful of your head. You got a nasty cut, but that will heal quickly enough," Dr. Masker said, walking me out to the waiting room.

"Thank you, Dr. Masker," I said, and Mr. Tenth came up.

"How is it?" Mr. Tenth asked.

"Six weeks in the cast, but she's fine. She'll heal in no time," Dr. Masker said. Then he walked away.

"Are you ready to go?" Mr. Tenth asked.

I nodded my head yes.

After Mr. Tenth stopped off at the local drug store to pick up the painkillers the doctor had prescribed for me, we got back to school. I told Mr. Tenth I was fine and I could walk back to my room. So he handed me the tiny bag with my painkillers inside and let me go off on my own. But when I tried to open the door with my keys, they kept dropping from my hand. When I finally got the key in, I sighed in relief and opened the door to find all my friends there, waiting for me.

"You really did break your arm. We thought Liam was joking," Sparnik said as I walked in.

"What happened to your forehead?" Liam asked.

"Just a cut; it's nothing," I said.

"So what happened?" Nicky asked.

"Well, I went out to the supermarket, and when I came back, Trent was here—"

"Trent Stone did this to you?" Liam asked, more than a little angry.

I took a deep breath and told them everything that had happened with Trent. The more I talked, the more anger showed on Liam's face. When I finished, I looked at Liam, and he looked back at me. Then he took my right hand and gently kissed it.

"Sparnik, watch the girls. Martin, Andy, and Nicky, do you guys want to help me with a project?" Liam asked, and they all nodded yes.

"Liam," I said, grabbing his hand. Then I whispered in his ear, "Liam, don't go. Stay with me, please," I begged.

"Change of plans, guys. I'm staying in tonight," Liam said. After he had a few seconds to think over my pleading request.

I smiled and mouthed a thank you. Liam brushed some hairs from my face.

"What do you want to do?" Liam asked.

"Let's just—" I didn't have time to finish; Andy walked over to us and cut me off.

"Hey, Liam, we're going to watch the football game. Do you want to come?" Andy asked.

"I didn't know there was a game on tonight. Who's playing?" Liam asked.

"I don't know; I just heard there's a football game on. So, are you coming or what?" Andy asked.

Liam looked at me, and then at Andy.

"Go watch the game, Liam," I said with a big smile, although I noticed something odd when Andy was talking about the game. I couldn't put a finger on it, so I just brushed the thought off.

"You sure?" Liam asked.

"Yeah," I said.

"Do you want to come?" Liam asked.

"I'm not a sports girl. I'll just stay here and read or something," I said.

"You sure?" Liam asked again.

"Ah, hello, it's me and a book. And don't worry—I'll try not to fall out my window again," I said with a little laugh.

"Maybe—" Liam started, but I cut him off.

"Go! Go before I make Andy drag you out. Have some fun; go team!" I said, throwing my right fist up in the air.

"Okay," Liam said.

"Bye. Have a good time," I called as everyone went out the door.

Just before I shut the door, I heard Liam say, "Do we have a plan?" That sounded odd. They had just said they were going to watch a game. *Well*, I thought, *it probably has nothing to do with me. Stop sounding so selfish, always about me. Whatever. They don't want me to know, so I'm staying out of it.*

After getting on my pink sweats with "Sassy" on the butt, I grabbed my favorite book, *Twilight* by Stephanie Meyer, to take my mind off the pain. My forehead was throbbing a bit, but I felt most of the pain in my left arm. Treelea had asked if I wanted some Advil she had in a bottle on the table near her bed. She said she sometimes had headaches, and I was wondering if it was because of all the animals she talks to. I told Treelea before she'd left with the others that I had painkillers but thanks anyway. After taking what was prescribed on the bottle, two kinds of tiny pills, I soon fell asleep, but crazy dreams gave me little rest. I was in Hoshi, running through Lycia Forest. I didn't know why I was running, but something didn't feel right. I heard no sounds other than my feet hitting the ground. Suddenly, that changed when I heard screams but not from in the forest. They seemed to come from in my head, as if I had left the dream and the voices had turned real. I grabbed the sides of my face as the screams rang in my head. Then something dark came over me, and all I could feel was the pain of others.

"With your powers, Anna, you can join with us. And you wouldn't have to feel this pain ever again," I heard a million voices say at the same time.

"Who are you?" I whispered, still feeling the pain of others.

"You know who I am, Anna," the voices said at once.

"Finbar," I said.

"Didn't anyone tell you not to speak my name? I don't mind, but your kind fears it. Fools!" the voices said, laughing.

"I don't fear you or your name," I said getting some of my strength back.

"It's been awhile since I've met someone who doesn't fear me."

"What do you want?" I asked in an angry voice.

"We want a partnership, your magic and our magic together."

"Why me?"

"You are very powerful, and we want to make sure you see your opportunity."

"What 'opportunity'?" I asked.

"Your opportunity to join us," Finbar said in his many voices.

"Go to ... Aaaah," I yelled when I heard the screams and felt the pain again. "Stop it," I said breathless.

I woke from the dream, sweating, out of breath, and with a serious headache. And I was starving. I looked at the clock and saw eleven thirty. *I know Liam thinks I'll stay here in my room, but I need to get some food*, I thought. Putting my book aside, I got up and walked out the door, heading for the kitchen. The big, dark, empty kitchen looked eerie and made me wish I knew where the light switch was—until I remembered my fire power.

"Fire," I whispered in the dark, holding my right hand out. Instantly, fire came to life in my hand, just a small fire ball, really all I needed. Then I almost forgot. "Wind," I called out softly, for it, too, I can control. And it answered back with a ruffling gust to my hair. "Warn me if someone comes here, please," I said softly, and it answered back with another gust.

Now I needed to find the refrigerator, which—wouldn't you know?—stood hidden way back in a corner, near the pots and pans. When I opened it, I could see only leftovers, some I could swear were moving. I was about to grab the milk when I felt a gust of wind. Shutting the refrigerator door and closing my hand to stifle the fire, I stood there in silence. Then I heard footsteps. Freaking out, I hid behind a counter. Just in time, too, for whoever it was had a flashlight. I heard the refrigerator open and someone going through it. Slowly stretching my head over the counter, I peeked to see who it was, but instead of seeing, I knocked a spoon on the counter to the floor. I ducked down right away. Then after I had let my heart slow down, I looked over the side of the counter again, but this time more carefully. Nobody. And the refrigerator door gaped wide open, spilling light all around.

Where was he—or she?

Has Finbar sent someone after me?

Is Trent following me?

Suddenly, in the middle of my silent questioning, a hand covered my mouth, stifling my scream, and an arm forced my body back against a muscular chest. As I began to struggle, an all-too-familiar voice spoke.

"Don't scream. It's me, Liam," Liam whispered in my ear. I could feel his breath on my neck as he very slowly loosened his grip from my mouth. But he never let go of me fully, and—I can't lie—I loved every second of being in his arms.

I turned around to face him as he still held onto me, and I closed my eyes for a moment. "Liam, you ... What are you doing here?" I asked, breathlessly with a smile. I couldn't stop smiling when Liam was around.

"Apparently I'm not the only one hungry tonight," Liam answered, putting his hand to my cheek and letting it slowly go down to my neck. As he did this, I bit my lower lip and looked into his eyes.

"You drive me crazy when you do that," Liam whispered, coming closer to me—if it were possible for us to get any closer to one another than we were at that moment. Then he gently pulled my head up, and in that magic moment we kissed. Willingly giving in to the emotions coursing through me, I felt like it was a wonderful, sweet, passionate, beautiful, enchanting, loving embrace.

Tink, tink I heard behind me, and both Liam and I turned to see what had interrupted us.

"Meow," a black and white cat said as it jumped up on a counter a little ways from us. Then it settled down and just sat there, staring at us with big blue eyes. *Nice try Sandy*, I thought. *The only thing you can't change is your eye color, unlike me. Well two can play at this game.*

"Oh, look how cute it is, Liam," I said.

"Yeah," I could hear Liam's anger, and he evidently didn't agree with me.

"Can you pick it up for me?" I asked, enjoying this too much on the inside.

"You want me to pick the cat up?" Liam asked, and I nodded my head yes.

Liam went over to Sandy in her cat form, picked her up, and came back to me.

"Oh, who's a cute little kitty?" I said, petting behind Sandy's ear, and Liam started laughing.

"Why are you laughing?" I asked, acting totally clueless.

"I think the cat's upset," Liam said, and when I looked at Sandy, she did look like an evil kitty.

"But it's soooo cute. Yes, you are," I said in baby talk to Sandy, who was getting more upset by the second.

"What do you think its name is?" I asked Liam.

"Ah ...," Liam said at a loss for words.

"Let's name it," I said, and Sandy looked up at Liam with wide eyes.

"What do you think of Fuzzy?" I asked.

"Why Fuzzy?" Liam asked.

"Its hair is a little fuzzy, so why not?" I said, and Sandy hissed at me.

"I don't think she likes it," Liam said, laughing.

"Well, what do you think?" I asked.

"I like the name," Liam said, and Sandy hissed at him, too. Then she jumped out of his arms and ran out of the kitchen.

"I guess I better go," Liam said.

"Oh," I said, only halfheartedly trying to hide my disappointment.

"Sorry," Liam said, slowly walking away from me.

"Good night, Liam," I said, walking out the kitchen door.

"Anna ..."

"Yes?" I said, turning around.

"I like the sweats," Liam said with a smile.

"Thanks," I said, wiggling my "Sassy" butt and walking away with a little hop. And as the door closed, I could hear Liam give a little laugh. But then I heard his voice become serious, talking to someone.

Fighting my curiosity, I continued on back to my room. As I lay in bed, I wondered, *Why did Sandy come in as a cat?* Then I thought I heard something move near me, and I sprang up fast and looked around my dark room with wide eyes. But I could see nothing there, so I lay back down on my pillows and soon enough went to sleep. I had pleasant dreams of Liam for a while, but then they turned back to Finbar and Lycia Forest.

A few days later, my arm was still hurting, no matter how many stickers and drawings people put on my cast. So I went back to Hoshi to get faster results from a healer.

"Pama, are you here?" I called when I reached the healer's cottage.

"Who's there?" someone asked on the other side of the door.

"It's Nature," I said biting my lower lip. The door opened, and before me stood a middle-aged woman in a bright yellow sundress, with necklaces of brightly colored beads hanging around her neck, and sporting dark blue hair.

"Nature, this is a surprise. What's the matter?" Pama asked.

I held out my left arm.

"Come on inside," Pama said, shutting the door behind me. I walked into a living room/kitchen area and sat down at a table with four chairs.

"Let me see your arm," Pama said, and I held it out to her again.

"Hmm … How did this happen?" Pama asked.

"Ah—" I hesitated, not sure where to start, but she cut me off.

"Never mind; don't tell me. I've got just the thing. Now let me find it," Pama said sweetly, getting up and looking around her cottage. A moment later, she came back with a cup of some liquid in her hands.

"Drink this and you'll be better in no time," Pama said handing me the cup.

I looked at it, and it looked and smelled innocent enough, like tea, so I drank it. It tasted wonderful, like root beer but better.

"What is that stuff?" I asked, finishing all of it.

"A family secret," Pama said, sitting in a chair across from me.

"What is—Mmm. It feels better already. Does it always work so fast?" I asked.

"Yes, usually, almost instantly."

"And what is it called?" I tried again.

"Hasn't got a name," Pama said, sipping her drink.

"Why doesn't it have a name?" I asked.

"What do you call something that can be anything?" Pama asked with a smile.

"What do you mean by that?" I asked.

"That 'stuff' can turn into your favorite drink and heal any wounds. But take too much, and it can kill you outright," Pama said, petting her white cat that had jumped up onto her lap.

"You have a beautiful cat. What's its name?" I asked, reaching over to pet its soft white fur.

"Her name is Blanchette," Pama said with an immense smile, looking at the cat.

"Blanchette, that's a lovely name … Wait a second—Blanchette—wasn't that the name of the cat in the fairy tale, *The White Cat*?" I said.

"Yes, in fact Blanchette here *is* the fairy tale," Pama said.

"Really? I thought in the end the white cat turned into a princess, married the prince, and lived happily ever after."

Pama started laughing behind her hand, and I'm pretty sure Blanchette was laughing too.

"Happily ever after? Do you really believe in that nonsense?" Pama asked, still laughing behind her hand until Blanchette meowed, and she stopped. "Actually, the story you know is partly true," Pama continued.

"What parts are true?" I asked.

"All of it except the 'happily ever after' part," Pama said.

"Well, if there was no happily ever after, what happened?" I asked.

"I'll tell you, but you can't tell anyone. Promise?" Pama said.

"I promise," I said, nodding my head once in agreement. Then Pama leaned in towards me and motioned for me to do the same. Almost close enough to touch noses; I waited for her to start the story.

"For this to work, you must take my hand and close your eyes," Pama said, so I did as she had instructed.

Six Siblings in Hoshi

"There were once six siblings who ruled Hoshi. It was said their beauty and power could stop anything or anyone," Pama began, and as when I had held Liam's hand for the stories of my friends, I now saw—and felt—everything Pama was describing. It was almost as if I was in the story.

"Lycia was the oldest, and the funniest." Pama's voice rang through my head as I saw a girl with blond hair so long it almost reached the floor, wearing a short opalescent colored dress with shorts and white sneakers, sitting in a grand castle room half filled with people.

"Next comes Palmsea (palm-SEE-a), the loudest and most outgoing of them all." Pama kept talking as I saw the next girl who wore a bright pink tank-top, bright purple short, and aquamarine colored sandals. Then I noticed her hair and gasped—the girl had navy blue hair.

"Pama, you're Palmsea, aren't you?" I asked.

"Yes," Pama said, and the girl turned around to show a younger Pama with a smile as bright as her clothes.

"Bryan is next," Pama said, and then I saw a young man around the age of twenty. He had shoulder-length, dirty blond hair, a trim and well-toned body, and an amazing smile.

"Do I know your brother Bryan?" I asked.

"You could. Why do you ask?"

"He looks like ... someone I know," I said, thinking of Liam.

"Bryan was a big flirt to all the women and women-creatures in Hoshi. Bryan and I always used to laugh about that," Pama said, and then I saw Pama jump on Bryan's back, for a piggyback ride.

"How old were you two then?" I asked.

"Bryan was twenty-one, and I was twenty-two, but we always acted younger. Lycia was twenty-four," Pama said, and we both started laughing as Bryan walked around the palace with Pama on his back. Then they went up to a girl with dark green hair, dark blue pants, a see-through shawl, and a long-sleeve, v-neck top that went way down south.

"What are you wearing, Linosa?" Bryan asked.

"None of your concern. I'm going out tonight, and that's more than you need to know," Linosa (lin-NO-sa) said.

"Not like that, you're not," Bryan said.

"I can wear anything that pleases me," Linosa said, putting her hands to her hips.

"You can't wear something that low-cut," Palmsea said, resting her head on Bryan's shoulder.

"Go and change into something else, Linosa," Bryan said.

"No. I like this outfit, and so does Eric," Linosa said.

"Who's Eric?" Bryan asked.

"Her new boyfriend," Lycia said, walking by, "her hot date tonight."

"Has anyone met this guy?" Bryan asked.

"No," Lycia and Palmsea said at once.

"As soon as he gets here, I want to meet him," Bryan said.

Linosa's face fell in disappointment, but then she looked outraged. "But he's going to be here any second, and we'll be late for the show tonight," Linosa said.

"Then you better get ready fast," Bryan said.

"But ...," Linosa said.

"Change, now. Go," Bryan said.

"Errrrrr ...," Linosa groaned as she walked out of the room.

["Linosa had a wicked temper, and sometimes she could create terrible chaos. She was eighteen back then," Pama said.]

"Has anyone seen Kittens?" a girl with bright red hair, an orange sundress with paint all over it, and bare feet asked.

["That was Amaryllis, but we called her Mary for short. She was fourteen back then, the youngest," Pama said.]

"Who's Kittens, Mary?" Pama asked.

"My pet, but I can't find her," Mary said, crawling on the floor.

"What does Kittens look like?" Bryan asked.

Screams echoed down the hall and into the room, and four maids came running into the room.

"Sir, there's a jaguar in the hall," one of the older maids said.

"Mary, is Kittens a jaguar?" Bryan asked, holding back a laugh.

"Yes, but she's really friendly. Here let me show you. Kittens …," Mary called, and then the jaguar bounded into the room. Bryan and Pama could not stop laughing as it walked to Mary, and Mary picked the young feline up off the ground.

"She's just a baby. I found her all alone outside yesterday," Mary said, holding Kittens like a baby. "Can I keep her?" Mary asked, looking at Bryan.

"I don't know …," Bryan said, and Mary's eyes widened.

"Oh, let her have Kittens; this could be good for her," Palmsea said to Bryan as she slid off his back.

"Well, all right, but you have to watch her. Promise?" Bryan said.

"I promise, I promise, thank you," Mary said, showing a smile so radiant it could outshine the sun and the moon together. Everyone in the room couldn't help but smile, and I couldn't either.

["Mary always had an infectious smile," Pama said.

["Can I ask you something personal?" I asked, and like hitting pause, everything stopped moving.

["Sure, I'll try to answer it the best I can," Pama said.

["Did you guys have parents?" I asked.

["We did once, but they died a few years after Mary was born," Pama said.

["I'm sorry. How did they die?" I asked.

["Sprats killed them," Pama said.

["What are Sprats?" I asked.

["They're half spider, half rat, and they're the size of a human," Pama said.

["I've never seen them before," I said.

["That's a good thing because they kill anything. And their webs are so strong nothing can cut through them," Pama said.

["So was Bryan like a father and brother?" I asked.

["Yes, and he was a lot of fun to be around," Pama said.]

Then the image of the castle came off pause, and the scene started playing again.

"What's happened, Blanch?" Bryan asked as a girl with beautiful white hair, a jean jacket over a red tank-top, brown short, and mud-covered blue sneakers came into the room with some blood on her face, hands, and legs.

["That's Blanchette or Blanch for short. She was sixteen back then, second youngest, and she always tried to be serious," Pama said.]

"I was hanging out with some friends in the village, when a guy a little older than us came up and started making fun of my hair. I told him to go away, and he pulled my hair, so I punched him in the face. He then punched me, so I punched him again, and we got into a little fight. But good news is I won the fight," Blanch said with a smile as Pama ran up to her with a cloth and ointments for her wounds.

The scene changed, but they all seemed still about the same age.

["All six of us cared for one another, but one spring day Mary disappeared. No one knew where she went. A few days after Mary went missing, someone found one of her dwarf friends, Seemsly, walking around the forest, talking to himself," Pama said.].

"He did it. He did something with our sister," Linosa told Lycia, Palmsea, and Blanchette. ['Bryan was out that day, looking for Mary' Pama told me.] "I say we make him tell us where our Mary is," Linosa said.

"You know we can't hurt Seemsly. He's our friend and Mary's as well," Lycia said.

"He was the last one to see Mary. Don't you think he would know something?" Linosa said, her temper flaring.

"We cannot be sure," Lycia said with her head down.

Then the scene disappeared altogether.

"Nature, I must stop here and tell you ... I feel something evil is coming," Pama said, staring at me.

"The fairies said the same thing to me, is it Fin—"

"Don't—"

"Fine ... Do you know what's going on?" I asked.

"Something evil ...," Pama whispered this time.

"I know that, but—"

"He's coming for you," Pama said, holding my hand.

"Why can't you say his name?" I asked.

"Hades was a taboo in the ancient world. For the Greeks, even to speak his name was dangerous in fear that it would call his attention. The Greeks feared death, and in some myths there would be heroes who would try to side-step it, but in the end Hades always found them. Finbar is the same way," Pama said.

"You must go," Pama said, getting up and walking toward the front door. I followed her.

"Wait what happened to you and Blanch and your other siblings?" I asked as Pama and I walked to the front door.

"I'll tell you some other time," Pama said.

"I'll be back soon," I said as I walked outside. Pama shut the door behind me so fast I jumped a little. I walked back to the forest and took out the stone, ready to go back to the other realm.

18

A Trip to the Beach

After getting back from Pama's house, I felt so tired that I immediately changed into my PJs and rested on my bed. My arm felt better—no longer painful—but it itched like crazy under the cast. Even though Pama had healed it, I had to keep the cast on so people wouldn't get suspicious. How would I ever have explained—one day I have a broken arm, and the next it's all better? I never could have without telling far more than I wanted, especially to a certain Mrs. Horn.

Pulling the covers up around me, I closed my eyes and began to dream. I was standing on a road to a small ranch with a barn to my left, a grassy open field to my right, and a house a little ways up the dirt road. I started walking towards the house, thinking that my dream wanted me to go there.

"Anna," my mom's voice called. I turned around but couldn't see her.

"Mom, where are you?" I called out, turning in circles, looking for her.

"Follow the sound of my voice," I heard her say from far away. I did what she said and walked in the direction of her voice for what seemed like an hour.

"Mom, I still can't see you," I said as I kept walking around.

"Over here, Anna," my mom called out softly from behind the house.

I walked around the building and found her there, sitting on a wooden bench built into the back porch of the house and basking in the rays of the setting sun. Her golden brown, shoulder-length hair moved lightly to her back as she turned to look at me, and then her face lit up with a warm loving smile as I came closer.

"Hi, Mom," I said with the same warm and loving smile as she opened her arms and we hugged.

"How's my youngest baby doing?" she asked.

"I'm okay. How are you, Mom?" I asked, sitting down on the bench.

"I'm fine. Just look at that beautiful sunset and all those glorious colors. How could someone look at that and not feel happy?" my mom said looking at the sunset then at me.

"Mom? Why are we on a ranch?" I asked.

"I told Tara to make your dream like this," my mom said, talking about my sister, Tara, who has power over dreams, including the ability to send someone's spirit to another in a dream. "I wanted to sit on a ranch. I like it here. Is that okay?"

"Sure. And I'm glad you're here, Mom," I said looking into her hazel green eyes.

"How's school going?" she asked.

"It's going well. How's everyone back home?" I asked.

"They're all fine ... although we have had a few problems, but nothing to worry about," my mom said, forcing a bit of cheerfulness at the end.

I turned away from the colors of the sunset to look at her. "What problems?"

"Just some small things ...," she said, but then her voice disappeared. Her lips were still moving, but I could hear no sound from them.

"Mom ...," I said, but she didn't hear me either. Then the sky started turning black, and my mom got up from the bench and started walking away.

"Mom!" I called as I got up and started following her. She walked off the porch towards the barn, and as I went to follow her, I took a wrong step off the porch and fell. I didn't hit the ground though but stayed in midair, just floating. I tried again to call out to my mom, but I couldn't—something was choking me, cutting off my breathing. I grabbed at my throat to try to release whatever was strangling me, but it didn't help at all. I could feel my body slowly going limp, and I closed my eyes, waiting, I don't know what I was waiting for, but I couldn't do much else.

"Anna!" I heard a familiar voice call my name. Liam! I tried to say his name out loud, but instead, my body turned to the side away from Liam, and I coughed up water. Water? My eyes snapped open, and I was looking straight at the school's pool, which was a few feet away from where I lay. *How did I end up here?* I asked myself. Then I turned back around to Liam and slowly looked him up and down. He was soaking wet, and he didn't have a shirt on, showing his muscles.

Liam then put his hand on my cheek and gave me a loving smile. "You scared me," Liam said, looking into my eyes.

"What happened?" I asked.

"I don't know. I saw you walking outside so I followed you. I mean, it's midnight I was wondering where you were going. You just stood by the pool talking to yourself for a while. Then you fell in. I came running in and jumped in after you," Liam said.

"Oh ... thanks," I said, knowing that those two words hardly did justice to what he had done for me. But I was still feeling overwhelmed and confused by what had happened, and coughing up so much water didn't help.

"You all right?" Liam asked as I started to sit up.

"Yeah ...," I whispered, now sitting fully upright. I could feel one of Liam's hands moving a little up and down on my back. I gave him a loving smile and leaned into him as he smiled back and moved closer to me.

"Can I ask you something?" I asked, resting my head on his shoulder.

"Sure," Liam said, kissing the top of my head.

"What are you doing up at midnight?" I asked.

"I was doing some work for my parents," Liam said with a little sigh.

"Like what?" I asked, glad Liam couldn't see the look of curiosity on my face.

"Just ... different things ... Baby, aren't you cold?" Liam asked.

I looked down at my wet PJs, then turned my head towards Liam again, and nodded yes. We got up from the ground, and we were just about to walk out when a spot of light hit over the dark pool.

"Who's there?" a man's voice rang out.

Liam pulled gently on my arm, and we quickly walked to the door leading out to the woods. Just as we made it to the door, the light from the security guard's flashlight turned on us.

"What are you two doing here?" he asked in an angry voice.

"Run!" I said to Liam, and we both ran out to the woods.

"Hey!" the security guard yelled after us, but we kept running. At one point I turned to look at Liam as I was running, but he wasn't there. I slowed down a bit and looked around some more.

"Liam?" I whispered in case the security guard was near. A shiver ran through my body, and wrapping my arms around myself, I kept looking for Liam.

"Boo!" Liam whispered in my ear.

I gave a little jump and then turned around to see him smiling at me.

"Where have you been?" I asked, smiling back.

"Didn't want security to catch you so I slowed down and then ran in a different direction to lead the guy away," Liam said with a proud smile on his face. Then he gently reached for my hand, and we walked back to the dorms.

"I'm going to head in and get some dry clothes on," I said as we stood in front of my room.

"You need any help?" Liam asked.

"With getting clothes on?" I giggled. "I think I can handle that, but thanks."

"I mean do you need any help because of your arm?" Liam said, nodding his head towards my left arm. I looked down at the wet cast covering my supposedly broken arm.

"Uh ... no, I'll be fine," I said with a half smile.

"Okay, then I'll go back to my room," Liam said, turning to leave.

"Wait," I said and Liam turned back to look at me.

"Yeah?" Liam said.

I leaned up and softly kissed his lips.

"Night," I said as I pulled away slowly and bit my lower lip.

Liam moved closer to me with a wickedly mischievous smile and leaned down till his lips were almost touching my neck. "Good night, Anna," he said and then kissed my neck once.

I turned my head slightly and closed my eyes for more. But when none came, I opened my eyes to see Liam pulling back. With that wicked grin still on his face, he turned and walked away to his room. With a slight giggle under my breath, I opened the door and walked into my room.

For six weeks, I had to pretend my left arm was broken. People's reactions to it only added to the horribly itching discomfort my encased arm felt. They stared at it whenever I walked by as if they had never seen someone with a cast before. The extra attention Liam gave me almost made up for the inconvenience. He acted the perfect gentlemen, opening doors for me, helping me with my books, offering to cut my meat at dinners. Not that he hadn't done some of that before, but he went out of his way just to help me while I wore the cast. I almost felt bad for pretending to have a broken arm while he went to such trouble for me. Almost.

I could hardly wait for the day when I'd get the cast off. When it finally arrived, Liam went with me even though I said he didn't have to drive me. He did it anyway, what a gentleman. Then Dr. Masker removed the cast, and—aaah—my arm could breathe again, and it felt so much lighter. After he examined my arm and he gave me a thumbs-up, Liam and I returned to Brownstone.

"I'll see you after your classes," Liam said as we got out of his car and headed for the school.

"Okay, see you then, baby," I said, giving Liam a light kiss on the lips as I walked on to my classes. I turned and stopped when I saw Liam walking back to his car.

"Where are you going?" I called.

"I have to do a few things for my parents," he said. Then before I could say anything, he opened the driver's door, got in, and drove off.

Wondering what mysteries he was hiding from me, I just shrugged my shoulders and continued on to classes.

"Psst."

I looked around my fashion class, but no one was looking at me.

"Psst."

Again I heard the noise. I could feel my eyebrows knit together as I looked around, finding nothing.

"Anna." Someone whispered my name, but from where? I looked out the open window, and there was Liam's smiling face.

"Liam ... Liam, what are you doing here?" I whispered with a shocked smile.

"I go to school here, Anna," Liam whispered with a smirk.

"Don't be smart with me," I whispered back laughing, while darting glances at the teacher, busy with another student.

Liam laughed too. "I'm here to get you," Liam whispered.

"But this class just started," I whispered.

"But I can't wait an hour for you to be in my arms."

I put my head to the side, smiling.

"What do you have in mind?" I asked.

Liam smiled. Then he picked up his cell phone and called someone. "She's in," he said, and he hung up the cell phone.

"What?" I asked.

"Just get ready to leave," Liam said with a big smile on his face. So I did as he said and put all my books in my bag.

Just then the door to the classroom opened, and Martin stomped in.

"May I help you?" the teacher asked. But Martin didn't look at her; he just kept walking until he came in front of Treelea.

"What the hell! I get a text saying we're over!" Martin yelled at her, looking livid.

"Martin, not here," Treelea said.

"Why not?"

"Because you're yelling at me in front of all these people!" Treelea yelled.

"I think it's time for you to leave," the teacher said, coming next to Treelea who was in the front row.

"Anna, let's go," Liam whispered from the window. I stood up and walked over to him, all the while keeping my eyes on the front-row fight.

"Are they going to be okay?" I asked.

Liam laughed to himself. "Anna! They're acting," Liam said.

"Why?" I asked.

"I'll explain later, but you need to crawl out this window now."

"What?" I asked shocked.

"Do you want me to come in and get you? I will if I need to," Liam said with a smirk.

I looked back at the class. Martin and Treelea were still arguing. Then I looked at Liam with a wicked smile on my face.

"Let's go," I said as I crawled out the window to Liam. He grabbed my hand, and we ran to his car.

When we were inside it, we both laughed.

"What was all that?" I asked still laughing.

"Martin and I wanted you and Treelea, so Martin texted Treelea, telling her the plan," Liam said.

"Oh, I see. And why wasn't I told about this?"

"'Cause I wanted to surprise you."

"So what was the master plan?" I asked.

"Well, Martin and Treelea would get into a big fight, I would sneak you out the window, and Treelea would ask the teacher if she could talk things over with Martin outside. That way I'd have you, and Martin would have Treelea. And … ta-da … here you are," Liam said.

I giggled and said, "So what are we going to do now, rob a bank?"

"As if the bank's going to need all that money, anyway," Liam said, raising his eyebrows.

I giggled again and then got serious and said, "Oh, you're joking."

Liam raised one eyebrow at me. "I wasn't," he said, and we started laughing again.

"Anyway, where are you taking me?" I asked.

"I thought we would just drive," Liam said, starting the car.

We drove on the highway for sometime. I could tell as Liam and I talked he was upset so I asked, "Are you okay, Liam?"

He looked at me with a half smile. "Yeah, why do you ask?"

"You just seem a little upset, that's all."

"It's just ... people want too much from me, and I don't think I can give them what they want," Liam said.

"I think you can do anything," I said, turning to look at him. Liam smiled his perfect smile at me.

I turned my whole body towards Liam and just looked at him. As darkness descended and time passed, I must've fallen asleep while watching Liam. When I woke, I felt a gentle kiss brushing my cheek. I opened my eyes, and there was Liam.

"I got breakfast for us," Liam said.

I sat up in the bed—BED?—and looked around the hotel room—HOTEL ROOM?—and then at Liam.

"Uh ... Liam how did we get here?" I asked, looking confused and wondering what exactly had happened the night before.

"You fell asleep in the car, so when we got here, I carried you in," Liam said with a smirk.

"And where is here?" I asked.

"Seaside, Oregon."

"We drove four or five hours to Seaside, Oregon?" I said, shocked.

"Yeah. I thought it would be fun," Liam said, getting up and standing in front of me.

"You're crazy ... but I love it," I said as he grabbed my hands.

"You're cute. You know that?" Liam said, looking down at me.

"So you said, but I don't believe you," I whispered with a big smile.

Liam, still looking into my eyes, gently put his hand on my cheek. I put my hand over his hand, turned my head slightly, and kissed his hand. Then I looked out of the corner of my eye at Liam. His shocking baby blue eyes never left mine. He reached with his other hand, cradling my chin, and kissed me. I could feel the blush work its way to my cheeks, I could feel my heart almost beat out of my chest, and I could feel the love and passion Liam and I felt for one another. I could never work this kind of magic with my powers. Nor could anyone else. What strength in something as simple as a kiss.

After breakfast, Liam and I walked the beach, holding each other's hand.

"So we don't have to worry about anything?" I asked.

"Nope, it's just us," Liam said, turning to stand in front of me.

"That sounds good to me," I said, wrapping my arms around his neck.

Liam smiled, and then he leaned in closer and kissed me. With perfect timing, Liam's cell rang. He stopped kissing me and pulled it from his pocket. He sighed and then answered it. "Yeah?"

Then I heard someone on the other end yelling at Liam.

"Who is it?" I asked.

"It's one of my older brothers," Liam said, rolling his eyes.

"What's his name?" I asked.

"Andrew. Why?" Liam asked, looking confused. I held my hand out for the phone, and Liam gave it.

"Andrew, your brother here needs some time off so goodbye," I said and hung up the phone.

Liam looked shocked, but then he smiled. "You realize he'll call back, right?"

I pushed the button that turned the phone off. "He can leave a message. Remember it's just us," I said with a smirk. Liam grabbed my hand, and we walked to the water.

I took off my sandals and waded in the gently breaking waves. I shrieked at the shock of the cold and then giggled. As the tide came in, one of my sandals dropped from my hand and started washing out to sea.

"My sandal!" I shrieked, splashing in after it. When I finally got it, I turned around to head back to Liam, but a wave hit me, sending me forward into the surf. The cold water splashed over me, and then I felt strong arms lift me gently out of the water.

"Anna, you okay?" Liam asked.

I looked up at him, put my head on his chest, and said, "I'm better than okay in your arms."

I didn't realize how far out we were until another wave hit us and we both went under.

"Don't get too attached to Liam, Anna," I heard under the water but couldn't see anyone or anything. When I reached the beach I guessed the waves had washed him to shore, for Liam was there smiling and dripping wet.

"Let's get something dry to wear," Liam said with a little chuckle as I walked towards him.

"I agree," I said, smiling, but that voice I had heard underwater kept ringing in my head. What did the voice mean by "Don't get too attached to Liam?" I tried to shake the uneasy feeling I had as Liam and I walked back to the hotel, but it just wouldn't go away.

"You can go inside. I'll get our stuff," Liam said when we were in the door of our room.

"Our stuff?" I asked trying to remember if I had brought anything besides my bag with my schoolbooks.

"I have a few T-shirts and other stuff in the car," Liam said.

"Hmm ...," I said.

"What?" Liam asked.

"Nothing, just kind of sounds as if you had everything planned, that's all," I said.

Liam smiled, "I didn't plan to come here, but I always keep that stuff in my car. Just in case," he said. Then he walked to the car, and I walked inside.

I grabbed a towel from the bathroom, wrapped it around my shoulders, and sat on the bed waiting.

When Liam returned to the room, he tossed me a T-shirt and a pair of cut-off jean shorts too small for men. I looked at the shorts and then looked at Liam with a questioning look.

"Treelea left those in my car a long time ago when all of us went camping," Liam said.

"Okay," I said with a smirk.

Liam moved closer to me until our bodies were almost touching, "You want to take a shower ... first?" he asked with a wicked smile.

I couldn't help giggle, which made Liam laugh, "Uh ... Y-y-you can take it first," I stuttered as his face came closer to mine.

"All right," he said, walking to the bathroom. "You can watch TV while you're waiting," he said still with a smile, then closed the bathroom door, and took his shower.

I started clicking through the channels, not really paying that much attention, until I found a channel with music videos. Lying on the bed, I closed my eyes and started mouthing the words to Shania Twain's "When You Kiss Me."

Halfway through the song I felt a kiss on my forehead, I opened my eyes to see Liam standing over me topless. I smiled, then grabbed his hand, and pulled him down to me. We kissed softly, one of his hands on my waist and one of my hands on his cheek. His lips trailed from my lips to my chin, stopping at my neck. I put my hand to the back of his head, running my fingers through his gorgeous dirty blond hair. His lips on my neck felt so amazing I sighed in delight. He must have heard since he laughed a little but didn't stop.

"Liam," I said, and he pulled back.

"Too fast?" he asked.

"No," I said with a giggle, "I just want to get some dry clothes on."

Liam looked down at my wet clothes from the beach sticking to my body, and then looked back at me with a wicked smile.

"I don't see anything wrong with these clothes," Liam said, moving his hand on my waist, up and down my side. I closed my eyes, and he started kissing my neck again.

"Not ... fair," I whispered, trying to stop my heart from beating out of my chest.

"What do you mean?" Liam asked in between kisses to my neck.

"Your touch drives me crazy. I can't think straight," I said.

"Really?" Liam said moving his hand on my waist slowly up my stomach. I took a deep breath, the blush on my cheeks burning hotter each second. Turning my head to the side, I tried to hide the deepening red. Liam's hand left my stomach and touched my cheek, turning my head back towards him.

"You do the same to me, hon," Liam said.

"I do?" I asked smiling.

"Yes ... although you blush more than I do," Liam said, and we both laughed a little. "Go take your shower. I'll wait here."

"Okay," I said, kissing him on the lips.

After I had showered and put on the shorts and T-shirt, I was in the middle of drying my hair when the lights in the bathroom went out. I reached for the light switch but, instead, felt a slimy hand. Repulsed, I backed away. Instantly a fire in my hand lit the room, and I saw what I had touched. The fire sparked as if it could tell I was fearful of the once human man before me.

"I found you," it said in a raspy voice, coming closer to me. I took a step backwards and tripped, landing flat on my butt.

"Anna, you all right?" Liam asked.

The thing turned towards the door and stared at it. I shot up from the floor and ran to the door.

"Yes," I said. Then turning around, I found the "man" behind me. I looked at him with eyes wide as he grabbed my arm and threw me across to the shower. Glass flew all around me when I hit the shower door, and then I fell to the floor. Looking up, I saw him coming towards me. I raised my hand to the water coming out of the broken showerhead and sent it towards the thing.

"Anna!" Liam rushed in just as the water engulfed the "man" and sent him away. "Anna, you're bleeding. What happened?" Liam asked.

"I ... I don't know," I said looking at my bleeding arm.

"Can you stand?" Liam asked.

"Yeah," I said, pushing off from the floor with my hands. My back and arms were in so much pain from the shards of glass that I didn't get an inch from the floor before my arms buckled and sent me back down.

"Would it hurt if I picked you up?" Liam asked, and I shook my head no. Liam put his arms around me and gently lifted me off the floor. He walked out of the bathroom and laid me down on the bed. I couldn't help but whimper a little when I pulled the piece of glass that was making me bleed out of my arm.

"Maybe I should take you to a hospital," Liam said.

"No hospital; I'll be fine," I said.

"That looks like a really deep cut. Is it painful?" Liam asked, worried.

"Nah, it's not that bad," I said but, *Ow! Ow! Ow! OW!!* I thought. Liam walked in the now damaged bathroom and came back with some towels. He grabbed my hand gently, examined the cut, and then started wrapping a towel around my arm.

"What happened?" Liam asked.

"The glass cut my arm," I said.

"No ... What happened in the bathroom?" Liam asked.

"What did you see?" I asked.

"I saw ... something or someone disappear in water, then you on the floor ... covered in glass and blood ..." Liam shut his eyes as if he would see it play over and over if he kept them open. "So what happened?" he asked again.

"I was drying my hair when I saw the ... thing. I still don't know what it is, but then it threw me across the bathroom, and I hit the glass," I said.

"How did it disappear?" Liam asked.

"Um .... someone in a mask showed up," I said, and Liam looked up at me shocked. I hated lying to him, but I couldn't tell the truth, not yet ... maybe not ever. "Yeah, I know it sounds crazy," I said with a half laugh.

"Nature," I heard Liam whisper under his breath. I'd rather have him think Nature saved the day instead of his "normal" girlfriend.

"The person in the mask sent the thing away," I said, and Liam smiled a little.

"Just as long as you're safe, babe," Liam said looking into my eyes.

"I think the person in the mask left something on the sink in the bathroom," I said, and Liam walked to the bathroom again. When he came back he had a small bottle in his hand.

"What do you think it is?" Liam asked, looking at the clear liquid in the bottle.

"I think it's for my arm," I said, and Liam looked up with a questioning look on his face.

"How do you know what that stuff is?" Liam asked, handing me the bottle.

"I don't," I said, opening it and drinking it.

"Anna!"

"I'm fine. In fact my arm is feeling better," I said.

After that, Liam and I decided to head back, not wanting to risk another attack. Once we were back, Liam told everyone in our group what had happened. I decided I needed a break from wild happenings and to go to Hoshi. I told Liam I was just going to see someone near the school who was like a mother to me.

"Okay. You want one of us to come along?" Liam asked.

"Oh no, that's fine. The woman I'm going to see doesn't like new guests," I said, which was true.

When I made it to Hoshi, I headed straight for Pama's house.

"Hey, Pama," I greeted, and then we both sat at her kitchen table.

"That ball of fire that appeared in this kitchen the other day and took the little bottle of my family's secret potion, was that you?" Pama asked with a smile.

"I needed it," I said.

"Obviously," Pama said, still smiling. So I told her everything that had happened while Liam and I were in Seaside and why I had needed her remedy for my arm.

"Trouble sure follows you around, and it always seems to hurt or break your arm. Maybe you should try to be more careful with your arms," Pama said.

"I had to call on fire to place the bottle in the bathroom so I could get better right away and Liam wouldn't worry," I said, and Pama nodded in understanding.

"So Liam thinks you're normal when your mask is off and doesn't know you're Nature?" Pama asked, and I nodded.

"I put a spell on my mask to shorten my hair whenever I wear it so people don't know who I am," I said.

"Hmm ..."

"What?" I asked.

"Be careful with that," Pama said with a look of concern.

"What do you mean?" I asked.

"Just be careful with lies," Pama said, and I didn't know what to say to that, so the conversation ended there.

Leaving Pama's house I went to the castle just to walk around and see if anything new was going on.

"Nature!" Liam called, walking towards me in the crowd.

"Hello," I said with a warm smile when Liam was standing in front of me.

"I owe you," Liam said.

"For what?" I asked.

"You saved my girlfriend, Anna," Liam said.

"She didn't need that much saving," I said with a wide smile.

"But still ... thank you."

My smile went down to a half smile as I said, "You're welcome."

"So what are you doing today?" Liam asked.

"I don't know. Why do you ask?" I said.

"I thought maybe you'd like to see something," Liam said with his perfect smile.

"What would that be?" I asked.

Liam grabbed my hand and said, "Follow me." We ran into Lycia Forest, laughing, the wind whipping back my hair. Then we slowed down, and Liam turned to face me.

"Wait here," he told me, and I nodded my head yes. He walked away, still looking at me, and then he was gone.

Content to stay there a while, I amused myself by watching some brightly colored spiders marching across the ground. Then a thought came to me. *I can control wind, fire, water, and nature, and that includes spiders. I can't talk with animals as Treelea does, but I can still communicate my desires to them.* I closed my eyes and let the wind carry my message to the spiders, asking if they could make me something to wear.

Immediately, the Ensin spiders went to work, weaving webs on the branches of a nearby tree. I smiled as they did their magical work. All at once they stopped, and I knew they had finished. But I could see nothing on the branches—or practically nothing, only a few webs. Then beautifully colored hummingbirds came down to the few webs on the branches, picked them up, and flew away with them. Up to the sky they went and through a rainbow, all the while carrying the spiders' webs. And when the hummingbirds came back to me, they had a beautiful sundress in salmon pink, light orange, aquamarine, topaz, and sapphire.

I gasped in surprise as they came closer. Oddly, the back of the dress was not finished. I was wondering why the spiders hadn't woven the back, but the hummingbirds, inches from me, seemed to insist I put it on. I held my arms out in front of me with a smile, and the hummingbirds slipped the sundress on. As they pulled the spaghetti straps up on my shoulders, I could feel the spiders start to weave the back of the dress, taking the two sides and putting them together. Then an orange spider started weaving a web on my left hand, and a bright pink spider started doing the same on my right hand. I watched as white and silver gloves took form on my hands. When they finished, both spiders did a "*Mission Impossible*" jump to the ground, joining the others. I looked in wonder at the snow-white gloves, decorated with flowers with silver centers. What an elegant touch—I hadn't even asked for gloves! And my outfit!—I hardly dared to touch the dress shimmering on my body.

"Gorgeous! This dress is gorgeous. Thank you," I said to the spiders and the hummingbirds.

Then suddenly they all left, as if something had frightened them away. But what could they be afraid of? The wind howled as a big gust of wind blew my lose hair off my shoulders and flapped my new dress. I knew something was coming, and the wind was trying to warn me. It was a beautiful day with not a cloud in the sky; the wind would never be so strong unless it was warning me. I had no time to waste and immediately climbed up one of the maple trees. Seconds later, a gray, white, and orange lynx walked under my tree but continued on, unaware of my presence. Soon after, when the wind blew a gentle breeze, I knew it was safe and let out a deep breath.

"Ugh," I groaned as my stomach twisted in fear, not because of the cat or my own fear; I was feeling it in someone else.

"RUN!" I heard a girl's frightened voice yell and saw two nymphs running.

Yes, her fear I felt, just as I can with any of nature's emotions. As a nymph and a part of nature, her feelings could be mine.

"Over here," I said, letting the wind carry my voice to the nymphs.

"I think it's Nature," one nymph said.

"Nature!" the other yelled.

I jumped down from the maple tree.

"Over here, girls!" I yelled. They ran to me, breathless, the flowers in their hair falling behind them as they ran.

"What's wrong, Olana?" I asked thirteen-year-old Olana, but she said nothing, stricken with fear.

"What's wrong, Olivia?" I asked Olana's twin sister.

"People … are … chasing … us," Olivia said, still trying to catch her breath.

"Who is chasing you?" I asked, but Olivia didn't have time to answer because at that moment three soldiers on horseback came towards us.

"Ah, there you two are. And I see you have a friend," a soldier with dark hair said with a smile.

"Are these the people that have been chasing you two?" I asked the twin nymphs.

They both grabbed my arms and nodded yes.

"Why were you chasing my friends?" I asked, glaring at all three of the unarmed soldiers. Dressed in T-shirts and jeans, they hardly looked like soldiers, but they wore the unmistakable sign of Hoshi soldiers—tattoos on their faces.

"We were just having a little fun, right, men?" the guy with dark red hair asked his two buddies. All three looked not much older than I was, maybe eighteen or so. The one who had spoken had a tattoo of a capital L with a dark angel wing and a dark fire design around it.

"Move aside," one of the other two commanded.

"No," I said with a firm voice.

"What's going on here?" a fourth male voice asked.

So focused on the soldiers, I hadn't even noticed Liam had returned.

"These soldiers were chasing my friends," I said to Liam.

"Is that so?" he asked, raising one eyebrow and staring at the soldiers.

"Like we said, we were just having a little fun," the dark red head soldier said.

"Well, fun's over, and you all need to leave," Liam said.

All three bowed their heads in a mocking way and said, "Yes, Your Highness." Then they rode off, and soon they were out of sight.

"Come on, girls. We'll take you back to the others," I said mouthing an "I'm sorry" to Liam.

"Nature, you can't," Olana said.

"Why not?" I asked.

Both the nymphs looked at Liam and then at me, and I realized they didn't want Liam to come for fear he would tell where the hideout was. "He won't—"

"Please?" both of them begged. Taking a deep breath, I closed my eyes and asked the fire if it could send them back to the other nymphs. When I opened my eyes, the fire was already sending the nymphs back.

"You okay?" Liam asked.

"Yeah. I've just never sent two at once before," I said, putting one of my hands to the back of my neck.

"Well I have a little something that might make you feel better," Liam said, gently taking my hand and leading me to a clearing.

"What are we doing here?" I asked.

"Just look up in the sky and you'll find out," Liam said.

I turned my gaze upward and waited. Just then, a giant cloud passed over us, but it didn't look like a normal cloud.

"That's the Cloud Dragon," Liam said.

"Whoa," was all I could say.

"I just thought you would like to see it," Liam said.

"I've never seen it before … Thank you," I said, looking at the Cloud Dragon and then at Liam.

"It's amazing, isn't it?" Liam said, and I nodded yes. "Nice dress, by the way," Liam said with a smirk.

"The Ensin spiders and the hummingbirds did it while you were gone," I said with a shy smile looking down at the dress.

"Is there anything you can't do?" Liam asked.

"Fly," I said sticking my arms out behind me, closing my eyes, and laughing. I could hear Liam laugh too. Then he picked me up.

"Do you count this as flying?" he asked, and I giggled more. As Liam and I looked at each other, our faces drew closer and closer, and we were about to kiss when Liam whispered something.

"Anna" he said, putting me back down on the ground. "I'm sorry," Liam said looking hurt.

"It's all right," I said.

"I just ... love her too much to do that to her," Liam said, and my breath caught in my throat at the word "love."

He loves me, he loves me, I thought, filled with happiness. But then I thought, *He loves the normal me*. And then Pama's words rang in my head: "So Liam thinks you're normal when your mask is off, but doesn't know you're Nature? Be careful with that."

"I must go," I said, starting to walk away.

"I really am sorry, Nature," Liam said.

I hid my face as I said, "You have nothing to be sorry for, but I must really go." When I was sure I was far enough from Liam, I called the fire to take me back to the other realm.

ANTH HAS A MESSAGE

"Did you hear?" Treelea asked me when I came into our dorm.
"No, what?" I asked.

"There's going to be a dance here at school," Treelea said.

"Really? When?" I asked.

"This Saturday and it's a costume party!" Treelea shrieked.

"Wow, that's soon."

"I know, but it's a dance."

"So what are you going as?" I asked.

"I have no idea ... Hey, maybe we should go shopping," Treelea said, and a big smile appeared on her face when she said the word "shopping."

"Sure," I said with a shrug.

Next day all of us went to the mall in search of a costume. The others went their own way, and Liam, Treelea, Martin, and I stayed together. By this time, I had forgotten all about the other day in Hoshi.

"Oh, boys," Treelea and I called from the dressing rooms.

We watched in amusement as their eyes quickly turned from shock and disappointment to wide-eyed delight. Treelea and I were wearing black dress coats for men, but we opened them up to reveal brightly colored bikinis.

"I like that!" Martin said. "How about you, Liam?"

"I don't know about that coat," Liam said with a smile.

I turned to the side and let the coat roll off my shoulders a little. Then I bit my lower lip, still looking at Liam.

"How do you like it now?" I asked.

"Well, you look so far away, right Martin?" Liam said.

"Yeah," Martin said, and they both started coming closer. Then in no time at all, Martin had Treelea, and Liam had me in his arms. He looked at me with longing, our faces inches apart.

"Dude, that's my sister," Nicky said, and everyone else was behind him.

"We leave you guys alone for a couple of seconds, and we come back to find this," Sparnik said, pointing to Liam and me.

"Go get changed, girls," Sandy commanded sweetly. (I think she still hadn't forgiven me about the Fuzzy incident.)

We went to our dressing rooms, but when I reached the door and turned around, Liam was still staring at me. So when I got into the room to change, I texted Liam. "I wore that for you. Now I want you to wear something for me."

"Yes, Ma'am," Liam texted back, and I couldn't help but laugh.

When I changed and walked out to the waiting area, everyone was there but Liam and Martin.

"What did you guys do?" Kara asked.

"What do you mean?" Treelea asked back.

"Liam and Martin are trying something on for you two," Nicky said, trying not to laugh.

"What are they trying on?" I asked.

"Oh, you'll see," Demaid said with a big smile.

"Oh, girls," Liam and Martin called behind us.

When Treelea and I turned around, we could not stop laughing. Liam was dressed as a bunny trying to be a clown, and Martin was a dachshund super hero.

"How do we look?" Liam asked, pinning his paws up to his chest and Martin beside Liam, pointing his dachshund nose in the air.

"You're so cute like this," I said, and Liam hopped over to me, making me laugh harder.

"What do you think of your boyfriend now, Anna?" Martin asked with a laugh.

"Well this might be hard to explain if Liam comes here and finds me with a bunny clown," I said, and everyone laughed. Then Liam picked me up and tried to kiss me.

"I am not kissing a bunny clown," I said, pushing Liam away. But that only made him try harder to kiss me.

"Just for you guys, we're renting these for the party," Martin said, and both Liam and Martin turned and wiggled their tails at us.

"But we want something from you guys," Liam said with a mocking smile.

"Oh really?" Treelea said.

"What?" I asked.

"We pick your costumes," Liam said.

"Fine, but nothing too revealing," I said, and Liam just smiled. So after Liam and Martin got their costumes, they started looking for outfits for Treelea and me. We must have tried on a million different costumes until Liam and Martin finally made a decision. Treelea got a purple mermaid with a scaly purplish-green tail/skirt and a seashell top. I was going as Scarlet O'Hara from *Gone with the Wind*, wearing a big fancy red dress. The dress looked more like Shania Twain's red salsa dress in her video, *Don't*, but I loved the way I looked in it.

"Hello, Miss O'Hara," Liam said in a deep voice when I came out with the dress on.

"Oh fiddle-dee-dee," I said, fanning myself, and Liam and I both laughed.

By the time everyone found a costume, we were all starving and headed for Print This, a diner/coffee house for teens where we got some drinks, burgers, and fries and then sat down.

"What costume did you guys get?" I asked Sandy, Sparnik, Nicky, Demaid, Andy, and Kara.

"I'm Little Red Riding Hood, the now-a-days," Demaid said with a smile.

"Meaning it's a low cut costume," Sparnik said rolling his eyes.

"I'm the Big Bad Wolf," Nicky said.

"There's a part the children's story doesn't tell, how Little Red Riding Hood was really dating the Big Bad Wolf on the side," Liam said.

"I was thinking about being Nature …," Kara said, and I choked on my drink.

"You all right?" Sparnik asked, and I nodded my head yes.

"I'm a belly dancer," Sandy said.

"And I'm a fire eater, well kind of, except for the fire," Sparnik said, tilting his hand sideways with a smirk.

"Can anyone guess what we are?" Kara asked, looking around at everyone.

"Kara's going to be a hot school teacher, and I'm her assistant, Andy said with a wicked smile on his face.

As we all sat there talking, a thirty-something-year-old woman, wearing a long multi-colored muu-muu, went on the stage near us.

"Hello and welcome to open mike night where anyone can come up and do anything. So everyone get up here and show us your talents," the woman said with a warm smile.

"What can you do, Anna?" the woman asked, and I froze.

"Do you know her?" Liam asked, looking at the woman and then at me.

"Ah …," I said at a loss for words. I looked at the woman closer, a light flickered for a second, and I saw her smile even wider. Then her teeth became larger, her muu-muu fell to the floor, and standing in front of us was a full-grown white tiger. I looked at my friends to see what they would do, but they weren't moving.

"Your friends are all right, for now," the tiger/woman said, coming closer to me.

"What do you want?" I asked.

"I am Anth. My lord has sent me to give you a message," she said.

"Finbar," I said, and her smile disappeared.

"How dare you use his name! For your disrespect, I should swipe one of your friends," Anth said, holding up a paw with extended claws to Liam.

"Do it and find out what happens," I said holding a fire ball in my hand, ready to use it.

"Easy. It was just a joke," Anth said putting down her paw, and I lowered my fire ball. After a moment of silence, she delivered her message, "My lord wants to meet with you."

"That's too bad because I don't want to meet with him," I said.

"You must," Anth said, getting angry.

"Well, tell Finbar I'm booked," I said.

"Are you mocking my lord?" Anth asked, showing her teeth.

"Easy there, kitty," I said, holding the fire ball up again.

"Very well, I'll tell my lord," Anth said, walking back to the stage. When she had resumed her human form again, she turned back to me and said, "Oh, Anna, I'll see you soon." Then another light flickered, and my friends were moving again.

"Anna, Anna," Liam called my name, but I just stared at my root beer.

"I need to go," I said throwing some money down on the table, grabbing my stuff, and before anyone could say anything, walking out the door. As I was crossing the parking lot, my mind was going crazy, trying to think of something normal. But it never did; I could think only about Finbar, Anth, and my magic.

Why, if Finbar is so strong, does he want me?

Is what I see in my dreams going to come true?

All that pain I felt, was that the creatures in Lycia Forest or all over Hoshi?

Are my friends in danger?

But more important, is Liam in danger because of me?

The questions filled my mind and, like unwelcomed visitors, refused to leave. Then Finbar's many voices came into my head. "I told you to join me," and the pain I had felt in my dreams came back to me, this time more powerfully.

"Anna! Anna, wake up! Are you all right?" I heard Liam talking to me, rubbing my face. I opened my eyes slowly to see Liam kneeling over me, and I was on the ground.

"It seems as if we're always in this position," I said with a little laugh.

"Yeah," Liam said, smiling.

"What happened?" I asked.

"You tell me. I came out to ask if you wanted a ride, and I found you like this," Liam said as I got up.

"I'm fine. You should go back inside," I said, putting my hand to my head. Feeling a little light-headed, I could feel myself swaying.

"I'm not letting you walk back like this. Come on. My car's over there. Do you need some help?" Liam asked, gently holding my arm as I stood unsteadily.

"Really, I'm fine," I said, taking a step forward and then stopping.

"Will you stop being stubborn and let me help you?" Liam said, and before I knew what he was doing, he picked me up in his arms and started walking to his car.

"Liam, put me down," I said, laying my head on his shoulder.

"Okay," Liam said putting me down for a second to open the passenger side door. Then he helped me in his car, shut my door, and went to the driver's side.

I don't remember what happened after that because I went to sleep. But when I woke up, I was in a bed not my own in a dorm room, also not mine but similar. The walls had posters of bands like Nickelback and Disturbed. Next to me in the bed, I found Liam. *He looks cute even in his sleep*, I thought as I reached up and softly rubbed his hair.

"Hello," Liam said with a smile, not opening his eyes. I leaned in and kissed his lips softly.

"Hello," I said.

"I see you're feeling better," Liam said, opening his eyes and kissing me back.

"Was I asleep a long time?" I asked when Liam stopped kissing me.

"No," Liam said.

"Did I do anything in my sleep?" I asked.

"Well you did hit me and kick me," Liam said, laughing.

"Oh no! I'm sorry," I said.

"It's okay," Liam said patting my head.

"Did I do anything else?" I asked.

"Well you did say my name and the word "secret" a few times. By any chance, do you want to tell me something?" Liam asked.

"I ..." I stopped myself and shook my head no.

"Sometimes I feel there will always be a part of you that you won't show me," Liam said, looking into my eyes.

I could feel tears coming. What could I do? I couldn't tell Liam about my powers. What if I told him everything and he hated me afterward? I couldn't risk losing him.

"Don't be upset," Liam said.

"I'm not upset," I lied, putting on a fake smile as I would a mask.

"When you're sad, your eyes turn brown. What's up?" Liam asked, and I just pressed my face to his chest.

"I'm sorry, Liam, I can't tell you because … you might hate me if I do and I might cause trouble for everyone else," I said, my face still pressed to Liam's warm body.

"Anna, you can tell me anything," Liam said, cupping his hand under my chin. I just smiled and nodded my head yes, then I leaned in and started kissing him.

SATURDAY NIGHT'S COSTUME PARTY

Before the costume party began, Treelea thought we could start the fun earlier by having all the girls in our group get ready together in our room. I'm sure Treelea thought she had a great idea, but she must never have thought how much space five girls plus all of their costumes and makeup and who knows what else would take up in our small room. Turns out that who knows what else took up a whole lot of space and we could hardly walk around without stepping on someone's precious costume or a little makeup brush.

Somehow we all managed, and, yes, I have to admit, we did have fun getting ready together, helping each other with makeup, and adjusting the costumes just so, even in that cramped room.

"So are we meeting the guys at the party?" I asked as Sandy, Kara, Demaid, Treelea, and I walked to the gymnasium where the dance was. I could already hear the music inside as we moved closer.

"Yeah," Demaid said with a smile, swinging her hips as we walked into the party.

We all grabbed a free mask at the door, and pretty soon we were all swaying our bodies to the music. But then I felt hands on my hips and turned around to see Alan Knife, one of Trent's buddies in a mask.

"What do you want?" I asked, pushing his hands away from my body.

But he grabbed my hand and pulled me to the crowded dance floor.

"Don't pull away. I'm here to give you a warning," Alan said, shaking his shoulder-long brown hair so it would cover his already masked face.

"What warning?" I asked.

Leaning in next to my ear, he said, "You can't tell anyone what I'm about to tell you. Promise?" Alan said.

I nodded my head yes.

"Tonight Trent and the others are planning to attack Liam," Alan said as we danced.

"Why are you telling me this? I thought you and Trent were buddies."

"Kelly and I are finished with Trent. He's going after our old friends, and we don't like it," Alan said, and I could hear the anger in his voice.

"Who's Kelly?" I asked.

"Kelly Graden is my girlfriend, and she's the only one besides me that you can trust."

"Why are you telling me all of this?" I asked.

"We think the only one that can help us is Nature," Alan said.

I froze.

"How …?"

"Relax; Kelly and I are the only ones that know," Alan said, pushing me a bit to get me moving again.

"Are you going to tell anyone?" I asked.

"No … Why would we do that to someone who might help us?" Alan said. Then he stopped and looked at me. "I know how you feel about Liam, so watch out for him and yourself. Thanks for the dance, Anna. Kelly or I will let you know if something new comes up," Alan said, turning around and walking away slowly.

"Where have you been?" Kara asked in the arms of Andy, moving to the music.

"Dancing with a friend. Where's my bunny/clown?" I asked, looking around the dancers.

"Who?" Kara asked with a confused expression

"Liam, where's Liam?" I asked with a little laugh.

"He's off dancing and looking for you," Andy said, kissing Kara's neck, making her giggle like a little girl.

"Thanks. Have fun, you two," I said, half-walking, half-dancing away to search for Liam. When I finally found him, I understood Kara's confusion—and why I'd taken so long to find him. Liam wasn't wearing a bunny/clown costume. He had on an old mob suit and a mask like everyone else. His new costume was a pressed, white-collar shirt under black suspenders, loose, pleated pants, shiny black shoes, and an old, dark brown paperboy hat.

"Hey, Anna, what's wrong?" Liam asked when he came up to me and saw the look on my face.

"Why aren't you wearing your bunny/clown costume?" I asked, sticking out my lower lip in a pout.

"Because there are two things I can't do in that costume," Liam said, grabbing my hand, and we started dancing.

"What's the other thing you can't do in that costume?" I asked.

Liam leaned in and kissed me softly on the lips.

"Okay you're off the hook, bunny," I said with a big smile, and Liam started laughing. Then when the song ended, we walked to the refreshments table for something to eat and drink.

"How do you like the party so far?" I asked Liam, and he shrugged.

"It's okay, but it would be better if something happened," Liam said.

"Okay," I said and kissed Liam on the lips.

Then I ran up to Treelea and whispered my plan. And then we both ran up to the DJ and told him what to play. He agreed and put on the CD as Treelea and I waited on stage for the song to start.

"Let's go girls," Shania Twain's "Man, I Feel Like a Woman" started out. Treelea and I started laughing and dancing in crazy ways on the stage, singing every word to the song off-key, and just having a fun time.

"Yeah," the DJ said over the mike, making Treelea and I giggle more.

Then Liam and Martin came over and got us off the stage, and we all danced together.

"Now, what do you think bunny?" I asked Liam, dancing dangerously close to him.

"Well …," Liam began, but his smile quickly faded as he looked behind me.

"What is it, Liam?" I asked, looking behind me, but all I saw were dancing kids.

"It's nothing … Do you want a root beer?" Liam asked, and before I could answer him, he walked away.

"Hey, where's Liam going?" Treelea asked, and I shrugged.

"He said something about a soda," I said. But then Alan's warning came back to me. "I have to go," I said to Treelea and Martin and started running toward the refreshment table when an arm grabbed mine.

"What's the rush, Anna?" Mr. Tenth asked.

"Nothing, sir," I said, walking slowly backwards.

"Really? You were running as if something's wrong. Are you all right?" he asked.

"Yes, sir. I was just looking for someone," I said glancing at the refreshment table, but Liam wasn't there.

"Would you like some help?" Mr. Tenth asked.

"Oh, no. I'll look for him myself, thank you," I said, walking away until Mr. Tenth turned around, and I ran out the door to the forest where I could already hear someone in pain. As fast as I could, I ran in that direction. When I got closer, I saw Liam writhing on the ground in pain and, next to him, a giant black panther.

"Liam!" I yelled as I got closer.

"Anna, stay back," Liam demanded.

"The hell I will," I said, kneeling beside Liam and checking his wounds. He had deep claw marks on his chest and right leg and more on both of his arms.

"Don't worry, Liam. I'll get you out of here," I said, trying to help Liam up.

"But we just started having fun," the panther said in Trent's voice, walking closer to us.

"Back off," I said, and Trent in his panther form laughed.

"What are you going to do?" Trent asked, coming even closer now.

"You'd be surprised at what I can do," I said, holding Liam close to me. Then the wind howled and rustled the leaves and branches until the trees themselves started moving.

"What is this?" Trent asked, looking at all the trees moving around us. Then a root came up from the ground and wrapped around Trent's front right paw.

"How …?" Liam whispered, looking up at everything that was going on. Then he turned to me. "The mask ...," Liam said, seeing my masked face, similar to another's.

"I'm sorry, Liam. This is the secret I couldn't tell you," I said.

"Nature … You're Nature," Liam said, and I nodded my head yes.

"So you're the all-powerful Nature? Well you didn't think I would come out here alone, did you?" Trent said, and at that moment, other beasts walked from the forest toward us—a brown bear, a black bear, two wolves, a lion, and a snake. Then Jenny Fair stepped forward with Sarah Pen, a classmate in my fashion class, and Alan Knife. All, except for Alan and the black bear, had wicked grins on their faces. *The bear must be Alan's girlfriend, Kelly Graden*, I thought.

"Trent, I thought you said you weren't going to hurt Liam," Jenny Fair said, hands on her hips, like a spoiled child.

"He's still alive for now," Trent said with an evil laugh.

I made the root grab tighten around his paw.

"Ow … Okay. If you want to play like that—get them guys," Trent said, and suddenly, all (except Alan and Kelly) charged Liam and me, stopping within inches of us.

"Are you going to fight all of us, Nature?" Trent asked.

I only smiled.

"Why is she smiling?" the brown bear (James Broader, who was in my English class) asked.

"She must think we're joking," Sarah said, frowning.

"I could claw that smile off," the lion (Ashley White) said.

"Why are you smiling?" Jenny Fair asked, and at this point they were all flaming mad.

"I'm not going to fight all of you," I said, looking around at everyone.

"What do you mean?" the snake (Jake Tellson) asked.

"You're right. You don't have a choice. You're trapped," one of the wolves (Classy Carve, or everyone called her C.C.) said.

"That's what you think," I said, still smiling.

"What are you saying?" Trent asked.

"Are you all watching real close?" I asked, and then fire blazed ten feet high around Liam and me. A few seconds later when the fire disappeared so had Liam and I.

A Poison No One Can Stop

"Nature, are you awake?" I heard Cat's soft voice.

"Cat is that you?" I asked, trying to open my eyes, and when I finally did, I saw all the nymphs standing around me as I lay on the ground.

"Are you all right, Nature?" Cat asked, and I nodded yes. Then the image of Liam and all his wounds came back into my head, and I sat up with a start.

"Easy, Nature. You hit your head pretty hard. Just lie back down," Rose said, and then she and Cat gently pushed me back to the soft grass.

"Where's Liam? Is he all right?" I asked, looking around at everyone.

"Are you talking about the boy we found next to you up on the hill?" Rose asked.

"How is he?" I asked.

"He had deep cuts so we got Pama to look after him. He's healing just fine so don't worry. But he needs rest, and maybe you should get some rest too," Cat said in a mother-knows-best voice.

"I am awake now, and I don't think sleep will help me. Thanks anyway," I said, sitting up and running my fingers through my hair.

"Is something wrong, Nature?" Sue-lea, another nymph, asked.

"It's nothing," I said, giving a fake smile.

"Okay ... Do you want anything?" Sue-lea asked.

"Can I see Liam?" I asked.

"I don't think you—"

"Let Nature see him," Scarlet demanded, stomping her foot once on the ground.

"Yes, let Nature see him. Are you really going to keep two people in love away from each other?" Rasie asked, and I touched my cheeks when she said the word "love" because I could feel them starting to burn.

"Cat, can I see him?" I asked, looking only at Cat as the others nagged her about Liam and me.

"Girls, please," Cat said in a soft but commanding voice.

All the girls became silent, waiting for Cat to say something.

"Nature, if you want to see the boy, you can. I will take you to where he's sleeping," Cat said, standing up, and I rose up with her. Then we both walked back into Lycia Forest, and right away I knew we were heading to Pama's cottage.

"Do you like this boy?" Cat asked as we walked on.

I nodded my head and smiled.

"What happened, Nature? Why does he have so many wounds? And why are you wearing that dress?" Cat asked.

I told her a short but detailed story of what had happened. By the time I had finished, we were stepping onto the front steps of Pama's cottage.

"Pama, are you here?" Cat called as she knocked on the front door.

Pama opened the door a few seconds later. "Come in, come in," Pama said to Cat and me, motioning us in with her hand.

"How is he?" I asked.

"He's sleeping right now and ..." Pama started to say something else, but then she looked at Cat with a worried look on her face.

"What's wrong?" I asked.

Pama and Cat exchanged glances, and then they both looked at me with sad eyes.

"Please tell me what's wrong," I said.

"The boy—"

"His name is Liam," I corrected Pama.

"Yes, Liam ... Liam is infected with a deadly poison. I believe the poison came from the claw marks on his chest," Pama said.

"What are you going to do?" I asked.

Pama looked down at her sundress, covered with cherry designs. "For once in my life, I can do nothing," Pama said with a sad expression, still looking down.

"No, there has to be something, anything ... What about that drink I had for my arm?" I asked as a little hope sparked in me.

"I don't have any more of it. I'm sorry, Nature," Pama said, this time looking directly at me.

"We are all sorry, Nature," Cat said, coming up beside me and hugging me with one arm.

"Can I see Liam?" I asked, almost whispering.

"Follow me," Pama said, taking my hand and giving it a little squeeze. Then we all walked down the tiny hall to the bedrooms.

"He's in here. I gave him a private room," Pama said when we stopped at a wooden door at the end of the tiny hall.

"I'll be with Pama if you need me. Take all the time you need," Cat said, petting my hair as a mother would do to a child.

"Thank you," I said, and they both nodded their heads and walked back down the hall to the kitchen. Turning, I faced the wooden door, took a deep breath, opened it, and walked into the room.

"Hey there," a weak voice called from the bed.

"Hi," I said, looking at Liam so weak, knowing I couldn't do anything. It made me want to break down and cry. Heartbroken, I looked down at the floor as I spoke.

"Anna," Liam said.

"Yes?" I asked.

"Why won't you look at me?" Liam asked.

His question stung. I had to look up at him, but I forced myself to hold back the tears I knew would fall if I let them.

"What's wrong?" Liam asked.

"Why do you think something's ... wrong?" I asked, my voice almost breaking at the end.

"You know I hate it when your eyes are brown. It always means you're sad. So tell me what's wrong," Liam said, patting the bed for me to sit down next to him. I walked over slowly and sat on the corner of the bed.

"Don't sit so close," Liam said jokingly, so I moved closer. He grabbed my hand, and a tear rolled down my cheek. Turning my head so Liam wouldn't see, I brushed it off.

"So ... you're Nature," Liam said, which caught me off guard.

"Um ... yes," I said softly. "I'm sorry I didn't tell you before."

"Well, it's not exactly a normal conversation you would just bring up anytime. 'How're your classes? Oh, by the way, I'm an enchantress named Nature in a land called Hoshi.' Yeah, I hear that all the time," Liam said with a little chuckle.

"Still ...," I said shaking my head.

"Babe, don't worry about it," Liam said, pulling gently on my hand until I was lying next to him. I looked into his blue eyes as he looked into mine, and I felt like a failure. I could do nothing. Pama could do nothing. They all said no one could do anything to save him. More tears rolled down my cheeks before I could stop them. Then before I knew it, Liam was trying to get up.

"What are you doing?" I asked, alarmed.

"Will ... you … just relax?" Liam said with another chuckle, but I could tell moving hurt him.

"I will as soon as you stop moving," I said, even though I knew that wouldn't stop me from worrying about him. He turned a little on his side to face me, putting his hand on my cheek to wipe my tears away.

"Do you know how much I love you?" Liam said, leaning in a little to kiss my lips.

"Only as much as I love you." I smiled for a second and then kissed Liam again.

"So are you going to tell me what's wrong?" Liam asked.

"I never want to lose you," I whispered softly, holding his hand.

"You won't lose me," Liam said with a warm smile.

"I know I won't," I said, kissing Liam one last time, then getting up, and walking to the door.

"Where are you going?" Liam asked.

"If you want something done right, you've got to do it yourself," I said. Then I walked out the door.

"Pama," I called, walking down the hall.

A second later, Pama came into view. "What is it?" she asked.

"Are you sure there's no way to save him?" I asked.

"The only way is with my family's secret remedy, but I don't know how to make it," Pama said.

"Is there anyone that does know?" I asked.

Pama hesitated and then answered with her head bowed low, "One person does."

"Who?"

"My sister Mary," Pama said as her white cat came up to her and stared at me.

"The one that went missing?" I asked.

"Yes," Pama said and then continued. "If you find her, she'll know how to help Liam."

"How am I supposed to find someone who's been missing for ... how long has she been gone?" I asked.

"Oh ... ten years now," Pama said.

"How am I supposed to find someone who's been missing that long?" I said.

"There's always Seemsly."

We all looked down at the white cat.

"Pama ... did ... did your cat just talk?" I asked, surprised.

"Yes, and I'm not Pama's cat. I'm her sister," Blanch the cat said.

SEEMSLY AND THE GIANT OAK TREE

"Seemsly?" I said.

"My story, Nature. Remember, the one who was wandering in the forest calling Mary's name after she disappeared?" said Pama.

"Yes, he was the last one to see Mary. He's a dwarf that lives a little ways from here," Blanch said.

"Then let's go," I said.

"We can't just go," Blanch said.

"Why not?" I asked.

"First of all, Seemsly is a little crazy, and second, some of us may be wearing inappropriate clothes for a visit with a dwarf. Nature … why are you wearing that dress?" Blanch asked.

In my distress, I'd completely forgotten about my attire. I looked down at my red dress and said, "I was at a costume dance."

Blanch put her paw over her face as she laughed.

"Fine, I'll go back to the other realm and change, and then we'll go," I said, walking out the front door and disappearing with the fire.

My aim was improving. This time, I landed right next to the school. As fast as I could, I ran up to my room.

"Anna!" I heard someone call my name, but I didn't turn around. When I reached my room, I put my key in, threw the door open, and ran straight for my jeans and black hoodie. Throwing my mask on the bed, I was going to get changed when I realized someone else had come in the room. Turning around, I saw Alan Knife.

"What's wrong?" Alan asked.

"I need to get changed," I snapped.

"Why are you like this?" Alan asked.

"I don't have time," I said grabbing a tank-top. "Do you mind?" I said, and Alan turned his back to me. I took off my dress, jumped into my jeans, and threw on my tank-top and hoodie.

"What happened, Anna?" Alan asked.

"You know what happened, Alan; you were there," I said, putting my hair up in a ponytail.

"Is Liam all right?" Alan asked as I grabbed my mask and put it on.

"No! But I'm going to fix that," I said, rushing past Alan to the door, but his hand caught my wrist.

"*We* are going to fix that. I'm coming with you," Alan said.

"No, you're not," I said, trying to pull my wrist free from his grasp.

"Yes, I am," he said.

I tried to push his hand off with my other hand, but he held on as if nothing was happening. "What are you made out of—steel?" I said, still trying to free my wrist.

Alan smiled.

"It helps to be super strong sometimes," Alan said, still smiling.

"You're super strong?" I asked, and Alan nodded yes. I called to fire and made it go to my wrist. The look on Alan's face said it was working, but he didn't let go. Instead he squeezed harder, as if holding on for dear life. I finally had to stop the fire, but by that time, Alan's hold was so strong it made me fall to the floor.

"You okay, Anna?" Alan asked, letting go of my wrist and standing over me.

"I've been better," I said, getting up.

"Let me help, Anna."

"I can get up on my own, thank you very much."

"No, I mean help you with Liam," Alan said.

"I don't want anyone else to get hurt," I said.

"They won't while I'm around," Alan said proudly.

"We need to tell my friends," I said.

"Why?" Alan asked.

"So they know what's happening to Liam," I said.

"Even I don't know what's wrong with Liam," Alan said.

"Urr. I've wasted enough time. Liam … he'll die if I don't find Mary," I said putting my hand to my head. "I need to GO!"

"I'll call Kelly and tell her to tell them to come to Hoshi," Alan said, phone in hand, already pressing in a number as we ran out the door. In gasps, he told Kelly the high points and then cut off the call. As we rushed down the hall, he asked, "Where are we going?"

"I have a faster way to Hoshi, but I don't like messing my room up," I said with a half smile. As we walked to the back of the school, I turned and asked Alan, "Are you afraid of fire?"

"Not even after what you just did. Why?"

"Then don't move—not that this fire will burn you," I said, grabbing Alan's hand and calling to fire to send us to Hoshi.

"Umph," I moaned as we hit the ground and Alan fell on me.

"Sorry," Alan said, getting up fast and then holding out a hand to help me up as well.

"Thanks," I said, lightly grabbing his hand and getting up.

"That was cool. Do you do that fire thing a lot?" Alan asked with a smile as we jogged to Pama's house.

"No, just sometimes," I said.

When we reached Pama's house I knocked on the door and waited. After a few minutes, the door opened to—no one. And then we looked down and saw Blanch.

"Sorry for the wait; the door wouldn't open," Blanch said, looking at me. Then her eyes stopped on Alan. "Who's this?" she asked.

"This is Alan, and Alan this is Blanch," I said, turning to look at Alan and seeing him just standing in awe.

"So, are we ready to go, or are we just going to stand here?" Blanch asked.

"No, we're ready, we're ready," I said.

Blanch nodded and then walked past us.

"Aren't the others coming?" I asked.

Blanch turned around. "Nope, just me," she said as she continued on. Dragging Alan along, I followed her into Lycia Forest.

"How far away is Seemsly's place?" I asked.

"I'll know it when I see, but I don't know how far away it is," Blanch said.

We had been walking for an hour when Blanch said we had reached Seemsly's, a giant oak tree with a door on it. We walked up, and I knocked on the door. When the door opened, I saw a dwarf with a grayish beard, dirty looking clothing, and kind brown eyes.

"Who are you?" the dwarf asked, hiding behind the door.

"Seemsly, it's me, Blanch. You remember me, don't you?" Blanch asked.

"Blanch, yes, of course. And what brings you here?" Seemsly asked.

So far, so good, I thought.

"We're here to ask you where Mary is," Blanch said.

The smile on Seemsly's face vanished, and he slammed the door shut.

"I've told you, Blanch, I can't tell you," Seemsly said through the closed door.

"Then maybe you could tell me, Seemsly," I said.

"Who are you?" Seemsly asked.

"I'm Nature," I said. I heard a click, and the door opened a little.

"Why do you want to know where Mary is?" Seemsly asked.

"Someone I care deeply for is ill, and unless I find Mary so she can help, I'm afraid something bad will happen," I said, dropping my head slightly.

"I'm really sorry, but I don't know where she is," Seemsly said.

"But you always say you can't tell us," Blanch said.

"Yes, well, I can't because I don't know," Seemsly said.

"He's lying," Alan said, making Seemsly hide even more behind the door.

"Seemsly, please tell me," I said.

"I want to, but Mary told me not to tell her family or to tell anyone else," Seemsly said.

"A second ago, you said you didn't know. Now you say Mary told you not to tell," I said, raising one of my eyebrows.

Seemsly looked nervous and was going to shut the door again when Alan's fist stopped it.

"You're going to tell us what you know," Alan said.

Seemsly looked up at Alan with wide eyes and then ran away inside his oak house.

"I think he's ready to talk," Alan said with a wicked smile. Then he walked into Seemsly's oak house.

"Alan!" I whispered, but he kept walking inside. Blanch and I turned to one another. "Come on," I said, and we both walked in.

Thank goodness Blanch was in cat form. The three of us barely fit inside the oak tree, huge though it was. We found Alan sitting in one of three chairs next to a small table and candles all around, giving a soft, flickering light. On a far end, I could make out a small bed with blankets and a pillow.

"Where's Seemsly?" I asked.

"Under his bed," Alan said pointing to a small foot sticking out near the corner under the bed.

"Seemsly ... Seemsly, are you all right?" I asked, looking under the bed.

"Mary?" Seemsly said.

I turned back and looked at the others.

Blanch looked with wide eyes. "He thinks you're my sister," she said softly.

"Play along," Alan whispered with a shrug, making Blanch hiss. "What? If she plays along, he might tell us where Mary is."

"Mary, is that you?" Seemsly asked.

"Um ... yes, Seemsly," I said, feeling a little guilty for lying.

"It's been a few days. I thought you forgot about me," Seemsly said, getting up from under the bed.

The rest of us opened our eyes wide in shock at his statement.

"A few days?" I said.

"Yup, it has been a few days. Your sister came by, but I didn't tell her anything," Seemsly said, and Blanch raised a claw towards him. I glared at Alan and then at Blanch, and he got my meaning. Taking off his jacket, he threw it over Blanch.

"What was that?" Seemsly asked, hearing Blanch hiss and claw Alan's jacket.

"I don't hear anything," I said, and Seemsly shrugged.

"Do you want anything?" Seemsly asked.

"Um ... yes ... I've decided you should tell someone where I am," I said.

"Why?" Seemsly asked.

"I just think it's time," I said, and Seemsly nodded.

"So what will you tell someone if they ask for me?" I asked.

"I'll tell them to go to the Myth Caves," Seemsly said.

"And what will you say if they ask why there?"

"I'll say ... I don't know. Why did you tell only me about the Myth Caves, again?" Seemsly asked.

"Ah ... because ... it's one of my favorite places," I said.

"Let's go," Alan whispered.

"Thank you, Seemsly. Now, I must go," I said, and before he could say any more, Alan grabbed Blanch, still in his jacket, and we all walked out the door.

"What did you do that for?" Blanch said, walking ahead of Alan and me.

"You were going to claw him," Alan said.

"I have every right to. He's seen my sister Mary and didn't tell," Blanch hissed.

"And if you had, we never would have learned where she is. Now we know where to look ... Blanch, have you ever been to the Myth Caves?" I asked.

"Nope," Blanch said, and I turned to Alan.

"I've never heard of it," he said, and I sighed.

"Liam's been asking for you," Pama said to me when we were back in her house.

I walked to his room, leaving the others in the kitchen.

"Hey, where did you go?" Liam asked when I walked in the room.

"I ... changed my clothes," I said, which was true.

"Oh," Liam said with a smile. I walked over and held his hand.

"How are you feeling?" I asked.

"I'm okay," Liam said with a weak smile. He was trying to put on a brave face ... for me. The smile faded from his face as he looked down at my wrist. "What happened?" he asked.

Looking down, I saw a red hand print from when Alan had grabbed my wrist.

"That's nothing," I said pushing my sleeve down my arm.

"But—"

"Shh, don't worry," I said, kissing Liam to stop him from asking any more about it.

There was a knock, and then the door opened, and in came Alan.

"Hey! Um … your friends are here," Alan said.

"Thanks," I said.

"What is he doing here?" Liam asked.

"Alan's here to help," I said.

"Help to finish me off, what your buddy Trent couldn't do it?" Liam said, anger rising even in his weakness.

"I'm here to help get you get better, and Trent is not my buddy," Alan said.

"He's telling the truth, Liam. Please don't get upset. It's all fine," I said, softly petting Liam's forehead.

"All right," Liam said, closing his eyes for a second.

"I'll be back after I talk to the others," I said, getting up slowly and walking to the door. I turned back when I was in the doorway and smiled at Liam, and then I left.

The others were talking among themselves, waiting outside because Pama's small house could never have accommodated so many inside.

"Hey, everyone," I said, and all of them—Treelea, Martin, Sparnik, Sandy, Demaid, Nicky, Kara, Andy, and Kelly—stared at me. I opened my mouth to speak, but no words came out.

"Liam's very sick," I heard Alan behind me say.

"What?" Treelea said, as shocked as everyone else.

"What happened?" Martin asked.

"Where is he?" Sandy asked.

"Liam's in Pama's house, resting. As for what happened, that doesn't matter right now. What is important is that I must find the only person who can save him," I said.

"You mean '*we* must find this person,'" Alan said, coming forward to look at me.

"No, I don't. I don't want anyone to get hurt," I said.

"I told you no one will when I'm around," Alan said.

"I can't take any chances. I'm sorry. I had to tell you all about Liam so some of you could watch him while I'm gone. The others can go back to the other realm. But no one is coming with me," I said firmly.

"You need my help, and you know it," Alan said.

"All I need is for someone to tell me where the Myth Caves are," I said turning away from Alan to look at my friends. "Does anyone know where they are?" I asked, and all of them shook their heads no.

"Why do you care so much about Liam?" Nicky asked.

"Nicky, I don't have time for games. You know Liam and I are dating," I said.

But he and everyone else only looked confused.

What don't you understand? I thought.

Alan coughed and whispered, "You're still wearing the mask. They think you're Nature."

"Oh ... sorry. I'm Anna," I said out loud to everyone.

But that made them look even more confused—and disbelieving. Finally, I pulled off my mask. "Now do you see?" I said as my neck-length hair instantly extended down to my shoulders.

"Anna ... you've been Nature this whole time," Treelea said.

"Look, all I care about right now is Liam getting better and for that to happen I need to know where the Myth Caves are," I said walking away into Lycia Forest.

"Where are you going?" Alan asked.

"I'm not just going to stand around, hoping someone will show up who happens to know where the Myth Caves are. I'm going to ask some of the creatures," I shouted back as I kept on walking.

SOMEONE'S MISSING

"Wait up," Alan said, walking beside me now.

"What are you doing?" I asked.

"What does it look like I'm doing? I'm coming with you," Alan said with a smile.

I stopped walking and crossed my arms, looking sternly at him.

"I just don't understand why you want to help this bad," I said.

"'And his heart grew three sizes that day,'" Alan said in a deep voice with a chuckle.

I shook my head with a little laugh. "Okay, Grinch, now tell me the real reason why," I said, but he just walked up to me with his hands shaped like a heart on his chest. "Fine, don't tell me," I said with a smile and started walking again.

"So where are we going now?" Alan asked in step with me.

"We're going to see the fairies first," I said.

"Why them first?" Alan asked.

"Because they're fast," I said.

"What does that have to do with anything?" Alan asked.

"If they don't know where the Myth Caves are, they might know some creature that does, and they can zoom to that creature, get me the information, and zoom right back."

"Oh," Alan said.

After that, we didn't say much more but picked up the pace a bit. About ten minutes later, we walked into a circle of trees where every branch was glowing with lights. As we got closer, we could see they were fairies. Before either of us could say anything, ten fairies came up and started flying all around Alan.

"What the ...?" Alan said, lifting his arms to try to protect himself.

"Down, boy," I said with a giggle. "They just want to get to know you."

And then a few fairies giggled too.

"Nature ... Girls, stop!" Hana said sweetly at first, but then, when she saw the fairies continued to bother Alan, she clapped her hands, and all the fairies pulled back.

"Hana, we need to ask all of you if you know where the Myth Caves are," I said.

Hana looked puzzled. "I have heard of that place, but I've never been there before," she said. Then she asked the other fairies, "Does anyone know where the Myth Caves are?"

"Hana ... Hana!" A light blue fairy came up next to Hana.

"What is it now, Oatin?" Hana asked, looking annoyed.

"I think I might know a creature who knows a creature that's heard of the Myth Caves," the light blue fairy said.

"Well that's not confusing," Alan said, and the other fairies giggled behind their wings.

"Can you go and ask those creatures?" I asked.

"Yup," Oatin said proudly with his hands on his hips.

"She means *now*, Oatin," Hana said.

"Oh, right!" Oatin said, flying away from us.

"Ow!" one fairy said as Oatin flew into her.

"Sorry," Oatin said, flying backwards, which made him bump into another fairy.

"Oatin, watch where you're going!" a guy fairy with a dark green glow shouted.

"S-so sorry," Oatin said and then finally made a clear departure.

"You'll tell me if you hear anything, right, Hana?" I said.

"Of course, Nature."

"Thank you," I said as Alan and I walked away.

"Where now?" Alan asked as we walked in Lycia Forest.

"The nymphs ... Well, maybe I should go by myself," I said.

"Why?"

"Because the nymphs don't trust anyone but me," I said.

"But everyone loves me," Alan said, making me laugh.

"Okay, I'll go see the nymphs later by myself. Right now, we can go see Nury. Hold on," I said grabbing Alan's arm as fire surrounded us, taking us to Nury's cave.

"Whoa!" Alan said, amazed by the piles of dazzling jewels and shimmering gold. Without thinking, he reached out to touch.

"Do and you'll find out what happened to the others," a deep voice said in the cave.

"Nury, it's me, Nature," I said, looking at Alan who had snapped his hand back as soon as Nury had spoken.

"Hello, Nature ... I see you've brought a friend for me. You're too kind," Nury said in his deep voice with a chuckle.

"Oh, Nury," I said shaking my head with a laugh. "He's just kidding, Alan. Nury is like a giant kitten."

"Only to my friends," Nury said, coming closer until his massive body was in view.

"You took me to a dragon!" Alan said, somewhere between astonishment and fright.

"Nury's a good friend of mine, oh strong and brave Alan," I said with a laugh. "I thought he could help us," I said, looking at Alan for a second before turning to Nury with a warm smile.

"And what is it I can help you with, Nature?" Nury asked, bringing his front legs up to rest under his chin.

"Have you ever heard of the Myth Caves?" I asked.

Nury looked deep in thought.

"Nature ... I mean, Anna, you better get back to Pama's house. Something's happening with Liam," Demaid said in my head.

"I'm sorry, Nury. Alan and I have to go," I said grabbing Alan's arm.

"What's up?" Alan asked.

"Demaid just told me something's happening with Liam. I have to go back and see what it is," I said. "We might be back, Nury. Bye for now." Then Alan and I were in the fire again, heading back.

"Demaid?" I called in my head, hoping she could hear me. My answer came back in a muffled scream—from Liam. "Liam!" I yelled running through Lycia Forest to Pama's house. I rushed through the door, down the tiny hall, and to Liam's room.

"He's in too much pain. You have to give him something!" I heard Sandy's voice when I ran in and saw everyone around Liam. Sparnik and Martin were holding down his arms as Liam turned from side to side, trying to get free.

"What's going on?" I yelled.

"Liam started clawing at his chest ...," Sandy said, trailing off.

"Liam," I called, but he didn't respond and only thrashed about, in pain and in frustration.

"It's all your fault he's like this!" Nicky shouted to me.

I froze, tears filling my eyes. I tried to hold them back, but they were already running down my cheeks.

"Shut up. It is not her fault!" Alan shouted back at Nicky.

"Nicky's right … it is my fault," I said looking at Liam. Then I turned and disappeared in the fire.

"Anna!" I heard Alan say before I disappeared fully. But my extreme sadness weakened my powers, and I got only a few yards from Pama's house. I sat on the soft grass, letting my tears fall and thinking how much I had messed up Liam's life. I put my hands through the blades of grass, and flowers flourished between my fingers. But as they were about to blossom, they stopped and went back into the earth.

"Even the flowers can tell you're upset," Pama said, sitting beside me.

"Oh, Pama, I don't know if I can do it. No one knows where the caves are. How am I ever going to find Mary … and the remedy? I'm killing Liam. I am. I did this to him, and now I can't save him. I can't help him. What am I going to do, Pama?

"I know you can do it, Nature. You just have to believe you can," Pama said with a one-arm hug and a smile.

"But … why are you here, Pama? Shouldn't you be with Liam?" I asked.

"We gave him something to make him sleep. Shouldn't you be with Liam, though?" Pama asked, and I looked down.

"Nicky was right. I am the reason Liam's like this," I said.

"You should come see him," Pama said, getting up and walking back towards the house.

After a few minutes of sitting there, I got up and started wandering around, away from the house. Trying to think of some other way to help Liam, I knew I couldn't think straight if I went back in the house. I came across a huge waterfall spilling into a rushing stream a hundred feet or more below. Across the watery divide, a fallen tree spanned the two sides of the waterfall and connected this part of the forest to the other side, known as Linosa. As I walked on the fallen tree, I heard a girl's scream and looked around for its source.

"Hang on, Kelly!" I heard Alan call from the top of the waterfall. Looking up, I saw Kelly hanging onto a branch. She must have slipped and was now trying to get back up over the side again.

"Alan!" Kelly screamed as the branch broke and she started falling. I closed my eyes and called to the water, which took hold of me on the inside. Making the water reach out like hands and I caught Kelly sending her gently to the ground.

"Kelly!" Alan shouted as he ran up to Kelly and me.

"I'm fine," Kelly said, a little shocked as she stared at me. "You caught me. Why?" Kelly asked.

"Why? Kelly! Why would I let you fall to your death when I could save you? I really had no choice but to step in, so to speak," I said with a half smile.

"Thank you," Alan and Kelly both said. Then Alan wrapped Kelly in a hug.

I turned as I got up and started walking back to Pama's house. Seeing Alan and Kelly hug reminded me of how Liam and I would hug, how every little kiss meant the world stopping for one split second. *I should go see Liam*, I thought. *No, I shouldn't*, I thought again, back and forth like a ping-pong ball my mind couldn't decide between seeing him and staying away.

"Poor Nature doesn't know how to find Mary so she can save her love," I heard a voice in the shadows of the trees near me. I looked to see a horrible wolf creature, its fur—more like just skin—was sticking to its skull, and it had an evil smile on its face.

"What did you say?" I asked.

"I can show you where the Myth Caves are," the creature said.

"Why do you want to help me?" I asked.

"Do you have a better plan—or know someone else who knows where the Myth Caves are?" the creature asked.

"No, but—"

"Then come with me," the creature said, cutting me off. I looked back at Pama's house where Liam was resting with my friends watching over him. Then I looked at the creature.

"Do you want to save your love or not?" the creature asked with a beastly smile.

"Let's go," I said to the creature, and we started walking away.

TRAVELING THROUGH MYTHS

"*A nna, what are you doing?*" Demaid asked in my head.
"*This creature is going to help me find the Myth Caves,*" I said in my head back to her.

"*Do you even know this creature?*" Demaid asked.

"*No, but it said it will show me the Myth Caves,*" I said.

"*This sounds bad, Anna. Can't you wait till someone you know comes and tells us?*" Demaid asked.

"*Demaid ... I don't know if Liam has that much time. I have to act now,*" I said.

"*At least let us come with you,*" Demaid said.

"*No, I have to do this by myself. I can't risk you guys. Demaid, just don't tell the others I'm gone,*" I said, and she said no more.

"*Sorry, Anna,*" Demaid said as I heard Pama's front door slam open.

"Run!" I told the creature, and we both started running. The creature took the lead so he could show me the way to go. When we came to the fallen tree next to the waterfall, I could hear shouting behind us.

"We have to cross into Linosa Forest this way," the creature said. Then it ran across. I walked out quickly on the fallen tree, but before I was even to the end of the tree, the creature pulled me to the other side so fast I gasped a little.

"You were taking too long," the creature said.

"Where do we go now?" I asked.

"We must go to the Abahs and pass their cave before we can go to the Myth Caves," the creature said as we started running again.

"Are you sure? There's no other way?" I asked, and the creature looked at me.

"Why? Are you afraid of the Abahs?"

"I'm not, but I hear they hate humans, and in case you haven't noticed, I'm a human," I said. Evil creatures that they are, Abahs live in cold, dark places because heat or light of any kind can kill them, melting their wax and clay bodies. I knew enough to avoid them.

"If we're fast enough, you won't have to worry about them," the creature said.

As I ran along with this creature I didn't know, my mind raced over disturbing thoughts. I knew better than to go with him, but I felt I had little choice. I would do anything to save Liam. As Nicky said, I had done this to Liam, so I had to help him. Before I came to Brownstone Boarding School, Liam and the others were fine. Then I came, and everything changed for them—not just changed but changed for the worse. If I had never come ...

I heard voices as we passed quickly by the Abahs' caves so fast I didn't get to hear what they were talking about. But they sounded angry about something, or someone. I felt nervous with each step I took, having heard only horrible stories about them and never having met any or been near their caves before. But thankfully we made it past them without any trouble and started walking to where the creature said the Myth Caves were. As we walked, a question came into my head.

"Do you have a name?" I asked.

"I'm called a Naio [na-EE-o] creature," it said. "Naio is a soul that's come back in its body after death."

"So do I just call you the Naio creature?" I asked. It shrugged its shoulders, and I could see some of its bone through the little bit of skin covering it, not a pretty sight.

"What are you doing?" the Naio creature asked, and I realized I had stop walking.

"Um … nothing. I was just thinking … how much longer do we have to go?" I asked as I started walking again.

"Not much. You'll know the caves when you see them," the Naio creature said, and I frowned.

"What do you …?" I trailed off as we came up to a giant cave. It seemed to glow, its ruby colored rock shining even in a little light. Walking closer, I could also see four faint drawings going all around the cave entrance.

"Told you," the Naio creature said with a sharp-tooth smile.

"Told me what?" I asked.

"That you would know it when you saw it. Welcome to the Myth Caves," the Naio creature said, motioning with a paw towards the cave.

I stared at the ruby cave in wonder.

"Well, I came here for a reason. Thank you for taking me," I said with a nod of my head as I started walking away from the creature to the cave. But the Naio creature started to follow, and I turned around.

"You need something?" I asked, not trying to be rude but wondering why the creature was still sticking with me.

"I'm going with you in the cave," it said.

"Oh no—"

"I must," the Naio creature said and then walked past me and leaned up against the cave. After a moment, I walked up to where the creature stood, and it waved its paw for me to go in the cave first. I took a deep breath and started to walk into the cave, but as I passed the drawings on the entrance, I saw something odd about them. I couldn't see that much of them because they had faded a little, but the drawing closest to me had only black spots—at first. I stopped for a second, and the drawing came to life in a beautiful sunset with all the yellows, oranges, reds, and pinks you could ever dream of, but it was raining too. I was going to touch the drawing, but it faded back into black spots again. Looking around at the other drawings, I wondered if they, too, could come to life just like the sunset with the rain. But I had more important work to do than look at pretty pictures, so I shook my head as if trying to clear it and walked on into the cave.

The Naio creature whispered to me as I felt along the wall of the cave. "I've heard stories about this place," it said.

"Oh yeah? Like what … have you heard?" I asked.

"It's a place full of what you humans call myths. It is said that when you come here, the myths you see will show you clues to what or whom you seek," the Naio creature said.

"How can you see anything in here with no light?" I said for it was really dark.

"It is also said that no light can show the inside of this cave for those who see fear will feed it," the creature said.

"Feed it? Feed what?" I asked, a little alarmed.

"No one knows for sure what that means," the Naio creature said. I stopped walking as my foot kicked a rock, and after a brief pause, I heard it hit water.

"What do we do now? I don't know if that's a safe drop or— AAAAH!" I screamed as I fell into the crevice of the cave, pushed by the Naio creature. When I hit the water, it was so cold I felt as if my lungs had frozen. A little light above the water was shinning through, but for some reason I didn't try to swim up.

"Give me your hand," a soft underwater voice commanded. I turned and saw a beautiful mermaid with dark brown flowing hair. "I will help you."

I looked at her in awe, my hand going towards her; then I stopped my hand and pulled it back to me before she could take it.

"You are smart, young one. Most would have given their hand because they cannot resist the beauty of the mermaids," said a man's voice. Its sweet melody rang in my ears.

In the next instant, I lay gasping for air on the cave's floor.

"Sorry about that. You see, I like to test those that come here with my mermaids. Few refuse their hand. The ones who give their hand find out why hardly anyone comes back ... Why did you refuse?"

I looked at the man now with his very tan skin and long dark hair. He looked kind as he smiled at me, waiting for an answer.

"I ... I didn't trust her," I said.

"Why? She is beautiful, after all."

"Beauty has nothing to do with trust. Yes, she is beautiful on the outside, but I do not know if she is the same on the inside. That is the part where I do not trust her," I said.

"I see," the man said, smiling.

"It's like, when most people look at the moon, all they see is an object in the sky. They do not see a friend that stays with you in the night. Even the wolves and coyotes howl to it as a friend. But you need to look beyond the physical and see its true self. Everything has a story or meaning, but no one nowadays takes the time to learn it."

"You seem to think, see, and understand a lot," the man said.

"I think I am talking too much," I said with a little laugh.

"Are you ready to find the clues you seek?" the myth man asked me, and I nodded my head. He put his hand to the cave wall and then motioned for me to come over. I rose from the cave floor, walked over to him, and stood there, waiting for something to happen. Then the ruby wall vanished, and in its place I saw only a black hole. I looked at the myth man, confused.

"You want to find the clues. There they are," he said, gesturing to the black hole like a game show host.

"I have to go in there?" I asked, a little shocked.

The myth man nodded.

I took a deep breath and then stepped into the black hole.

"In return for our freedom, we present each of you with a special gift."

I turned around to see the speaker, a Cyclops, the rest of the Cyclopes, the Hundred-handed Giants, and what I took to be some of the Greek gods. I froze, not knowing what to do.

Glad I paid attention in World Mythology, I thought

"To you, Zeus, we give the gift of thunder and lightning in the form of a thunderbolt, an invincible weapon against any enemy. We will make more of these for you when we set up on Mount Olympus.

"To you, Poseidon," the Cyclops continued, "we give the trident. Not only is it a superior fishing spear, but you will also find it a most effective device for shaking the earth and creating great waves at sea. Until then, its three-barbed prongs will make it a useful weapon against the Titans."

Oddly, a piece of paper was sticking to one of the prongs of the trident. Then I realized that was the first clue, and I would have to figure out a way to get it.

"And to you, Hades," the Cyclops concluded, "we give the helmet of invisibility. In times to come, the hero Perseus will need your weapon to kill the monstrous Gorgon, Medusa. Until then, it will serve you well against Cronus and his Titan allies."

As everyone was in high spirits, I quietly walked behind Poseidon and slipped the paper off the trident. Just as Poseidon was turning around, the black hole sucked me from that scene and sent me to a cave. At first I thought it had sent me back to the Myth Caves. But when I saw the giant serpent with a hound on its throat and a girl plunging her sword first into the back of the monster's head and then its neck, I knew it had sent me to clue number two.

"Poor girls!" the girl said softly, bending down next to some skulls and bones on the ground. The serpent lay not too far away, dead from her attack. "The monster killed you because you were too timid to put up a fight! How pitiful!"

Under one of the skulls, I saw another piece of paper, another clue. I sprinted over as if the clue would dematerialize if I waited too long. The girl looked at me as I picked the paper up from under the skull.

"Great work, Chi Li," I said with a big smile. Chi Li looked at me in confusion, but before either of us could say anything more, the black hole sucked me back.

Next it sent me to a room full of giants in the midst of a wedding. I took a closer look at the bride and recognized no ordinary woman giant but Thor, disguised as Freya. Thrym, the Frost Giant, had Thor's hammer and refused to return it until he had Freya as his bride. Loyal wife to Odr, Freya would marry no other. So Loki came up with the idea that Thor should dress as Freya to fool the Frost Giants. Finally, I discovered my clue on Thor's sandal. Sticking the other clues in my pocket, I started to sneak to Thor, who was wolfing down the feast set up by the giants. I hesitated, waiting for the right moment to remove the paper.

"Has any other bride ever had such a great appetite?" Thrym asked. "Has any other bride ever taken such big mouthfuls of food or drunk as much mead?"

The handmaid, who I remembered was Loki, replied, "Freya has so longed for her wedding day that she has not eaten for eight long days!"

A few seconds ticked by, and I wondered if I had missed my chance. The talking continued, but I paid no attention; all I wanted was the clue.

"Bring forth Thor's mighty hammer in order to bless the bride. Lay Mjollnir upon her lap, and wish us joy as we join hands and make our marriage vows," Thrym said.

I had no time to lose and grabbed the note. Backing away, I knocked lightly into Loki, but he looked at me as Chi Li had, with utter confusion, in seeing such a person at the wedding feast.

"You're quite devious, aren't you?" I said to Loki, and we exchanged smiles. Then the black hole took me away, undoubtedly leaving him wondering even more.

"Welcome back," the myth man said when the black hole finally deposited me at the Myth Caves.

"Uh ... thank you," I said, brushing myself off from all the stones and dust that had fallen on me when I returned.

"Did you find what you were looking for?" the myth man asked with a smile.

"Hope so," I said, holding up the last clue.

"Take your time reading them," the myth man said, walking away and leaving the cave.

I sat down on the cave floor. Extensive handwriting in a neat and tight script covered both sides of all three pages. I started reading what I guessed was the first page.

> Everyone warned me never to go to the Cloud Dragon.
> I asked them why, and they said that everyone who goes
> to it is never seen again.

> But I wasn't going to listen to the townspeople. I wanted
> to be near the Cloud Dragon. Early this morning, I left
> my family a note saying not to worry and I would be

back. I didn't say what time; I didn't know. In fact, the only thing I did know was I'd find the Cloud Dragon. So I made my own way up the mountains to where the Cloud Dragon sometimes stopped. I followed the path for what must have been hours. Just when I was going to rest for a bit, I heard something a little ways away from me on the top of the mountain. So I walked a little faster along the trees. I knew it was the Cloud Dragon. Nothing else would be up here. Everyone stays away from this mountain because the Cloud Dragon lives here, everyone except me.

I heard a man's voice ahead of me call "Oran," but I didn't see anyone. I kept walking, looking everywhere for whoever had just spoken. Then I heard it again, telling Oran to come out because the man didn't want to play hide-and-seek anymore. Then a young man in his twenties stepped into my view. He had dark brown hair—I couldn't see the color of his eyes—and a navy blue T-shirt and jeans. We both froze where we were and stared at one another. Then I turned and ran—I don't know why—down the mountain.

He called for me to wait, and he ran after me. But I didn't stop running. I

The first sheet ended there, in mid sentence. I had no better idea who had written it than I had when I began. Maybe the other two would clue me in, I thought, and picked up a second page and began to read.

didn't know what to do. The next day I got up and realized I had to go back. And, of course, Lycia had to ask what I was doing with all the food I was packing. What could I say? I just told her I was going to have a day out. Then before anyone could say anything more, I grabbed my bag and ran outside.

As I walked up the mountain of the Cloud Dragon, I kept my eyes open for the man I'd seen the other day. But not long into my walk, I tripped over someone, and I fell on top of him, into the person's arms. I looked down at the person and realized it was the guy I was looking for. As I stared at him, I wondered why in the world I'd run away from someone so handsome. While he held me, he asked if I was going to run away again, and I just shook my head no. Then he laughed and said that was good because he wasn't in the mood for running. Resting in his arms, I sure didn't feel like running away either.

I apologized for running away the first time, that I hadn't expected to see anyone on the mountain and got frightened when I saw him. Then he asked why I'd come again if I was so scared. But I said I wasn't afraid anymore and I'd brought some food for him. He thought that was strange, that I'd bring food for him, but he sure didn't mind eating it!

We talked a bit while he ate the sandwiches. He told me his name was Ensin. Then he asked me why I'd come to the mountain the first time. I told him that I wanted to see the Cloud Dragon that I didn't believe all those stories people told about it. Ensin thought that was funny, that I'd do something so different. Actually, he said I was different. I didn't know if that was good or bad, so I asked him, and he said I was different in a good way. I liked that, and we both laughed about it.

That ended the second sheet. Obviously, this was someone's journal. But whose? People don't write their names on each page, so I wondered how I'd find out. Then I remembered "Lycia" on this page. Mary's sister. Could this be …? Maybe the third page would tell. I picked that one up and read on.

I like Ensin. A lot. I've been seeing him every chance I can.

Today he came to see me near my family's castle. We were in the forest by the castle, but that didn't hide us. People would still be able to find us and see us together, but I thought we would be okay there. I mean so what if people saw Ensin and me together. Then Ensin told me—and I could hardly believe it—that someone had found out about us. Oran, the Cloud Dragon, had heard some people talking about making sure he stayed away from me.

Someone wanted to hurt Ensin? No, I couldn't think about that. I almost cried. Then Ensin took me in his arms and said he never wanted to leave me that he would stay with me forever, that no one could keep us apart. I loved hearing that, but I don't want him to get hurt because of me, and I told him so.

Then he said I should go with him to his castle. I'd still be able to visit my family, but they'd never be able to come to us. We'd have to keep that a secret. When I asked where his castle was, he whispered in my ear, even though no one was around us. The Myth Caves! The door to his castle is hidden in the Myth Caves.

I don't know what to do now. The only way to

The third page ended. I looked up and around right away. *She's here!* I thought. *Mary's been so close, right here in this cave.* I just had to find a way to get to her. Then I realized the myth man hadn't come back. I jumped up and walked to the opening where I had last seen him. Looking around the opening, I saw a hallway. I found it odd that a tile floor with marble walls was inside a cave. Starting to walk down the heaven-like hallway, I kept my eyes open for signs of the myth man. I passed so many rooms, all very large, but I had a strong feeling the myth man wasn't in any of them, and as far as I could tell, they were all empty.

Or most were empty. I came upon one with a bright orange book in the middle of the floor. Looking out of place in the room, it had to have something to do with the myth man or Mary. I took a step into the room and just missed getting stabbed by a falling icicle so big and sharp it cracked the tile floor. Checking the ceiling for how it had come down, I saw thousands of icicles hanging a hundred feet above. I jumped out back to the hallway and another icicle fell. Backing up till I could feel the wall on the other side of the hall, I focused on the book as I started running full speed into the room, the size of a football field. As I ran to the middle of the room to the book, hundreds of icicles fell all around me. I zigzagged back and forth, trying to avoid the giant ice needles. One sliced my upper right arm, and I crashed to the floor. As I looked up to the ceiling, another icicle broke off right above me. Out of nowhere, impossibly strong hands grabbed my waist and pulled me back just in time as the icicle dropped a few feet away from my feet.

"This is a poor way to kill yourself," someone whispered in my ear. I turned to see Alan's smiling face.

"What are you doing here?" I asked, shocked.

"I followed you here."

"How—" But I stopped as I saw another icicle falling above Alan's head. I pulled Alan close and held my hand up to the icicle as fire shot out of my hand and melted it, sending icy water on Alan and me.

"Brrr! That's cold!" Alan said, getting up and then helping me up off the ground.

"How did you get past the mermaids?" I asked.

"We can talk about that when we're not in a room like this. Come on. Let's get out of here," Alan said, grabbing my arm and pulling me towards the door.

"Wait!" I said, trying to pull my arm back.

"What?" Alan asked.

"I came in here for that book," I said, pointing to the orange book fifteen feet away.

Alan groaned a little and shoved me towards the hall.

"I'll get the book. Just get out of here!" Alan said as a giant icicle came between us.

I kept turning around as I ran to the hallway. Alan grabbed the book and was now heading back when I was halfway to the door. The floor shook under my feet, and then it caved in, bringing me down with it. While falling down the black hole, I tried to grab onto something, but it was too dark to see anything. I hit the ground hard, landing on the broken icicles and bits of tile.

"So your lord wants us to kill a human?" I heard a voice a little distance away. I could see some shadows moving and tried to find a weapon or anything to protect myself with.

"My lord wants you to bleed the human," the familiar voice of Anth purred in the darkness. I heard someone next to me and froze.

"Alan?" I whispered softly. The person next to me moved a little. Then I felt a hand brush against mine.

"Why bleed?" said the same voice as before, the one I didn't know.

"My lord feeds off fear. If the human bleeds, the fear comes," Anth said, and I could tell she was smiling.

"So this sacrifice will make all of us human?" the voice asked.

"Yes," Anth said. I turned my head to my left and saw crystals hanging on a wall, the moonlight reflecting off them. It was just enough light for me to see Anth in her tiger form, a room full of creatures that looked like humans, and Alan, lying next to me, not moving. Forgetting the pain I felt, I jumped up and looked at Alan.

"He's all right," one of the creatures said.

I looked up and saw what had to be the Abahs. "What did you do?" I asked them, kneeling over Alan.

"Which one do we bleed, the boy or the girl?" a very tall Abahs asked, ignoring my question.

"We have no use for the boy. Do what you want with him. We need the girl. But make sure you don't kill her when you bleed her," Anth said, smiling at me.

"Anna …" I heard Alan's voice and looked down to see his eyes open.

"Alan, are you all right?" I asked.

"My head broke the fall," he said with a little chuckle.

For one second I smiled; then looking back up at the Abahs, my smile vanished.

"Alan, can you stand?" I asked, resting my hand on his shoulder. Before I could call fire to help us, two Abahs came up behind me and cuffed my wrists.

"Just to warn you," the Abahs all smiled as the taller one of them said this to me, "you can't get free of those cuffs. Every time you use your powers, they take away some of your energy. So you see you won't be able to get out of here," he finished.

"I won't, but he will," I said, and before they could grab Alan, I called the fire to send him away. "Alan, tell Demaid to listen for me," I said just before Alan disappeared and left me with the Abahs and Anth.

CAPTURED

"Why did you do that?" one of the Abahs women asked. "Nobody hurts my friends. You want me? Now you have me," I said with more confidence than I felt.

"Anna, what did you do?" Demaid asked me in my head.

"Is Alan safe with you?" I asked, avoiding her question.

"Yes. But why did you do it?" Demaid asked again.

"I saved him … Demaid could you do something for me?" I asked.

"What is it?"

"Could you and some of the others try to find Mary … to save Liam?" I said, looking down at the cuffs.

"How are we supposed to do that?"

"I'm guessing that orange book Alan has is the rest of Mary's diary. It might say where she is."

"She's your problem now; remember just keep her alive," Anth said, looking at me once before turning and walking away.

"Demaid you might want to block me out sometimes," I said as the very tall leader of the Abahs came towards me.

"Why?" Demaid asked in a worried voice. The Abahs leader raised his hand and hit me across the face so hard that I fell on my side.

"Anna!" I heard Demaid almost scream in my head.

"I'll be fine, Demaid. Please, just find Mary so she can save Liam," I said. Then looking up at all the Abahs' smiling faces, I shut my eyes tight.

"Okay …," Demaid said.

"Demaid, get out of my head for right now … please. I don't want you to see, feel, or hear anything the Abahs—"

"The Abahs? Oh, Anna—"

"Please. Now!" Without another word between us, Demaid left me. When I could no longer sense her in my head, a feeling of total aloneness washed over me like a wave of sorrow.

❧

"Liam," I whispered in the dark cave the Abahs had put me in.

"Demaid, are you still there?" I asked in my mind.

"Yes," Demaid answered back.

"How is he?" I asked. I felt so drained that speaking in my head was getting difficult.

"Not good," Demaid said in a sad voice.

"Demaid, don't tell him or show him how bad it is, please," I said. Thinking of Liam seeing everything that had happened to me hurt more than any of my wounds. I didn't want Liam seeing my body like that, with so many cuts. The thought made my heart ache with sadness. Liam was the reason for my trying to be strong. I only hoped the others would find Mary so he could be saved.

"Okay," Demaid said.

"But tell him I haven't stopped thinking about him," I said, trying to smile but my face hurt too much.

"I haven't stopped thinking about you either, babe." Instead of Demaid's voice, I had Liam's in my head.

"Liam, is that really you?" I asked, the happiness in hearing him giving me a little more strength.

"Yeah, it's really me," Liam said.

"How?" I asked.

"Demaid has some serious power; she's in both of our heads so we can talk to each other," Liam said.

"Thank you, Demaid," I said.

"I don't know how long this will last so forget about me and talk to each other," Demaid said.

"Anna," Liam said.

"It sounds like heaven when you say my name," I said with a little smile, and I could tell he was smiling too.

"I wish I were with you," Liam said.

I could hear his pain—and his attempt to cover it—and my heart ached for him.

"No, not here. I don't want you in this place. I wish I were with you, too, but not here," I said, trying to fight the tears in my eyes.

"If you don't like the place you're in now, just get out," Liam said.

"If only it were that easy," I said.

"Can't you do that fire thing and get out?" Liam asked.

"No … I can't," I said, hating myself for being so weak.

"You're not weak," Liam and Demaid said together.

"You only feel weak because of what the Abahs are doing to you," Demaid said.

"The Abahs!" Liam said. Even in his weakness, I could sense the force of his words.

"Demaid!" I said.

"Oh, I'm sorry," Demaid said.

"What are the Abahs doing to you?" Liam asked concerned.

But before I could answer Liam, four Abahs came towards my weak body on the cave floor and looked at me.

"Demaid, you and Liam get out of my head," I demanded.

"What's wrong, Anna?" Liam asked.

"Demaid, now! Now! Understand?" I asked.

"Yes," Demaid said.

"What's going on, Anna?" Liam asked, worried.

"Demaid!" I almost yelled in my head.

"Anna—" And Demaid cut Liam off.

I looked at all four of the Abahs, smiling in anticipation. Closing my eyes, I saw Liam's face and kind smile. Then one of the Abahs kicked me in my side. I grabbed for that spot, and another one clawed my right leg.

"Ahh!" I moaned in pain, tears running down my cheeks. They only laughed at me. I touched my right leg and felt blood. A blow to my face this time rocked me on my back. I grabbed my head in pain, sobbing behind my hands. One of the Abahs pushed my hands away and roughly grabbed my chin so I was looking right at her.

"You should be happy we don't kill you now," she said to me.

"But … Anth and Finbar need me … and you all … need them to … become human," I said through breaths.

"Oh, didn't you hear?" she asked.

"We Abahs no longer follow under Finbar's rule," one of the Abahs men said. "We don't need Finbar to become human. We're saving you only until our leader decides we should kill you. You should feel honored."

"Why is that?" I asked, knowing I had no reason to care.

"You're dying for us—so we can be human," the woman said with an evil smile.

"But you're forgetting one thing," I said.

"And what is that?" another of the Abahs men asked.

"You can't kill me," I said, and they all looked at each other confused.

"What are you babbling on about?" the woman asked.

"You would be killing everything I can control, which means water, fire, wind, and nature. If you did become human, you would die because you wouldn't be able to survive without all of that." As I said this, they all looked a little scared, but then the woman smiled.

"She's lying," the woman said, and everyone turned to her.

"No, I'm not," I said.

They looked to the woman for a decision about my truthfulness.

"Can't you see? She wants us to believe this lie so we won't take her life. Nice try," the woman said to me. "But not good enough."

And the others turned to me with a knowing smile.

"I'm not lying. I'm telling the truth," I said, but they just smiled.

"No matter what lie you tell us, you're still going to die for us," the man who first spoke said to me.

"Are you all that dense you don't believe me?" I said.

The woman answered by coming up to me, but before she could strike me—

"Ahh!" she cried out as my leg came up and kicked her. She fell backwards, and immediately, the men descended and started hitting me. I covered my face, but someone pulled my arms down, and they struck me again and again. Then the woman walked back to me, the men parting for her, and she hit me full in the face. Everything went dark after that.

My Name Is Mary

"You poor girl," a woman's voice whispered. I opened my eyes to see a dark shadow kneeling over me.

"Who are you?" I asked.

"My name's Mary. I believe you were searching for me … Well, here I am," the woman said, and I tried to see what she looked like in the dark.

"Why are you here?" I asked.

"You were searching for me."

"No, I mean why are you here playing games on me?"

"Games?"

"You're not the Mary I'm looking for, but nice try," I said.

"Sorry. Just taking orders," the woman said.

"From whom?" I asked.

"Me," a small light appeared just then as a girl in her late twenties with bright red hair walked up to me. The other woman bowed her head in respect, and the girl nodded once then looked at me.

"Mary," I said, and the girl smiled.

"Even as weak as you are now, you knew it wasn't I," the real Mary said.

"How did you know I was searching for you?" I asked.

"Ensin told me when you found the pages to my dairy," Mary said.

It took me a few seconds to put the pieces together. "Ensin was the one to show me the myths," I said.

"Yes. When you were reading the pages, Ensin told me, but when we both came back, you weren't there. Then a few of our spiders told us the Abahs had played a trick on you, making you think you were still in the Myth Caves. You were really in the Abahs' cave," Mary said, kneeling down now to look at my injuries.

"So that orange book Alan and I found isn't your diary?" I asked.

"No, in fact, wherever that book is it'll soon turn to earth," Mary said. I looked at her in confusion. "The Abahs made the book out of earth to fool you," Mary continued.

"Alan took the book just as I sent him back," I said.

"No matter. We're here to get you out. Come on," Mary said as she and the other woman tried to help me up.

"I can't leave," I said.

"Why?" they both asked.

"The Abahs put these cuffs on my wrist. No magic can break them, and I can't use my powers to get them off. It takes my energy when I try," I said, and they both laid me back down gently

"What are we to do?" the other woman asked.

"I don't know …," Mary said with a sigh.

"You both should go," I said and they both looked shocked.

"We're here to help you," Mary said.

"You can help me by going to your sister Pama's house and treating a guy who's very sick. He needs your special family remedy that cures anyone of anything and that only you can make," I said.

"All right," Mary said with a nod and then continued. "But we'll come back for you."

"No! And tell my friends to stay away as well," I said, trying to sit up but stopped when I got a head rush. Just then I heard a sound that must have been the Abahs.

"You have to go now before the Abahs see you two!" I said. The woman looked at Mary, Mary looked at me with sad eyes, but then they both left. As I watched them leave, I felt a tinge of happiness knowing Liam was going to be all right.

"We have some exciting news," one of the Abahs women said, walking towards me.

"What now?" I asked with a sigh.

"Tomorrow we're taking the cuffs off you," she said.

I looked at her shocked. "Really?" I asked.

"Yes ... We can't have our sacrifice wearing those," she said with an evil smile.

I closed my eyes so that I wouldn't have to see their wax and clay faces.

"Did you say tomorrow?" I asked, my eyes opening wide.

"I did. You're going to be sacrificed tomorrow night," the woman said.

"Why tomorrow night?" I asked.

"Tomorrow night is the first time in twenty years that the moon will not be in the sky in Hoshi. Your powers won't work, cuffs or not," one of the Abahs men said, stepping forward to tell me.

"How do you know my powers won't work?" I asked.

"Someone came to our leader and told him," the woman said.

"Who?" I asked.

"We cannot say, but he knows about you," the woman said.

"Why did he tell you about me?" I asked.

"We made a trade," the man said.

"What trade?"

"If he told us about you and how to kill you we couldn't—"

"Enough!" the woman interrupted. "You're telling her too much."

"Don't you think I have the right to know why someone would want to help kill me?" I said.

"No," the woman said, still smiling.

"Fine. Then leave," I said, turning my head to the other side where I couldn't see them.

"How dare you order us out!" The woman said coming closer, but the man stopped her.

"Let's go," the man said.

"You're taking her order as if she's our leader?" the woman said.

"This is her last night. Let's give her that," the man said, and I turned to see him standing between the woman and me. After an angry sigh, the woman looked at me one last time and then left.

Only the man now remained with me. As he turned around, I noticed something strange about him, but I couldn't quite tell what. He knelt beside me and brought his hand up to my face. I flinched away as he raised his hands, palms towards me. But no blows came.

"Easy. I'm not going to hurt you," he said.

"How can I trust you?" I asked, remaining wary.

"You can't," he said with a smile.

"But—"

"I used to be human," he said.

"What?" I asked, a little shocked.

"A long time ago, I fell in love with a wonderful girl. But our love soon turned to fighting. So one day I told her it was over. She told her father who was a demon, and he turned me into one of the Abahs," he said.

I just lay there, listening to his story and wondering if he was telling the truth or playing some kind of cruel joke. *But how can something like this be a joke?* I thought, but still, I didn't stop thinking he was lying. Then another thought came into my head, and I had to voice it.

"So the only way for you to be human again is to kill me?" I asked, and he looked away from me.

"You have to know I don't want you to die," he said.

"Yet you're not going to do anything to stop them," I said back.

"What can I do?" he asked, sounding upset.

"George, you're not supposed to be in here by yourself," a man's voice rang out through the cave.

"I have to go," George whispered to me as he got up and walked away.

"George," I called quietly, and he turned around. "I know there's nothing anyone can do." He closed his eyes and continued out.

"*Anna?*" Liam's soft voice woke me. I opened my eyes and was a little sad when I didn't find him next to me.

"Liam," I whispered feeling hollow.

"I didn't want to wake you." Liam's voice came again to me, this time with a shock. I wasn't just thinking of Liam too much, daydreaming to keep my mind off … Knowing he was really talking to me brought tears to my eyes once again.

"How are you feeling? Did Mary come to see you?" I asked.

"Yes, she's here now. I'm doing better now that Mary's given me that remedy," Liam said, and I sighed in delight.

"I'm so glad," I said.

"How are you holding up?" Liam asked.

"Don't worry about me. I'm just so happy you're all right, Liam."

"Baby, what's going on?"

"Nothing," I said.

"We're coming to get you soon," Liam said, sounding happy.

"What!" I said so shocked I almost yelled it out loud.

"Yes! Did you really think we would leave you?" Liam asked with a little laugh.

"Liam, don't you dare come here," I said, and his laughter stopped.

"What? … Why?"

"I don't want any of you to come here. Don't. It's not safe. Not at all. If you do—"

"Anna we're—"

"No Liam!" I commanded. Then after a while, I realized what I had done. *"Liam?"* I called. No answer. *"Liam, I'm sorry."* Silence again. *"Liam, please talk to me,"* I said but heard nothing back. By this time, my heart felt as if someone had ripped it out. *"Can someone please talk to me?"* But no one, not even Demaid, answered.

"Oh, once again Nature is so sad," an evil voice said in the cave.

I lifted my head and looked around but couldn't see anything.

"One would wonder why. I mean, after all, she only wanted her lover to get better, and now he's doing just fine."

"Who's there?" I asked, not scared but angry.

"Don't you remember me?" the evil voice asked. Then the Naio creature stepped into my view.

"You!" I said, and the Naio creature smiled.

"Hello again."

"What are you doing here?" I asked.

"I came to see you on your last day," it said with the same forced smile.

"Why don't you ... Wait. Were you the one to tell the Abahs how to kill me?" I asked.

But the Naio creature only looked at me in an almost mocking way.

"Answer me!" I demanded.

"No, someone else had the pleasure of doing that," it said, looking at what was left of his paw. I looked away in disgust.

"Do you know who told them?" I asked.

"You mean you don't know?"

I shook my head, which gave the Naio creature great delight.

"At least I know more than you on this. I'm surprised. I thought they would've told you. After all, you know this person so well," the Naio creature said, drawing out this torture.

"Who is it?" I asked.

"Hmm ... I wonder if I should tell you. The person must have a good reason not to tell you—"

"Just tell me!" I almost yelled.

"Well, I'll give you a hint. It's a guy who told the Abahs," the Naio creature said.

"What guy?" I asked.

"Are you sure you really want me to tell you?"

"Yes."

"'Cause I could just call for the Abahs, and we could ask them."

The Naio creature's smile was starting to irritate me more than the Abahs'.

"Just tell me who the guy was."

The Naio creature chuckled a little as he said his name. "Nicky."

I was taken aback. My eyes grew large; then I closed my eyes and shook my head.

"You're lying," I said.

"No, I'm not," the Naio creature said.

"No ... Nicky ... he wouldn't ... Would he?" I whispered to myself.

"Oh, he did," said the Naio creature, trying to make everything worse.

"Why would he?" I asked, finally looking up.

"He made a pretty good trade with the Abahs."

"What was the trade?" I asked.

"That if he told them how to kill you the Abahs wouldn't bother him or anyone else he knows again. Apparently the Abahs have given him nothing but trouble, so he must've thought this would stop them from hurting him and his friends."

"Do the others know what he's done?" I asked.

"Who are you talking about?" the Naio creature asked with a sarcastic smile.

"My friends, do they know Nicky made that trade?" I asked.

"Ah, that I don't know. Perhaps you'd like me to ask them?"

"No!" I said.

"Why don't you want some of your friends to know what he did?"

"Everything is already bad enough. He saved them," I said, sighing a little at the end.

"He told the only creatures stopping you from freedom how to kill you," the Naio creature said, coming closer and lowering itself on its paws to the ground.

I put my head down. I realized Nicky had done this to save the others, but still I asked myself if this was also some kind of payback for my part in Liam getting hurt. Nicky had yelled that this whole thing was my fault, and I had agreed with him. Was it not my fault for all the attacks? Was it not my fault that Liam got hurt? Was it not my fault that I was here in the Abahs' cave?

"The only one who is to blame for all this … and soon … for my death, too … is me," I said, thinking about how no one would answer me back now. Would they even care if they knew what Nicky had done?

"Fine, I won't tell your friends now," the Naio creature said.

"And you never will," I said firmly, looking back up at the now frowning Naio creature.

"Fine," the Naio creature muttered like a sad child.

"Tell me … When will the Abahs come and get me?" I asked.

"You've been asleep for most of the day. They should be coming in about an hour."

"I've been asleep for most of the day?" I said, shocked, and the Naio creature nodded.

"The Abahs wanted you well rested, so they made sure you slept all day. How odd that you would sleep in, knowing this is your last day."

"As if it makes a difference," I said with resignation. "Wait! Did you say I have an hour until the Abahs come to get me?" I asked.

"That's what I said," the Naio creature said, examining its claws.

"Are you going to help me out of here?" I asked, and the Naio creature laughed.

"Is that why you think I'm here, to help you get out?" it asked, still laughing.

"Then why are you here?" I asked.

"I like to talk. But now I'm done," the Naio creature said, getting up and walking away.

"Where are you going?" I asked in a small voice.

"Leaving. I would say see you later, but since your death is tonight and I won't be there, I must bid you goodbye."

Then the Naio creature walked away, and I could see nothing but darkness.

❧

An hour went by with only my thoughts to keep me company. I wondered what my friends were doing right now. Probably sitting around Liam's bed in Pama's house and making sure he was getting better. I also wondered what Liam was doing, now that he was getting better. The thought of Liam brought back so many wonderful memories. *What better way to spend my last hour*, I thought, *than remembering those times I spent with him—walking with him to class in the mornings, just hanging out with each other after classes, skipping class.* And then I thought of the more special moments—his lips moving softly with mine as we kissed, his hands holding mine as we walked along, him wrapping his arms around me in a loving embrace. With a sigh, I closed my eyes and tried to feel him still with me.

"Is she still sleeping?" A woman's voice broke the silence in the cave, sounding almost insulted that I should pass my final moments in such a state.

I opened my eyes to see eight Abahs looking at me. Some were standing not too far away from me, and the others were sitting on giant boulders scattered around the cave.

"Her eyes are open. She must be awake," said a man sitting on one of the boulders.

"What do you want?" I asked, sitting up slowly. I knew they had come to get me, but I wanted to show no concern or fear to them.

"It's almost time. We have come to get you ready," another woman said, smiling without kindness in her voice or expression. Then one by one, all the Abahs on the boulders got on their feet and walked toward me.

"Coby, would you like to go first?" the first woman who had spoken asked as one of the Abahs men stepped forward.

From what I could see in the dim crystal light, he looked to be in his late thirties and had the same black hair that all the Abahs had. Coby smiled and nodded, then came up to me, grabbed a handful of my hair to pull me up, and threw me to the cave floor. I felt as though I had no more bones to break. And then he delivered a powerful kick to my side and laughed. I had hardly the strength to cry out.

"Easy there, Coby. Save some for the rest of us," the woman said, and I could hear the pleasure in her voice. I could also hear when Coby started walking away and someone else walked over to me.

"What ... are you ... doing?" I gasped, taking in deep breaths.

"We need you very weak for later tonight," the woman said as another Abahs came up and hit me. One by one all eight took turns to pummel me, although, in truth, I lost count after the fourth attack. After what seemed like a lifetime, someone new came into the cave and told everyone to stop.

"It's time," said a voice so rough that it gave no hint of either man or a woman. Strong arms grabbed mine and lifted my upper body up from the ground, and then they dragged me out of the cave. The cold night air stung my face, but still I looked up to see what I was about to face.

BECOMING THE SACRIFICE

With no moon that night, I could barely make out the scene before me in the last minutes of sunset. I guessed that more than fifty Abahs stood staring at me. Those that had dragged me out brought me up to what looked like stairs carved in the giant boulder where a few more Abahs stood. As they moved me up the stone steps—for in my condition I never could have climbed them alone—I recognized the leader of the Abahs. Much taller and more muscular than the rest, he stood out from all the others. He moved closer until he stood before me, looked at me for a second, and then turned to his people. The Abahs holding my weak body dropped me to the ground and bowed to their leader.

"Do you know why you are here?" the leader asked, turning to me once again.

I looked up slightly at his smiling face and said nothing.

The two Abahs next to me picked me up again, and one yelled at me, "Answer him!"

I stayed silent still.

SLAP! I fell as the two dropped me at the leader's strike to my face.

"Fine. Remain silent if you wish," he said to me. And then, talking to my guards, he commanded, "Make the sacrifice kneel before me."

I lay on the ground, neither willing nor able to move

"Kneel!" the leader commanded me.

One of the two that had held me up kicked my back and shouted, "Kneel!"

"Ugh!" I groaned in pain when he kicked my back. One of them grabbed my hair and pulled me up to kneel. My whole body swayed the pain so intense I almost felt numb. I looked up to see the leader holding an eight-inch blade in his hand.

"Now it's time for us Abahs to become human. Any last words, oh mighty Nature?" the leader asked with a mocking smile.

"You make fun of me now, but if you kill me, you will kill all of nature. I have warned you, yet you still do not believe me. I hope you stay wax and clay creatures forever," I said breaking my silence and infuriating the Abahs leader.

"I've had enough of you and your lies!" the leader shouted, bringing the blade to my throat. I closed my eyes when the cold metal touched my skin. No tears came to my eyes, for the days when I had cried had made me stronger. The wind blew my hair to my back, and I welcomed the reminder of my friend the wind, even though I now had no power over it. Deep within, I had a hollow feeling as if I couldn't feel anything. I don't know why, but at that moment the image of Liam and me came into my mind, only it was as if I was looking from someone else's point of view because I saw Liam spinning me around in his arms and then I looked behind me at all my friends—no, not all; one was missing from the smiling group.

"*You are one of us, Anna,*" Demaid's voice said, breaking through the silence, and she sounded so happy.

"*I've only brought heartache,*" I said in my head.

"*You've brought happiness,*" Demaid said, but now with a hint of sadness in her voice.

"*It doesn't matter now, but thank you for talking to me,*" I said. But the hollow feeling just kept getting worse. I could feel the blade press deeper into my throat and then silence.

"What is this?" the leader's voice asked in the silence.

I opened my eyes and followed the Abahs leader's eyes. Some kind of fight was going on in the crowd of Abahs, but all I could see at first was a group of Abahs clustered together. What I heard next I was not prepared for.

"Anna!" Liam's voice rang out through the cold night air, my eyes widened, and my heart leaped with joy. Liam was fighting through the Abahs to get to me, and behind him, I could see my friends. He had said that he and the others would come to get me, but I hadn't believed him. Now, in the moment of seeing Liam, I forgot about my pain and started to go down the steps towards him. But my weakened body could hardly hold me up, and I stumbled. Still, I kept going—until someone knocked me on the side of my head, making me fall hard to the ground.

"Where do you think you're going?" the leader of the Abahs said, standing over me. Then he reached down and grabbed my throat, squeezing the air out.

"Li … Liam," I choked out his name in a whisper, even though the Abahs leader was slowly cutting off my breathing.

"No matter what, tonight I will become human," the leader said as he lifted me up off the ground, my feet kicking weakly. In his other hand, he held the blade, brought it closer, and cut my cheek. I tried to cry out in pain, but it sounded more like a gasp of air. Just then a little light blue spot flew in the leader's face. He dropped me to the ground and started clawing at it.

"Run, Nature. We can give you only so much time," Hana said as more colorful lights came over the Abahs leader. With the fairies as a distraction, I got up and tried to move towards the fighting. But Hana flew into my face and stopped me.

"What are you doing?" Hana asked.

"I need to help Liam and my friends," I said, moving to the side. But she moved with me and blocked me.

"Nature, you can't even stand right now, let alone fight. You would be helping your friends if you got out of here and to a safe place," Hana said.

I looked past her to the fight, then sighed, and turned around. WHAM! A strong fist connected with my face, and I hit the ground hard and grabbed my face. It hurt, but nothing seemed broken. I looked up to see my attacker, the leader, standing over me, still smacking away the fairies. Trying to get up once again, I started stumbling away. I looked back every once in a while, but it was no use for, even with the fairy lights, the night was too dark, and I was too far into the forest to see much. A dark shadow showed up a few feet away from me, and I started backing up and then stopped.

"Anna?" the shadow said, and I stumbled forward to that familiar voice with a huge smile across my face.

"Liam!" I almost shouted as I threw my arms around him in a hug, and he did the same. "Are you all right?" I asked.

"Shouldn't I be the one asking you that?" Liam said with a chuckle. I pulled away just a little to see his face.

"I thought after the way I told you to stay away from here and then didn't hear anything more that you were mad at me," I said, looking down.

Liam touched my cheek ever so lightly, aware of the abuse I had suffered, and made me look into his eyes.

"I could never be mad at you, baby," Liam said, smiling.

"I never want to lose you," I said, leaning in towards Liam and kissing him softly on the lips once, then hugging him again.

"You won't, babe, anymore than I'd just let you go," Liam said, hugging me back and gently petting my hair.

"You should go to Pama's house. I'll tell the others that you're safe, and then we can all go," Liam said, pulling a little away to look into my eyes.

"I'll go with you," I said, looking back into his amazing blue eyes. Liam shook his head no.

"I might have to fight again when I go back, and you're in no condition to join in that," Liam said, and I looked down.

"Liam," a voice said behind me. I turned around and froze.

"Nicky, you okay?" Liam asked as Nicky came closer to us.

"Yeah, I just … came looking for you, Liam," Nicky said.

"Why?" Liam asked.

"The others and I are pulling back. I got away to find you. We need help with the Abahs," Nicky said, looking only at Liam as he spoke.

"I'll go help them. Can you take Anna back to Pama's house?" Liam asked, and Nicky nodded.

I looked at Liam and held his sleeve. "Don't go," I whispered softly to Liam.

"I have to help the others, Anna. You know I can't leave them," Liam said with a confused look on his face.

"Then I'll come with you," I said, taking a step forward only to have Liam gently grab my hand and stop me.

"No, you're going to Pama's house with Nicky. Don't worry, Nicky will take care of you," Liam said with a kind smile as he started walking away.

"Yeah, he'll take care of me … mob style," I muttered as Liam ran into the forest back to where the Abahs and our friends were fighting, leaving just Nicky and me.

When Liam was out of sight, Nicky looked at me. "You ready to go?" he asked, taking a step towards me.

I took a step back. "You didn't really come out here to find Liam, did you?" I asked, and Nicky stopped walking.

"What are you talking about?" Nicky asked.

"Save it! I know you were the one to tell the Abahs how to kill me," I said, and Nicky looked shocked.

"How do you know—"

"Someone told me," I said cutting him off.

"Look, Anna, you have to understand. I was trying to protect the others," Nicky said.

"You didn't have to sell me out to the Abahs just to protect the others," I said, feeling more than a little angry as the memory of my beatings and my near escape from a bloody sacrifice flooded over me.

"You don't know anything," Nicky said, looking away.

"I know you gladly traded my life to the Abahs," I said.

"I had to, or they would've gone after Demaid," Nicky said, looking back up at me with a pained look.

"Why would they go after her?" I asked.

"Because I know how to stop powers," Nicky said.

"I don't understand. What does that have to do with anything?" I asked.

"The Abahs already had you. They wanted to kill you, but they couldn't do that while you had control of your powers. So they found out about what I can do and asked me—"

"Telling her lies, are you, Nicky?" said the Abahs leader as he stepped out from the darkness.

"How long have you been standing there?" Nicky asked.

"Not long, but long enough. Good work, Nicky. I could see it on her face that she was starting to believe everything you were saying." And the Abahs leader stepped even closer.

"This ... was a trick?" I said, looking at Nicky and the Abahs leader.

"No!" Nicky said.

"That's the reason he got what's-his-name out of the way. Your boyfriend would've tried to save you, and Nicky couldn't just stand by as one of his best friends got hurt. That's why he made up the lie," the Abahs leader said.

I felt betrayed once again.

"He's the one lying, not me!" Nicky said.

"You may have tricked me once ... but I won't let you do it again," I said as I turned around to escape them.

"Don't listen to him. He's just lying so he can make you weaker!" Nicky shouted as he came after me.

"How could he make me weaker then I already am?" I asked, slowly moving away. I knew I could never outrun them, not with my beaten, broken body. But I could at least keep some distance from them as I kept them talking.

"He's making you think all your friends are turning on you," Nicky said.

"You've already turned so how do I know the others haven't as well?" I said.

"I told the Abahs about you because I was trying to save the others, but now that they are safe, I don't have to help the Abahs," Nicky said.

"Then tell me this. How did he know to find us here? Is that what you mean when you say you're not helping the Abahs?" I asked.

"I don't know. Maybe he followed one of us," Nicky said. "All I know is the others would never turn on you and I won't anymore either," Nicky continued.

"You shouldn't have betrayed me in the first place," I said.

"I know," Nicky said, sounding upset.

I tried to make sense of all of this. Who could I believe? Anyone? No one? Maybe the Abahs leader did follow one of us. But did that mean I could believe Nicky was telling the truth? How could I believe anything he said after what he had done? He could be saying all this to help the Abahs finally kill me. But maybe he was telling the truth. How could I tell?

"Nicky, she's not going to listen to you anymore. You've done your part; now I'll do mine and finish her for good," the Abahs leader said.

I continued inching away, not sure where I was going, especially in the deepening darkness, but trying to keep at least an arm's distance between them and me. Still they kept with me.

"AHH!" I gasped loudly as my foot came to a cliff's edge, stopping abruptly as it sent stones and dirt over to the depths below.

"You'll go no further, now," the Abahs leader said, still smiling as I faced them.

"What do you mean the others are safe now?" I asked Nicky and ignoring the Abahs leader.

"I put a charm on all of them, and it's powerful enough to make sure they don't get injured." Nicky said.

"Why didn't you put that charm on them before you sold me out to the Abahs?" I asked.

"Because I didn't know I could until Mary came to Pama's house to help Liam and told me about it," Nicky said.

"Where is Mary now?" I asked

"I don't know. She could still be at Pama's house. What does it matter?" Nicky asked, looking confused.

"Just wondering," I said, barely making out the cliff's edge behind me in the moonless night.

"How long will it take?" I said.

"How long will what take?" the Abahs leader asked.

"How long will it take for Nicky to run back to Pama's house," I said.

"I'm not going anywhere," Nicky said, standing his ground.

"What if one of us got hurt? Then would you go get Pama and Mary?" I asked.

"That's not going to happen," Nicky said.

"What if it did?"

"It's not!"

"You feel sure about that?"

"Will you two stop this!" the leader of the Abahs said in frustration.

"Well, Nicky, are you sure about that?" I asked.

"Yes," Nicky said.

"Enough!" the Abahs leader said, rushing towards me.

"Very well," I said, looking at Nicky one last time before turning around and with a relaxed attitude stepping off the cliff.

"ANNA!" I heard Nicky yell, but then the wind blowing past me silenced his voice. As I was falling, my arms stuck out from my sides like a bird's wings, and I closed my eyes, feeling the cold air blow my hair up. I felt a massive claw gently grab me, and I smiled as I opened my eyes to see Nury.

"Nice catch, Nury," I said, and he smiled back at me as we flew away from the cliff.

"Where to?" Nury asked.

"Far away from the Abahs," I said, closing my eyes.

"I know where," Nury said after a moment of silence. Then away he flew, flapping his huge wings faster and faster.

Magic Mirror

Nury took me back to his cave of treasures and told me I would be safe there as long as I didn't leave. While he went to tell the others where I was, I amused myself, playing with his jewelry and gems and other precious items. I figured Nury wouldn't mind as long as I didn't take anything. First, I picked up a gold chain with a clear diamond crystal, almost like a teardrop, hanging off it. Then I found a gold hairpin decorated with light and dark blue crystal flowers. They were both so beautiful I couldn't resist putting them on. I looked around some more and found something of tarnished silver. Picking it up gently, I discovered it was an old mirror with designs carved all around the frame. A thick film of dust coated it, and as I traced my fingers over the designs, I brushed the dust off and then blew it off the face of the mirror. Taking a good look at myself, I saw ugly cuts and bruises all over my whole face. I turned away for a second, afraid to bring up bad memories, but then turned back and lightly felt my face. I grimaced at even that slight touch, so I put my hand down and just looked at the necklace and hairpin.

Out of the corner of my eye, I thought I saw movement in Nury's pile of treasures, but when I looked in that direction, I saw nothing new. Continuing to examine the two pieces of jewelry, again I caught something moving. But rather than turn to it, I kept my vision steady and figured out where it came from. The mirror! As it lay on the pile next to me, a face not my own appeared on it. I held the mirror a little ways away from me so my own reflection would not show and then looked in it again. A girl's head, turned sideways, she was looking somewhere else.

"Hello, Lynnie," a young man's voice said.

Concerned, I looked all around the cave before I realized it had come from the mirror. Then a teen guy in blue jeans, a black hoodie, and bare feet walked into the mirror's view and up to the girl. Taller than the girl, he bent down to kiss her forehead and then hugged her.

I closed my eyes. The strain from all I had endured was finally hitting me. Now at a place where I could rest safely, my body started relaxing. Despite my will to remain awake, I felt myself drifting off.

"Please, help my daughter," a third voice, soft and of an older woman, came from another direction.

As if in a dream, I lifted the mirror up again, looking at it, confused. The couple had wandered off, and in the distance I saw her.

"Is your daughter Lynnie?" I asked.

"Yes ... she—"

I could no longer fight it. I felt my head swaying, and then I collapsed on Nury's pile of treasures while the mirror slipped from my hand.

"You have to help her ... You have to ... help her ... Please ... Anna ... Anna ... Anna ... You all right?"

Voices swirled in my head. Was I dreaming? Was Demaid talking to me? Or—

"Anna!"

That voice I recognized. I opened my eyes slowly and found Liam's worried face turn to happiness as his great smile spread across it.

"Mm," I nodded my head once and smiled. "Just tired," I said as if I were a young child.

"Do you—Anna, try to stay awake," Liam said gently as my eyes started to close.

"It hurts," I said, keeping my eyes open just a little.

"I know you're tired," Liam said, moving his hand to my forehead and rubbing it softly.

"My head I mean," I said, closing my eyes as I moved one of my hands to the back of my head and winced as I touched a sensitive area.

"What's wrong?" Liam asked.

"Just a little sore ... nothing ... much ... Where are the others?" I asked curling my fingers into a fist, still behind my head.

"They're at Pama's house," Liam said.

"Is anyone hurt?" I asked.

"Only a few cuts here or there, but other than that, everyone's fine. I think everyone just wants to head back to the school," Liam said with a reassuring smile.

"Why aren't they back yet?" I asked.

"They're waiting for us. When we couldn't find you at first, we all started searching for you. Then Nury flew down a few days later and told us," Liam said.

"I've been here for days!"

"Yeah. Didn't you know?" Liam asked.

I shook my head. "The night Nury brought me here, I tried on a few pieces of jewelry, looked in a strange mirror, and then I fell asleep. But for days? Has it really been a few days since the night with the Abahs?" I asked.

"Yes," Liam said, now sounding concerned.

"Well, I guess I needed some rest," I said with a little laugh to make Liam think it was no big deal. "Liam ... exactly how many days?"

"Three days," Liam said, still worried and not giving in to my attempts to make light of my extended sleep.

"You can go tell the others they can go back to the school now that you've found me," I said with a reassuring smile.

Liam went to get up and stopped, still looking at me with concern.

"Is there something you're hiding?" Liam asked.

"What are you—"

But before I could finish my sentence, Liam reached for my hand that was behind my head and gently pulled it into view.

"Anna, why does your hand have blood on it?" Liam said, staring at my fingertips, spotted with fresh blood. Then he looked into my eyes for an answer.

"It's nothing, Liam," I lied, looking down.

"Please, stop hiding things from me," Liam said, and I could just hear the sadness he was trying to suppress.

"I'm sorry. I just don't want you to worry over little things," I said.

"If you're hurt, I need to know," Liam said.

I nodded my head and then winced a little.

"The blood came from a wound on the back of my head," I said.

Liam got up and went behind me. I felt him lightly part my hair to look for the wound.

"Is it bad?" I asked.

"It won't be for long. We just need to get you to Pama's house. She can fix you there. I think we should go now," Liam said, coming back around to face me.

Liam helped me out of the cave and to Pama's house where she told us that the blood I lost from the wound in my head plus the beatings by the Abahs had caused me to pass out for those several days. But under her and Mary's attention and the secret remedy, I quickly healed, and they told me I could go back with my friends to the school.

"But before you go, one of your friends asked to have a word alone with you," Mary said before I could get off the bed I had been lying on.

"Who?" I asked, now sitting up and resting my back against the pillows.

"I'll go get him now," Pama said, leaving the room.

"I better go, too," Mary said, her hand turning the doorknob.

"Who is it?" I asked again.

"You'll see," Mary said, and then she, too, walked out of the room. A few minutes later I heard a knock on the door.

"Come in," I called lightly and then jumped to my feet when I saw Nicky come in.

He shut the door behind him and looked at me. "How are you feeling?" Nicky asked.

"I'm fine," I said even though I was feeling a little dizzy from jumping off the bed. Pama and Mary had warned me about moving too fast at first, so I wasn't concerned.

Nicky nodded once, still standing near the door. Then he looked down and whispered, "I'm sorry, Anna."

"Just don't try to have me killed again," I said, walking towards the door slowly so I wouldn't get dizzy again.

"Um ... Anna?"

"Yes?" I asked, stopping just before him and the door, but keeping my distance.

"Could I ask you a favor?" Nicky said.

"This is rich! You almost have me killed, and now you want a favor!" I said and then continued, "Well what is it?"

"Don't tell the others what I did," Nicky said.

"Oh I get it! That apology was fake, wasn't it?" I said.

Nicky looked up at that moment, "No, I meant it. I still mean it," Nicky said.

"Yeah right! You just don't want to look like the bad guy," I said. Before Nicky could say anything I continued, "Well, don't worry; I'm not going to tell anyone."

A look of surprise crossed Nicky's face. "You're not?" he asked in disbelief.

"I'm not, but don't think you're off the hook with me just yet," I said moving past him, opening the door, and walking out.

When we all got back to Brownstone, Treelea decided to switch rooms for the night so she would be staying with Martin, and I could have the room with Liam. Liam and I spent the whole time just looking into each others eyes and talking about the days we were apart.

"The others said it took two days for Mary to make her remedy, and then, when they finally gave it to me; I started feeling better right away. I never stopped thinking about you, so when I felt well enough to stand, I said we had to get you back. The others told me to wait, but I couldn't, not after that last time we had talked. You had sounded so bad," Liam said, wrapping his arms around me and pulling me closer to him.

"You were on my mind the whole time too," I said, cuddling into him.

"I'm so glad you're back in my arms again," Liam said, looking down at me with a loving smile. I smiled the same way back, then leaned up and softly kissed his lips. As we kissed I could feel Liam's hand slowly move up and down my waist. I moved one of my hands and gently laid it on his cheek. Then I felt a chill on my back and shivered a bit. Liam moved his hand from my waist and brought the covers of my bed up around us.

"You cold, babe?" Liam asked as he pulled away slightly to smile at me.

"Just a little," I said, smiling back at him and trying to act all cool. Then I wrapped my arms around his waist.

Liam chuckled a little when I did that.

"Liam?" I said.

"Yes?"

"I love you," I said, gently grabbing one of his hands and holding it close to me.

"I love you too, baby," Liam said and leaned down and kissed the top of my nose.

I giggled slightly then cuddled into him again. Liam's strong hands were gentle as he rubbed my hair. His magic touch felt so good. I closed my eyes and soon fell asleep to peaceful dreams.

This is one of the miracles of love:
It gives a power of seeing through its own enchantments
and yet not being disenchanted.

❧ C. S. Lewis

About the Author

Tiffany Leahy first started writing this book when she was 12 years old. Her greatest loves are reading and writing stories. Tiffany discovered this passion for writing stories when she was quite young, and just started writing her thoughts and stories in notebooks.

Teachers and family read some of her writings and encouraged her to write these stories down for a book.

Tiffany's love for mythology is well defined and laced through her stories thus where the name "Annadyomene" came from. Tiffany also shares a love for animals and travel. Tiffany's travels have taken her to Ireland, England, Spain, Holland, and Africa, among visits throughout the United States, Hawaii, and Canada.

Tiffany is the youngest out of four children. She currently lives with her family outside of Seattle, WA.